CONTENTS

IV
NOVELLA

NEW HORIZONS

Items should be returned on or before the last date shown below. Items not already requested by other borrowers may be renewed in person, in writing or by telephone. To renew, please quote the number on the barcode label. To renew online a PIN is required. This can be requested at your local library.
Renew online @ www.dublincitypubliclibraries.ie
Fines charged for overdue items will include postage incurred in recovery. Damage to or loss of items will be charged to the borrower. *rent 2024*

ISBN: 978-1-906018-06-1

A CIP catalogue for this book is available from the National Library.

Cover image courtesy of George McConkey, Abbey Street Howth, Co. Dublin.

Published by Original Writing Ltd., Ireland, 2007.

To the memory of my parents,
Michael and Catherine O'Malley.
May they rest in peace.

ACKNOWLEDGEMENTS

The author wishes to record a special word of thanks to Dublin Corporation for their financial support towards the cost of this publication.

INTRODUCTION

I first met Desmond O'Malley in 1999 when he set up the Dubliners Literary Circle. He soon gathered together a group of committed people. These have stayed with the Circle ever since. Some four years later he retired from work and began to apply his drive and energy to other activities of a more creative nature. We heard of short stories, poems and, to cap it all—a novel. He also found time to write some literary essays. The result is the published work we now have before us.

His mental energy is huge as evidenced by the wide range of topics that appear these stories and poems. Romance, homelessness, poverty, loneliness, a maritime tragedy, alcoholism, faith and belief, all feature in this collection. But it will be apparent to readers that Des is also very conscious of our Celtic heritage, as evidenced by his long epic *Flight of the Spirit*.

It has taken quite an effort on his part to bring these stories to the stage of publication. Twenty-one short stories, a novella, five poems and three essays are a very substantial work to put before the public as a first collection for their pleasure and stimulation. It is important to mention pleasure because it is so easily overlooked by the more theoretical of our critics. Des believes in reading for pleasure. He has a few more short stories in reserve and will soon write more. He has also in the past few months set up a forum for aspiring writers of any age.

Sophie Tucker used to sing "Life begins at forty." For Des life, (well, a new life) began at sixty. We will hear more from him. In the meantime there is this collection *New Horizons* to be enjoyed by all.

Alan Finnegan,
Dublin 2007.

I
POEMS

Ireland's Eye

At last I'm here. O calm, peace, repose,
a breath of thee is mine while I rest upon
this jagged hill until I rise and go. Yet I
will stay awhile and cast longing eyes
upon that distant jewel that from this
curious sea looks to a moody sky.

O Irelands eye, true golden gem of our fair
Emerald Isle, what magic is in your make?
That I should long to leave my short repose,
to take myself to your serene embrace as
you rest in the magic of immortal time?

O that I had wings I would fly across this
silent sea, and there I'd lay my body down
to rest—a rest the longing of ten thousand
years now past.

Alas, alas! No wings have I and so these noble
thoughts must pass on by, and I must rest
contented on this jagged hill and dream and
dream, and in my dreams be with my Irelands eye.

A Country Scene

Grey stones and small, scattered along
muddy banks; bright scenes of bluebells
and cowslips graced those banks; a
Kingfisher flew by turns building its
summer nest as clear water rippled away.

In tree tops jackdaws, ravens, all sang
and chirped! A colony there, many birds
in gathered host; great family talk: they
sang. And hawthorn bushes, thick along those
flowery banks—in full blossom, absorbing the
midday sun.

Ripple, ripple—splash, splash, clear waters
flow as frogs, curious ever, hop here and there.
A hawk appears! Silence reigns; now all to
ground—hush. How beautiful is the silence of
this country scene? Bright sunshine blankets all
the land, and the green foliage of Oak and Ash
hangs gently in the summer air.

Thoughts beautiful pervade my mind as I rest
on grass full green: silence everywhere, broken
only by the ripples of this clear watery scene.
Here no thoughts of anguish invade the peace of my
soul; the silence only broken by this gently flowing
stream; the singing of the midday birds, they lull
me to a peaceful rest. I watch; I wait. Time.

O that times gracious hours would fill our lives
with scenes like this; that cares would float
away like these watery ripples below! That in our
daily lives when uncertain times threaten sorrow to
our lives, such scenes as these would bring to our
striving hearts, our frightened souls—the fullness of
eternal peace.

Flight of the Spirit

The story of a lost Youth.

I

The morning rose, the sun was up. A youth set forth
in search of life's immortal soul; to look upon the
world at large, to adventure over hill and dale, in
soothing sweetness—to play: his spirit, the world
his own. Swift as an arrow this agile youth set forth.
He crossed a stream, feet firmly place on solid ground...

II

...he stood there by a grey, and misty wood, and, like
a young sapling tree, he faced the world. His glowing
eyes searched o'er that land; his feet firm in muddy soil,
the company of so many scattered stones that lay upon
the ground. Suddenly the silence of the morning was
shattered by the screeching of a black Raven, whose...

III

...flapping wings sent a sudden noise across the woodland
scene. The youth's keen eye turned sharply to the right,
and keenly did he watch this black messenger, in its ease
of flight. "O Raven spirit I watch you as you fly," he cried.
"Are you some messenger of life and death, from out this
woodland scene? Do you, as in days of old go as the...

IV

…Raven did, when upon brave Cuchulain's warlike form
it heralded that great warriors death? Or has some
mystical force this morning called you forth—some
truth for to unfold?" The youth watched the sky closely, as
this black messenger soured above this wooded scene.
Slowly he advanced towards this silent wooded glen;
a soft blowing breeze did suddenly arise, while the tree
branches swayed to…

V

…and fro and hundreds of Oak, Ash, and Willow leaves
did gently rustle in the wind. He heard their gentle call,
which was like music to his ears; "What music do you
make," he cried, as they gently echoed out their universal
song—a solace to his soul. He paused, listened, when
suddenly there before his eyes stood a female form of
beauty so profound, whose long black hair did mark her
with a princely air. The youth, transfixed, stood and stared
upon this strange sight, a comely maiden all dressed in
Celtic green, so like, he thought, an ancient Irish warrior
queen. Suddenly, she beckoned him forth, thus: "Come,
o gentle youth. Come away from this wild and unhappy
world and dwell amongst these happy trees—in…

VI

…my woodland glen of eternal youth. Come." As he
watched and listened to her call, the Raven was nowhere
to be seen; the leaves continued to rustle in the wind,
ebbing and flowing this way and that. Silence reigned. Fear
gripped the youth as he stared at the scene that lay before

him, unsure of what to do. Again he cried out: "Who are you o fair and beauteous one, and whence come…

VII

…you to this wooded glen?" The maid replied: "I am the maiden of the wooded glen. Here I dwell among these trees so fair; here I dwell in peace and harmony among my friends the Oak, the Ash and the Elm. From my true spirits home have I come to dwell amongst these trees where once my Celtic ancestors lived. Look now and see my Celtic dress, my garments of Royal green, and stare you now upon my Royal…

VIII

…stance, for I was once a great warrior queen. On Tara's Royal hill I once did dwell among noble warriors great and tall. But come, come," she cried, "Enter now this haven of universal peace, this place of eternal youth, and stand by my side: come." Still the youth paused, hesitated. Again a soothing gentle breeze blew up, and the gently rustling leaves sent forth their chanting song that was magic to his soul. As in a trance…

IX

…he stood transfixed to the ground, enraptured by the gentle music of the leaves: their soothing notes true music to his soul. Suddenly he advanced forward towards the woods, and the comely maiden stretched forth her hand and gently led him on. Once more the wind it ceased to blow. And the swaying branches with their rustling leaves

did cease their soothing song. Silence reigned. As they both
went deeper and deeper into the…

X

…woods, suddenly the trees seemed cold and bare, and
the youth did think that they softly whispered in his ears,
"Back, back! O fair and noble youth; do not enter this
wooded glen of deep despair." They both disappeared.
Shortly the silence was shattered as two Raven birds in
hasty flight did quickly emerge from the wooded heights;
and on that sunlit morn did hover about In graceful flight,
though soon they disappeared from out of…

XI

…sight. Alas! The youth was seen no more. And despite
a thorough search throughout the wooded glen—aye and
around the countryside too, the youth was never seen
again. Years passed, yet it was said by the village folk where
once the youth did live, that by moonlight, on autumn and
Winter nights, a sole Raven was often seen in apprehensive
flight! Aye, and screaming a bird-like sound, like a spirit
soul in great distress; and…

XII

…on early summer mornings, too, more than one or two
reported it, that from this wooded glen a single Raven
did come forth in a most strange and anxious way, as if
struggling to communicate—and find its way. Soon all
local villagers began to speculate: what can this be, how
strange to see a black Raven in midnight flight! And more
strange too, was what this Raven used to do, for at the

youth's old parents' home, each morning at the stroke of dawn, upon the gatepost—there did land screeching and howling to all indoors, till soon it was put to flight. Then early on an Autumn morn, the youth's aged mother from her cottage did come out, and there upon the garden lawn close to the gate, stretched out—as if in silent sleep, this noble youth, her son—lay dead, some thought asleep. Great anguish gripped her soul, as she raised her son—so very, very cold…

XIII

…and her warm tears they fell upon his youthful face, as she hugged him warmly in a firm embrace. "My son! My son," she cried aloud. "Why did you stray so far out in the world and leave us so; where did you go these many years past, and now return—but dead." Throughout the village great sadness reigned at this turn of events, so very strange. Though this noble youth had at last been found, though dead—was thought a matter most profound: not having aged was stranger still…

XIV

…many wept at this most strange death, but few could understand it yet. At the graveside upon the hill, a great crowd gathered there, and the youths aged parents they wept aloud while a heartrending sadness pervaded the crowd. Tragic it was to see such a noble youth now laid low. Flowers they laid upon the grave, till soon they drifted all away; yet not before they all did see a Raven descend from a nearby tree, land upon the grave, look here and there, then quickly fly away.

The Burden Of The Thinking Man

Who can fathom the depth of my soul's sorrow,
or restore again the lost moon-beams that once
charmed the cockles of my heart. No blackbirds song,
nor skylark's melody on high can move the cloud of
darkness that engulfs my soul! Woe is me!

Would that nature had robbed me of an understanding
mind! That foolishness had come to warm my painful
hours; for I lament the hour wherein I was born a
thinking man: that understanding had gripped my
mortal frame, oppressing me with visions that gave
grief and sorrow to my being!

Lament, lament! Cold comfort now that I of mortal
flesh must walk the joyless path of times immortal
hours! Speak not to me of human suffering, for pain
has been the heritage of my soul.

When the flowers bloom in May, and I walk abroad
through fields of green, and though my eyes, wet by
tears that bring sadness to my soul, yet shall I plead
of immortal time to lend solace to my life. For I am
human, and though burdened with a thinking mind,
whose cosmic visions transport me to new worlds
beyond, yet would I wish to be of simpler nature, now.

When falling autumn leaves delight my being, and winter
snows on country lanes add courtship to my time, then
could I live my life and, shrouded in plain garments
know life's happiness—the true inheritance of my being.

Plead in joy and happiness you that walk by me on paths
of stony grey; think not of me as you would of others,
for I carry that unseen burden that weighs heavily upon
my soul;
that weight that robs me of a lasting peace—it's the
burden of the thinking man!

Evergreen

By Rock Bawn's fair banks I strolled the grassy green.
My heart was lifted high again as I looked upon this
stream; I listened to the rippling water as it raced upon
its way, and recalled your soft and gentle voice, and the
singing birds that day.

My heart it raised a faster beat as I watched the waters flow,
no more I thought of death, or of earthly human woes. A
rabbit hopped along those banks, a gentle peaceful scene; it
tipped-toed between the bluebells as it went along its way.

I stood upon that humped-backed bridge, and thought of
my fair love, who died just aged sixteen. O fairest flower of
Rock Bawn's Vale, I see you standing there, your beauty—
a rival to the bluebells in the evening summer air. I
remember how the birds did sing as we walked this Vale
then, and your loving smile, your golden hair—seemed to
charm the very air!

As we paused upon that bridge to watch the waters
flowing past, you so enthralled my soul that day, I thought
my heart would burst. I held your hand, united we were
one, no happier beings did grace that scene, in the evening
setting sun.

But hollow is this scene now as here alone I stand, reflecting on those former times, and you firmly in my arms. O where are you my fair loved one! Could I but see you once again! To hold your hand, behold your smile, in this green and happy land.

But gone you are to a great and wide unknown, no more along these flowery banks, will you and I now roam. So rest in peace my departed love in that graveyard upon the hill, and think of me who loved you always in Rock Bawn's vale of green.

II

ESSAYS

Jane Barlow

1857–1917

JANE BARLOW, POET AND NOVELIST was born on the 17th of April 1857 at Clontarf Dublin. She was the eldest daughter of the Reverend James William Barlow, later Vice-Provost of Trinity College Dublin, and of his wife, Mary Louisa, who died in 1893. Her father, James died in 1913.

She was frail in body and of slight build. She was educated at home and quickly became a frequent contributor to the Dublin University Review after 1866 and had her first poem published in 1886. She quickly attained notoriety from her literary endeavours after the publication of her book, *Bogland Studies*, which appeared in 1892. This contained narrative poems in the native peasant dialect. In the same year she published *Irish Idylls*, a collection of rural tales. Set in the village of Lisconnel these dealt in a sentimental way with the local peasantry, and were much admired by Lady Gregory.

She never married and lived alone for most of her life in "The Cottage", Raheny. Douglas Hyde once described her as "the great incognita." She was avidly fond of hill walking and numbered among her friends and acquaintances, Katherine Tynan, who spoke of her as "very shy and difficult to talk to." Tynan was a great admirer of her work and the two became great friends for over twenty years. Sarah Purser, the artist also became a good friend and corresponded with her for many years. In 1894 she painted her portrait, and also completed portraits of her father and mother.

A quiet, shy, and reserved person, she produced some fine literary works which attained recognition both at home and abroad. She had, says George A. Greene in *A Treasury of Irish Poetry* "in a few years gained for herself a well-deserved reputation among Irish writers in prose. It is not merely the peasant dialect that is faithfully and picturesquely reproduced, but the working of the rural mind and the emotions of the heart, fully and sympathetically understood. It may be doubted, indeed, whether anyone has to the same extent sounded the depths of Irish character in the country districts and touched so many chords of sympathy, humour, and pathos."

Her literary works included *Bogland Studies*, and *Irish Idylls* (1892), *Kerrigans Quality* (1894), *Lisconnel*—her second series of stories—and, in 1895, *Maureen's fairing*. In 1896 she finished *Mrs Martin's Company*, a second collection of stories. In 1911 she wrote a novel, *Flaws*, in which she satirised middle and upper-class protestants in southern Ireland for their snobbery and petty jealousies. In the same year she wrote a play entitled, *A Bunch of Lavender*, which was staged on the Abbey Theatre but was not a success.

She also contributed numerous pieces under the pseudonym Antares Skorpios, both to the Dublin University Magazine, and the Saturday Review, including a sketch entitled, *Rescues*, which appeared in April 1917. This described the effect of the famine and evictions of 1845 from the viewpoint of a returned Australian emigrant; in this she was critical of the landowning class.

Her talent may be gleaned from the following excerpts from her book of poems published in 1916, entitled *Between doubting and daring*.

From *A dream by the wild water:*

> Still-looked, yon star o'er the wild water
> through deeps of night, from a bourne
> unknown, dim-flickering rays down the
> void vast hollow sends thrilled afar where
> no thought dare follow.

From Over-hasty:

> Low down in the vale he was leading his flock,
> where sleepeth blue shadow beneath the cold rock,
> when off up the hill rang a call fluted high,
> till echoes around him grew rife far and nigh:
> Haste thee, shepherd, haste hither!

From *A want-Wit*:

> The long straight pastures threaded on the stream
> all night beneath soft rain—showers lay a dream,
> but waked when rose-red clearance still increased
> beyond one low grey cloud that rimmed the
> east in stonewall country -wise . . .

From, Harvest, a. d. 1914 (by the wayside.)

> O'er harvest hills soft haze of shimmering heat
> folds blue and dim; glows fiery sheen of wheat

at core of amber sunbeams; kindled white the
road creeps in beneath green shadow plight
of woven branches…

Her writing was much admired in America where several
of her works went into many editions. She subscribed to the
foundation of the Irish Abbey Theatre. Her last novel, entitled
In Mio's Country was published shortly after her death. She
died at St. Valerie, Bray County Wicklow in April 1917.

The single greatest tribute that can be paid to Jane Barlow
is the brilliant way she captured the dialect of the rural folk
of Ireland. Her book *Irish Idylls*, published by Hodder and
Stoughton, received several reviews as follows:

The Saturday Review wrote: "It serves as an effective setting to the sketches of the inhabitants and the simple record
of their lives, in which the author shows such power and
observation as entitle her to rank among Nature's sternest
painters, yet the best."

The Guardian went further and described it as "A book
of great and unmistakable merit. And further: Indeed, Miss
Barlow may be compared with Mrs Gaskell, while she has
in addition all the advantages which Irish humour and Irish
pathos—each so different from and so superior to its English
counterpart—can give her."

In 1895 W.B. Yeats choose as his best Irish book of the
day *Irish Idylls*, praising Miss Barlow's "mastery of the circumstances of Irish peasant life."

In the magazine, 'Speaker,' A.T.Q.C. described it as a
"Notable Book," and, "As the performance of a new writer
it is nothing less than wonderful."

To read Miss Barlow's writings is indeed a delight; her
writings added greatly to Irish literary history in the 20th

century. Like Moore, Synge and many others she has left us a fine record of the character of rural Ireland and its people. As an Irish writer's she has much to offer, and is an author whose literary remains are well worth reading.

Mary Tighe (née Blanchard)

1772 to 1810

Poetess

MARY TIGHE WAS BORN ON OCTOBER 9TH 1772 in Dublin. She was the daughter of Rev. William Blanchard, a Church of Ireland clergyman, who was also librarian in March's library from 1766 to 1773.

His wife, Theodosia Tighe was a granddaughter of John Bligh, first Earl of Darnley. They were married in 1770 but three years after the marriage he died having contracted a malignant fever. She was left to rear their two children. Mrs Blanchard was a good manager and donated a large portion of her fortune to charity. In 1775 she joined the Society of Methodists and founded in Dublin the Home of Refuge for Unprotected Female Servants which she saw grow from strength to strength.

Mrs Tighe was an acquaintance of John Wesley. She gave her daughter a strict religious upbringing. On the 6th of October, 1793 Mary Blanchard married Henry Tighe, her first cousin. He was a member of parliament, representing Inistioge in County Kilkenny until the passing of the Act of Union in 1800. The marriage was childless and said to be unhappy. In the early years of the 19th century the couple spent some time in London where Mary met several literary friends, notable among them was Thomas Moore who was a keen admirer of her writing. She had been writing poetry since before her marriage; however nothing was published till 1805.

Her great work, *Psyche*, or the legend of love is a poem of six canto's comprising 372 verses written in the style of Edmund Spenser. It was published and privately circulated in 1803. I hope the reader will be able to capture its sheer beauty in the following sample verses:

Psyche Canto 1. Verse 1.

Much wearied with her long and dreary way,
and now with toil and sorrow well nigh spent,
of sad regret and wasting grief the prey,
fair Psyche through untrodden forests went,
to lone shades uttering oft a vain lament.
And oft in hopeless sighing deep,
as she her fatal error did repent,
while dear remembrance bade her ever weep,
and her pale cheek in ceaseless showers of
sorrow steep.

Canto III. Verses 1.

Oh! Who art thou who darest of love complain?
He is a gentle spirit and injures none!
His foes are ours, from them the bitter pain,

the keen, deep anguish, the heart-rending groan,
which in his milder reign are never known.
His tears are softer than the April showers,
white-handed innocence supports his throne,
his sighs are sweet as breath of earliest flowers,
affection guides his steps, and peace protects his
bowers.

Verse 2.

But scarce admittance he on earth can find,
opposed by vanity, by fraud ensnared,
suspicion frights him from the gloomy mind,
and jealousy in vain his smiles has shared,
whose sullen frown the gentle godhead scared;
from passion's rapid blaze in haste he flies,
his wings alone the fiercer flame has spared;
from him ambition turns his scornful eyes,
and avarice, slave to gold, a generous Lord denies.

Canto V. verses 1.

"Delightful visions of my lonely hours!
Charm of my life and solace of my care!
Oh! Would the muse but lend proportioned powers,
and give me language equal to declare
the wonders which she bids my fancy share,
when wrapt in her to other worlds I fly;
see angel forms unutterably fair, and hear the
inexpressive harmony that seems to float in air,
and warble through the sky.

Might I the swiftly - glancing scenes recall!
Bright as the roseate clouds of summer eve,
the dreams which hold my soul in willing thrall,
and half my visionary days deceive,
communicable shape might then receive,
and other hearts be ravished with the strains,
but scarce I seek the airy threads to weave,
when quick confusion mocks the fruitless pain,
and all the airy forms are vanishing from my brain.

Thomas Moore, writing in 1802 and after reading *Psyche* wrote:

Tell me the witching tale again,
For never has my heart or ear
Hung on so sweet, so pure a strain,
So pure to feel, so sweet to hear!

Mrs Felicity Hemans visited Woodstock in 1831; She had been so struck by the poetic splendour of Psyche, she penned the following lines as a tribute to her memory:

Fond dreamer! Meditate thine idle song!
But let thine idle song remain unknown;
the verse which cheers thy solitude, prolong;
What through it charm no moments but thy own,
though thy loved Psyche smile for thee alone,
still shall it yield thee pleasure, if not fame;
and when, escaped from tumult, thou hast flown
to thy dear silent hearth's enlivening flame,
then shall the tranquil muse her happy votary claim!

Again after visiting her tomb she wrote:

> where the dust had gathered on beauty's brow,
> where stillness hung on the heart of love,
> and a marble weeper kept watch above.

And further:-

> Yet, ere I turned from that silent place,
> or ceased from watching thy sunny race,
> thou, even thou, on those glancing wings,
> didst waft me visions of brighter things!

Her works included the following: *The Vartree*, a delightful poem set in the Wicklow countryside, from which the following verses are drawn:

> Sweet are thy banks, o Vartree! When at morn their sweet verdure glistens with the dew; when fragrant gales by softest Zephyrs borne unfold the flowers, and open their petals new.

> How bright the lustre of thy silver tide,
> which winds, reluctant to forsake the vale!
> How play the quivering branches on thy side,
> and lucid catch the Sun-Beam in the gale!

> "How soothing in the dark sequestered grove
> to see thy placid waters seem to sleep;
> pleased they reflect the sombre tints they love,
> as unperceived in silent peace they sleep.

And speaking of the animals grazing:

> Beneath the fragrant lime, or spreading beech,
> the bleating flocks in panting crowds repose:
> their voice alone my dark retreat can reach,
> while peace and silence all my soul compose.

She moves on the to reflect on the vanities of
human society:
> Where folly lures thee, and where vice ensnares,
> Thine innocence and peace no longer stake,
> nor barter solid good for brilliant cares.

On one occasion while away from home in 1799, and staying
at Scarborough, England, in a reflective mood she penned
the following beautiful lines:

> As musing pensive in my silent home
> I hear far off the silent ocean's roar,
> Where the rude wave just sweeps the level shore,
> Or bursts upon the rocks with whitening foam,
> I think upon the scenes my life has known; on
> days of sorrow, and some hours of joy, both
> Which alike time could so soon destroy!
> And now they seem a busy dream alone; while
> On earth exists no single trace of all that shook
> my agitated soul, as on the beach new waves
> forever roll and fill their past forgotten brother's
> place: but I, like the worn sand, exposed remain to
> each new storm which frets the angry main.

In 1805 she suffered a severe attack of consumption. According to Moore she struggled to hold on to life. She was advised to go away to the Madeiras.

Eventually she pulled out of her illness and lived for a further five years, ending the last few months of her life as an invalid. Here she remained at her brother in law's estate at Woodstock Co Kilkenny, eventually dying on March 24th 1810. She was buried in Inistioge churchyard, Co Kilkenny.

Just before her death she penned the following lines:-

"Odours of Spring, my sense ye charm
with fragrance premature,
and mid these days of dark alarm
almost to hope allure.

Methinks with purpose soft ye come
to tell of brighter hours,
of May's blue skies abundant bloom,
her sunny gales and showers.

Alas! For me shall May in vain the powers
of life restore, these eyes that weep and watch
in pain shall see her charms no more. no, no;
this anguish cannot last - beloved friends -adieu!
The bitterness of death were past could I resign
but you. But oh! In every mortal pang
That rends my soul from life,
That souls, which seems on you to hang
Thro' each convulsive strife, even now, with
Agonising grasp of terror and regret,
To all, in life, its love would grasp clings

Close and closer yet.

Yet why - immortal, vital spark, thus mortally
opprest? Look up, my soul, through prospects
dark, and bid thy terrors rest.
Forget - forego thy earthly part, thine heavenly
being trust. Ah! Vain attempt! My coward heart
still shuddering clings to dust!

Sir James Mackintosh, spoke of her poem, *Psyche* as, "of sur-
passing beauty, and beyond all doubt the most faultless series
of verses ever produced by a woman."

Mrs E. Owens Blackburne, in her epic work *Illustrious
Irishwomen, Vol. 11*, on reading her works, said, "her soul
was like a star, and dwelt apart." And speaking of *Psyche*
in particular, she said "it stands alone in the literature of
Ireland —pure, polished, sublime—the outpouring of a
trammelled soul yearning to be freed from its uncongenial
surroundings."

A contributor to the Quarterly Journal, Vol. V. 1811 in re-
viewing *Psyche*, wrote as follows: "The most obvious char-
acteristics of the poem before us are, a pleasing repose of
style and manner, a fine purity and innocence of feeling, and
a delightful ease of versification. Passages certainly occur,
distinguished by force of expression, or by considerable de-
scriptive energy; but these are not predominant, and their
effect is quenched by the not uncommon intervention of
languor. With several individual exceptions, therefore, the
poem is, on the whole, pleasing rather than great, amiable
rather than captivating." "Still," continues this correspond-

ent, "in the address affixed to the poem by the editor, we are told that even in the life-time of the author, 'it was borrowed with avidity and read with delight.' And, 'that the partiality of friends has already been outstripped by the applause of admirers.'"

Of her death Moore penned the following lines:-

I saw thy form in youthful prime,
nor thought that pale decay
would steal before the steps of time,
and waste its bloom away, Mary!
Yet still thy features wore that light
which fleets not with the breath,
and life ne'er looked more purely bright
than in thy smile of death, Mary.

Mary Tighe was a charitable woman; from the profits of her poem *Psyche*, which incidentally ran into four editions, she had built an additional section to the Orphan Asylum in county Wicklow, called the Psyche ward. She was much admired in her day. For a time she lived in Dominic Street and Gardiner Row in Dublin, eventually moving back to Woodstock in county Kilkenny. Her poetry was of a pleasing nature. Finely strung together, it showed a sensitivity of soul which won her many admirers. Like many other writers of the Anglo-Irish tradition, her poetic genius is deserving of our attention—if not our admiration.

Margaret Woffington

An actress for all seasons.

MARGARET WOFFINGTON WAS BORN IN DUBLIN sometime between 1714 and 1720 of humble parents. Her father was a bricklayer who died from a building site accident when she was but a child. She received some rudimentary education but after his death had to give up schooling. Her mother opened a shop on Ormond quay, and to help her Margaret walked the streets of Dublin in her bare feet, little dish in hand calling out, and "All this fine salad for a penny, all for just one penny!" Unfortunately this venture was not a success. It was a hard time for the future actress; a time she would reflect on in later years when she would take her mother by carriage around the city.

Madam Violante, a dancer and tightrope walker lived along the quays. She managed a troupe of child actors who would perform in an exhibition booth she had in Fowne's Court, Temple Bar. Her shows were very successful and eventually she moved to larger premises off George's lane, now South Great Georges Street. One day Madam Violante noticed young Margaret as she was drawing water from the river Liffey for her mother. Immediately struck by her youth and beauty, she visited Peg's mother and proposed taking her on as an apprentice. Having reached agreement Margaret joined the troupe. She was taught dancing, singing and acting, which would eventually lead to a brilliant theatrical career. Unfortunately the dancing and tumbling show performed from the booth began to lose public appeal; changes were required, and quickly. It so happened that at this time the Beggars Opera was all the rage in London, so with her company of young actors she decided to produce it here in Dublin. At just twelve years of age she got her first part in a Dublin production. From here her career went from strength to strength.

Her first major appearance was at the Aungier Street theatre on September 1st in 1735, where she appeared as Dorinda in the John Dryden and William D'Avenant adaptation of the Tempest. During the next two seasons, 1735–36, she played in a variety of roles, including Arabella in Henry Carey's, *The Honest Yorkshire Man*, and Rose in George Farquhar's, *The Recruiting Officer*. This latter play was one with which she would be long associated.

In January 1738 the Dublin Theatres were closed owing to the death of Queen Caroline of England; she at once left for Paris, France, where she joined a Company led by a Mons Delamine—a brother of William Delamine—with whom she had danced at Aungier Street. She did not return to Dublin till September 1739. Again in 1748 she crossed over to Paris with Owen Swiny to study the acting techniques of the actress, Marie Dumesnil. Here she met the dashing professional swordsman, Signor Domenico Angiolo. He accompanied her back to London, where, for a period of time they were lovers.

Returning to Dublin she now began to play parts from which she would score her best successes. These included playing Phyllis in *The Conscious Lovers*, Lappet in *The Miser*, and the title role in *The Female Officer*. These latter roles were played wearing breeches! She also wore breeches in the role of Harry Wildair in *The Constant Couple*, all of which parts were a great success with the Dublin audiences.

In the 1739-40 season she was also cast in several other roles, including Silvia in *The Recruiting Officer*, Nell in Charles Coffey's *The Devil To Pay*, and Phyllis, in Richard Steele's *The Conscious Lovers*. The failure of an amorous relationship with a lover named Taafe, prompted her to emigrate to London. Here John Rich at Covent Garden Theatre engaged her at 5 guineas a week. She gave ten outstanding performances of Sir Harry Wildair, in *The Constant Couple*.

W. R. Chetwood, who wrote a history of the stage in 1749 in commenting on her role as Harry Wildair, said: "This agreeable actress, in the part of Sir Harry, upon coming into the green room said pleasantly, 'In my conscience! I believe half the men in the house take me for one of their own sex.'

Another actress replied: 'It may be so but in my conscience, the other half can convince them to the contrary!'"

Her career now advanced by great strides. She appeared in Covent Garden Theatre, London, as Silvia in the play, *The Recruiting Officer*, where her beauty raised great excitement. Swarms of gallants vied for the beautiful young actress' attention when she appeared. Two of the more prominent were, Colley Cibber, who was aged 71, and Owen Swiny, who was 61.

Charles Hanbury Williams, another great admirer addressed the following lines to her:

If when the breast is rent with pain,
It be no crime the nymph should know it,
Oh Woffington, accept the strain pity,
Though you'll not cure the poet.

In the summer of 1742 she paid a return visit to Dublin in the company of David Garrick. Together they had a most successful season. As the popular journals of the day recorded: "Garrick fever had come to Dublin Town!" They returned to London and lived together for a couple of months; however, they never married.

Geo Faulkner, writing of her in the Dublin Journal was euphoric in her praise. He wrote, "The celebrated Mrs Woffington's performances in Smock Alley theatre continues to draw the most crowded audiences hitherto unknown." and "her unaffected ease and vivacity in comedy, her majestic pathos in tragedy, shows her to be an exact imitation of nature; in Caesar's phrase, 'She came, was seen, and she triumphed.'"

Peg, as she was now popularly called, was the acknowledged belle of Dublin society. Thomas Sheridan introduced her to the Beefsteak Club, which met every Saturday morning to the rear of Wellington quay. This was an all-male club and no women were allowed in. Its membership was comprised of the most influential members of Dublin society, including members of Parliament. Her popularity may be gauged from the fact that not only was she made an honorary member—but was also elected president! This set the tongue's of fashionable Dublin society wagging; Peg was in no way bothered by the loose gossip of the town.

She returned to Drury Lane Theatre London, where she considerably extended her repertory, including playing Rosalind in Shakespeare's *As You Like It*, and Nerissa in *The Merchant of Venice*. Whether in comedy or tragedy, she proved herself adept in whatever role she took on.

Despite having many lovers she never married. Always fiercely protective of her career, she was determined to remain mistress of her own fortune. She lived at a time when actors and actresses were viewed poorly in the social pyramid of 18th century England. Her sense of independence and the fact that she endeared herself to all classes with whom she came in contact, were hallmarks of her whole life.

She wasn't slow to help others less fortunate than herself. On one occasion while in Dublin she loaned the famous Gunning sisters evening gowns to attend the Lord Lieutenant's annual Ball in Dublin Castle. Maria Gunning later became Countess of Covington, while her sister, Elisabeth became Duchess of Hamilton and Argyle. She made many friends and the skill and professionalism of her acting made her a theatre legend.

Nevertheless, she was not without her critics. Her coarse Dublin accent, despite her hard work to refine it, settled uneasily among the refined talkers of the upper class theatre-going public.

Nevertheless when John Rich of Covent Garden Theatre first met Peg, he described her thus: "A more fascinated daughter of Eve never presented herself to a manager in search of rare commodities. She was as majestic as Juno, as lovely as Venus, and as fresh and charming as Thebe." He hired her at once.

Of her many performances in the theatre under his management, the London Daily Post and General Advertiser published the following rhyme in her honour:

When first in petticoats you trod the stage,
Our sex with love you fired, your own with rage:
In breeches next, so well you played the cheat –
The pretty fellow and the rake complete – each
Sex was then with different passions moved: the
Men grew envious and the women loved!

Edmund Bourke, writing to Matthew Smith in 1753 said of her "she is of low origin, it is true, but talents and nature often avenge themselves on fortune in this respect." She literally took London Town by storm with the quality of her performances. Her role as Harry Wildair in *The Constant Couple* dressed in all male attire caused a sensation. Tate Wilkinson recalled that "She had a new suit for the role, and looked quite the man of fashion!" A critic writing in the London Magazine and praising her performances, penned the following lines:

Delightful Woffington! So formed to please!
Strikes every taste, can every passion raise;
In shapes as various as her sex's are – and
The entire woman seems comprised in her.
With easy diction and becoming mien,
Distinguished shines and shines in every scene,
The prude and the coquet in her we find,
And all the foibles of the fairer kind.

Despite some who criticised her easy-going approach to life, and the fact that she would not marry, her popularity with London and Dublin society was huge. Henry Seymour Conway, writing to Horace Walpole, said of her: "So you cannot bear Mrs Woffington; yet all the town is in love with her."

Her sister Polly, whom Peg had sent to be educated in Paris, returned to England; she tried her hand at acting but was not a success. Instead she married the Honourable Robert Cholmondeley, the second son of the impoverished Earl of Cholmondeley in St. George's chapel Mayfair, on November 30th 1746. The father of the bridegroom at once remonstrated with Peg over the marriage; she replied to the good Earl, "Mr Lord I have much more reason to be offended at it than your Lordship, for I had before one beggar to maintain, and now I have two."

Peg Woffington's career as an actress was one of outstanding success. Despite her social origins and the fact that she was a humble Dublin washerwoman's daughter she nevertheless demonstrated an ability to hold herself excellently with all classes in society. Her talent, charm, and generosity of heart commended her to all who knew her; she was charitable in an exemplary way, and, of the twenty-six benefit performances held for her ailing colleagues, she performed in no less that twenty-four. As an actress she ranked among the best of her profession, performing alongside such giants of the stage as David Garrick, Mrs Prichard, and Richard Brinsley Sheridan.

Whether on or off the stage she was a free spirited person; she had a fearless and a deceptively winsome manner, which concealed her resolute determination to have her way: she preferred the society of men—finding most women tedious and frivolous.

In her relationship with her fellow actresses none was so

fiery as that between herself and Kitty Clive; they were both giants of the stage, and according to Thomas Davies, "No two women ever hated each other more unreservedly than these great dames of the theatre."

The final word must be left to Theophilus Cibber, who, writing in 1748, said: "I know none since Mrs Oldfield who have shown themselves so equal to characters of an elevated rank; she has grace in her gesture, an ease in her motion, very fitting the deportment of a woman of quality; her attitudes are quite picturesque yet, by an early transition from one to the other, and a proper application of them all, they seem to be the work of nature only."

In 1757 she collapsed on stage having suffered a paralytic seizure and never acted again. She retired to her home in Teddington a short way from London, where she died three years later on March 28th 1760. She was buried in Teddington Parish Church where a tablet was erected to her memory. She died a rich woman. In her will she left the bulk of her fortune to her sister who, like her mother she had supported during her life.

Margaret Peg Woffington was just one of many who left Dublin to seek their fortunes in England. Like Spranger Barry, John O'Keefe, Richard Brinsley Sheridan, Dion Boucicault, Thomas Sheridan, to name just a few, she proved by her talent and acting ability a true credit to her profession—something more than the "Stage Irishman" caricature so amusing to certain theatre-goers of the time. Given the many acting roles she played so successfully, it can truly be said that Margaret Woffington was indeed, "an actress for all seasons."

III

STORIES

An Everyday Occurrence

MRS BENSON LEFT 44 HOLLOWAY STREET at 2:30 PM that Wednesday afternoon. It was a bright, sunny, autumn day. In the nearby school the children were beginning to leave for home, while across the street Mrs Clancy stood waiting at the 66 stop for the bus that would take her into town to see her sister. Regularly each Wednesday, at precisely this time, Mrs Benson would see her and give her a friendly wave.

There was nothing unusual about the day and Polly Benson was looking forward to her stroll. About twenty minutes into her walk she suddenly noticed John Anthony, the village postman, struggling up the street. He seemed quite dazed and unable to control his bodily movements. Polly rushed forward and caught him by the arm.

She cried out, "Are you all right, Mr Anthony?"

He was unable to control his bodily movements, and with a struggle, he replied "I…I'm…okay Mrs Benson. I'm okay, thank you."

He then fell against the garden hedge fronting the street housing, crying out as he did, "I'm after being attacked by two youths and robbed of the mail."

Mrs Benson immediately cried out for help.

"Help, Help! Someone!"

The teachers coming out of the local school heard her screams for assistance. Immediately two of them, a Miss Johnson and a Mrs Cooney rushed to her aid.

"Good God, Mrs Benson, what is the matter?" cried Miss Johnson.

"It's the postman, Mr Anthony—he's been attacked and robbed. Quickly, someone call the police—and an ambulance."

Miss Johnson, using her mobile phone, dialled the local station. Within minutes a patrol car arrived, followed shortly by an ambulance.

By now a small crowd had gathered, and while the police and ambulance personnel were attending to Mr Anthony, there was much speculation among the onlookers as to where and why he had been attacked.

"Terrible business," cried one local resident.

"A body is not safe walking the streets nowadays—even in daylight."

"Disgraceful!"

"And where are the police when you are looking for them?" asked another.

"Nowhere," remarked a third resident.

"Terrible, terrible!"

All expressed the hope that he did not sustain any serious injuries.

The postman was placed in the ambulance and, accompanied by one of the police officers, was whisked off to hospital. The small crowd slowly dispersed.

As Mrs Benson continued on her walk one of the teachers remarked, "And did no one see where the poor gentleman was attacked?"

"I've no idea, replied Mrs Benson. But it is a terrible business. No-one is safe walking the streets nowadays. One only has to look at the police crime statistics to see that such attacks are an everyday occurrence. It's a disgrace, that's what it is—a disgrace."

Bidding the teacher a good day, Mrs Benson, still slightly shaken from the experience, carried on with her walk.

Passage Of The Dead

AT AROUND 7:00 AM ON THAT COLD December morning the tragedy had been reported over the national airwaves.

"Freak 30 foot wave sweeps passengers from deck of the midnight ferry crossing the Irish Sea. Intense search for bodies throughout the night; hope of recovering those washed overboard being hampered by rough seas."

This news bulletin was reflected in the headlines of the morning papers. All Cork was stunned by the news. By early morning anxious relatives were gathered by the quayside awaiting the arrival of the ferry, the Sunbeam Ark. At 10:35 AM on what was a cold, misty morning, the ship slowly sailed into Cork harbour.

On shore, an anxious crowd waited patiently for their loved ones to disembark. Many had relatives returning home from England for Christmas. Standing huddled together, the anxious expressions on their faces said it all, as they waited for the ship to dock. The captain with two of his officers came down the gangplank to speak to the crowd; they went into some detail about the freak waves that had struck the ship during the night expressing deep sorrow for the deaths that had occurred. Six stretcher-bearers then disembarked bringing three covered bodies ashore. These were reverently laid out on the quayside for collection by the medical authorities that were already racing to the scene.

The assembled crowd suddenly surged forward, a sea of anxious faces, each wondering whether a son or daughter would be among the dead. Only three bodies had been recovered. The captain, stepping forward, informed the crowd that an exact number of those missing would be made known shortly. Just then an ambulance raced down the quayside screeching to a sudden halt. A team of medical personnel began to take the bodies into the ambulance for return to the city morgue.

Suddenly the anxious crowd began to roar "Uncover the bodies! Uncover the bodies!"

They rushed forward and hurled the ambulance men out of the way and uncovered each stretcher. A hushed silence came over the crowd, as all looked upon the prostrate bodies. A scream suddenly broke from an old lady standing close by, "My daughter, my love, sweet Jesus how could this happen, how could this happen?"

Falling upon her knees, and weeping bitterly, she raised the dead girl and wrapped her arms around her. All about her were beset with deep emotion upon witnessing this most tragic scene. Meanwhile as the rest of the passenger disembarked all were reunited with their relatives and loved ones; slowly the crowd began to drift away. As they did so, many were seen to make the sign of the cross, thankful that a son or daughter or other relative had not been drowned.

The ambulance personnel returned to their duties and the bodies were put aboard the ambulance and taken back to the city morgue. The old lady, in a most distressed condition accompanied them. Once again, as so often in the past, the cruel Irish Sea had again claimed her victims. Driving down the Cork quayside the driver noticed a hunched up figure sitting in a doorway. As the ambulance passed the figure of an old man with an unshaven face stood up. Staring at the driver he was seen to make the sign of the cross; then, once more slump down into the corner again. Soon a bright, morning sunshine broke through the grey overcast sky brightening up an otherwise dull quayside. As the ambulance sped away nothing was heard now save the deafening aura of silence.

The Awakening

DECLAN RYDER SAT PENSIVELY ON A STOOL in Matchers Pub. It was 6:45 PM. He had come into town a little earlier, this afternoon. Normally he would not arrive till around 8:00 PM. He had been sitting at home somewhat bored. Each week the routine was the same: up in the morning, wash, have breakfast, potter around the house, go into town, come home, have dinner and tea, watch television, then back to bed. It was a boring life. Retirement was not all it was made out to be!

The problem was that he had few friends. At fifty years of age life was passing him by. He never married. Nothing exciting ever happened in his life. He was a lonely man. When he had worked as a hotel porter it was great. It got him out of the house, but accept for that cur of a supervisor he worked under, he enjoyed the work immensely. Now he was retired. No job. Not good.

The town was in a bustle. Temple Bar was thronged with visitors, Spanish, Italian, French, and of course English. The tourist season was well under way. Declan looked around the bar, it was very crowded.

He thought of his mother and father, both passed on; and

of the 40s and 50s when he and his brothers were reared up. Those were happy times. Coming and going to school, sure they hadn't a care in the world.

His father had worked very hard just to earn a few pounds, and his mother equally hard keeping the house together. They had a hard life. No twice-yearly trips to the Costa del Sol for them! You were lucky if you visited Connemara once a year.

A tear came to his eye; he struggled hard to hold it back. A growing man crying in public! What would everyone think? And yet what would the wider public know or care about him. Anything? Nothing? He took a large gulp of his pint of Guinness.

How strange life is, he thought. Millions of individual human beings occupied the planet, every one with a distinct personality. Did they care whether he lived or died? No! Here he sat in Matchers pub surrounded by people. Outside thousands more hustled and bustled about their business unaware of his existence. He thought of God's plan for the human race; had he a plan? Sipping his pint, he quietly sang that Irish song, *She Moved Through the Fair*. He thought of Kathleen O'Meara—his Kathleen!

What a fool he had been to let her emigrate. Australia, twenty-seven years ago. Should have married her. Loved her. Fool to have let her go. He struggled with his left trouser pocket. Yes, got it. Her last letter dated March 20th, 1968. He always carried it around. Held the letter for several seconds afraid to open and read it. Every time he did he cried like a child. Sad.

He thought of Alan Sillitoe's book, *The Loneliness of the Long-distance Runner*. He enjoyed that book. This evening he too felt like a lonely, long distance runner. After glancing briefly at the letter he put it back into his pocket. He enjoyed the thoughts of his own company. He was communicating with himself, like Mr. James Joyce, in *Ulysses*, the stream of consciousness, and all that. That was nice. Wasn't he one of those millions of people who occupied the planet? Week after week he struggled to cope with life. It wasn't that he had insufficient food to eat, or proper shelter. He owned his own house; he was well nourished. He had plenty of fuel to keep his fire alight. His retirement pension was satisfactory. Yet there was something more to life, some greater purpose, a greater destiny that he must fulfil If only he knew what is was! The question nagged at him continously. He could be lonely, yes. He had few friends. He was different. So what? Some called him a snob. Not true. Different, yes: a snob— no! Anyway, was it a crime to be different; or to be a snob —No! He was a troubled man. If only he knew where life was leading him. He was fifty years old; time was moving on. Terrible feeling.

The voices that cried to him in his head, his inner thoughts, confirmed this. He was alive, physically—but spiritually? He was not sure. He felt lonely; would he overcome his lone-liness? Who knows; he wasn't sure about this, either. He drank a further mouthful of Guinness. Nice.

He thought of the planets. Of Jupiter, Saturn, Mars, and all the thousands of stars that lit up the skies at night: how won-derful. What great secrets they must hold! Time would tell. Sipping his drink he pondered what he should do for the rest of the evening. Go dancing? No. Long past that!

Did not want to get drunk. It was five hours to mid-night…five hours to kill. What now? Go home? Home to a dreary house, where the only companionship was the four walls, the television set…and…No! Kathleen…should have married her: big mistake. Folks all around him were chatting and laughing with their wives or girlfriends; friendship, companionship, tonight? Not likely. His only companions were his innermost thoughts. He thanked God for his spirit—the spirit that made him feel alive. He didn't know why this spirit gave him life; gave him that warm feeling that sustained him in this valley of loneliness.

Millions of people in the world…would someone say hello to him, communicate with him? If only. He decided that he would go home and read a book. That would engage his thoughts. His reading would be a companion to his soul. Yes! He would engage his spirit; have a speaking contest: that would be great. Maybe indulge in his favourite hobby—experimental mathematics. (A:B inversely proportional to C.) Yes, he loved to dabble in numbers (Y squared over M (proportional) to X/R = to the power of Q). Wonderful!

He grew excited at the thought of this. The written words in the text would speak back to him, communicate in a most friendly manner: how nice that would be. So, what author would he read? Several names came into his mind: Shaw, Joyce, Greene, O'Casey? He rejected all four. Thackeray, William Makepeace. Yes, a fine conversational writer, he thought. He stayed in Dublin one time, mid-nineteenth century. Fine Hotel. Brush held up window! Loved the town. Now…which volume? Ah, yes. Got it. It would be *Lovel the Widower* and particularly the chapter entitled, 'The Batchelor of Beak Street'. It was decided. It would be Mr Thackeray. He would not be lonely or drunk again: Mr Thackeray would be his boon companion. He would introduce him to all his friends, like Mr. Denis Duval, Miss Prior, and lots more. It would be wonderful! He would finish his drink at once; withdraw from this crowded, noisy environment: this valley of a thousand voices—none of which spoke to him. He would go straight home. Fine.

Having finished his drink he made his way towards the exit. As he did so the barman cried out "You're away, sir?"

"Aye," returned Declan, "Away home. Visitors, you know. Mr Thackeray, a great conversationalist. He's expected with some friends later on. Must be off. Good night."

Just as he was about to pass out through the exit, Declan turned and smiled across at the barman, whom he noticed was quietly smiling also.

Dance Of The Angels

It was a bright, autumn evening outside the Grisham Hotel, as Rachel Curley stood at the bar waiting for a vodka and orange. Her thoughts ranged over many things, including the loveliness of the bride and how well she and her husband John looked on this most important day of their lives. They had been married just four hours earlier and on this, the occasion of their wedding celebration, she was very happy for them both. She was particularly happy to see the large number of staff that was present from the job. There was Timothy Baskin, the print room supervisor, Robbie Mitchell, head packer, and Kathleen and Michelle Parker—the "terrible sisters" who worked in the production department. Both looked provocatively gay in their low-cut tight fitting dresses. Kathleen's boyfriend, Mark Ryan was here also and seemed to be watching her every move! He was too possessive. She did not like this.

She noticed also Stephen Doyle who was the floor supervisor in the company. Standing five foot, ten inches tall, of stocky build with closely cropped black hair, he had a commanding aspect about his personality. Quiet, unobtrusive in company, he was admired by all. Standing at the far corner of the bar, she stared down at him as he chatted with some of the other guests. She heaved a sigh as she thought how painful being in love could be. She loved Stephen, yet, so far she failed to get him to ask her out on a date; she was determined that on this occasion she would not fail.

The barman brought her drink and placed it on the counter, "That will be four euro and eighty cents, Miss."

Rachel handed him the money. Just then the band struck a series of musical notes, and all the guests were invited to dance. This was quickly followed by a call for the bride and groom to lead the floor.

"Bride, Bride and groom, please," shouted the best man.

Tall, handsome, and in an immaculate wedding dress of satin and lace, the bride, accompanied by her husband, walked to the centre of floor and started to dance. Looking at Stephen, Rachel's heart sighed as the band and lead singer opened with that favourite wedding song, "o how we danced on the night we were wed."

The emotional effect was almost too much to bear. She swallowed her drink quickly and, calling the barman, ordered the same again. Meanwhile the happy couple whirled around the dance floor in an ecstacy of romantic happiness.

Rachel tried to manage a smile. She stole a glance in Stephen's direction. " I must have him. I will have him," she cried. All the guests formed a circle round the happy couple, and with great verve danced and sang…"O how we danced on the night we were wed"…Rachel noticed that Stephen hadn't joined in. He was still engaged in conversation with his work colleagues. She walked over to him.

"Well, what's the story lads, no one dancing?" she cried.

"We're not dancing Rachel, perhaps later,," Stephen retorted.

"Oh, come now!" urged Rachel, "this is a wedding - not a wake! You guys need to shake a leg; get into the swing of things. Think of the bride and groom, for God's sake."

Stephen smiled. Turning away he continued on with their conversation.

Rachel was offended, but pretended not to show it. Instead she taunted and teased him for several minutes in order to get him to dance, but without success.

Spotting her friend, Rose Tierney, she joined her, "Men! They have so little understanding of us women; they would break your heart."

Rose smiled as she spoke, "You're right, if we were foolish enough to allow them."

The barman interjected, "Your drink Miss."

Rachel took the drink and paid him.

"So, Rose, are you enjoying the wedding?" Rachel asked.

"Yes," replied Rose, "And you?"

Rachel stared at her friend for several seconds before replying, "It's okay, you know…I'm glad for Karen. She has always been a good friend. I hope they will be very happy together."

"You don't sound very enthusiastic," cried Rose, "Something bothering you?"

Looking in the direction where Stephen was sitting, Rachel apologised to Rose for the tone of her reply, "I'm sorry Rose, my mind is elsewhere just at the moment."

"I can see that," replied Rose, "So what are you going to do about it?"

"I'm going to get that fellow to dance tonight if it kills me!"

"Men, they have as much understanding of us women as I have about sending a rocket to the moon—none!"

"Spoken like a true Celt," retorted Rose, "I'm going

to make sure you succeed. How do you feel about that?"

"Great, wonderful," exclaimed Rachel. "Like Josephine after she captured Napoleon's heart! Lets do it!"

By now the two friends were becoming slightly inebriated. As the music grew livelier they approached Stephen and his friends. Rose asked Robbie Walsh to dance. He immediately obliged. Stephen continued talking. Rachel interjected, "What is the matter with you, Timothy Blake, got lead in your feet? And you Stephen Doyle, surely you want to dance? To the brides happiness—no?"

Stephen did not reply. Rachel fumed, but determined to persist. By now the music had reached fever-pitch. The floor was packed with dancers. She began to dance on her own. She danced back and forth towards Stephen, who quickly began to take notice. Several dancers watched as she hovered ever closer to him, her body swaying and undulating to the rhythm of the music. Staring intently into his eyes he became visibly uneasy; he began to shuffle about. He ordered another drink. He stood close to his friend Timothy Blake, but they did not converse. Rachel continued to taunt him.

"Dance, dance," she cried, "to the honour of the bride and groom."

All the while she was looking at him in a most bewitching manner. Stephen grew intense; he blushed; he was visibly unsettled—his spirit stirred on fire, the look in his eyes reflected the awakening of his innermost soul.

Rachel danced faster and faster, round and round, at times only inches from Stephen. Her whole body trembled; her eyes reflected the volcanic light of her soul, which seemed to mesmerise not only him, but also some of those dancing nearby. Suddenly the expression on Stephen's face changed. Staring at Rachel he began to feel a stirring in his body, an intensity of feeling in his soul that he had never felt before. She appeared to him like a flower—bright, beautiful, a daffodil oscillating back and forth in a gentle breeze; her red lips like the petals of a summer rose, enchanting in the beauty of their radiant glow. He was seized with a desire to possess her. Rachel slowed the tempo of her movements; she moved close to him again, looking deeply into his eyes. Then, taking him by the hand she led him into the centre of the floor. The band began to play that enchanting Irish air *She Moved Through the Fair.*

Dancing slowly, they embraced warmly. Noticing her friend Rose, she smiled and winked at her. Then, resting her head on Stephens shoulder, Rachel uttered to herself, "now my love you are the endearment of my soul, the love of my life. Now I too dance the Dance of the Angels!"

White Feather

MICHAEL DONOVAN ROSE EARLIER THAN usual on that bright Spring morning. It was just like any normal Friday morning, save for this difference: today was his seventieth birthday. Today he would treat himself to a large brandy, and treat his favourite pigeon to some real Indian maize. He had nick-named this pigeon White Feather and had been feeding it for several weeks on bread crumb; today it would receive a real nutritious meal.

On each Friday morning he would leave his apartment at 9:45 AM and go to 10 o'clock mass in the local church, after which he would spend some time talking to friends and neighbours, before carrying on to the post office to col-lect his pension. Quiet and reserved, he did not socialise much, and the one hobby he always enjoyed was when he was able to keep and race homing pigeons. In his youth he had raced them and, by all accounts, had won many prizes. Now, living in an apartment he was not allowed to do that. He missed his hobby.

This particular morning was to be very special. He felt great, and was looking forward to visiting Conways pub for his brandy, and of course seeing his favourite pigeon White

Feather. Having attended mass he walked on to Wickers pet shop, where, from his limited pension, he intended to buy a two euro bag of Indian maize. As he made his way there his thoughts roamed over many things; three score years and ten, that is mans' life; sometimes it is four score years and ten. Lots of birthdays too. He wondered: do pigeons have birthdays? Must have. But who wonders or cares about that? No one. General public, what do they care about pigeons? Filthy things—dirtying all over the place! Get rid of them! Strange, can anything God created be called filthy, dirty?

Soon he came in sight of Wickers pet shop. He entered and was greeted by the man himself.

"Top of the morning to you Michael," cried Wicker. "You're out and about early."

"Aye," replied Michael, "have some important business to attend too this morning."

"Oh? And what would that be could one ask?"

Donovan looked about the shop searching for the pigeon corn, and for a few seconds did not answer, "I'll be visiting a good friend later this morning; celebrating his birthday same as myself."

"I didn't know it was your birthday."

"It is an' all," replied Donovan. "Seventy years of age I am today and as fit as a fiddle, thank God."

"Well congratulations!" exclaimed Wicker, "and may God grant that it will be a happy one. In the meantime what can I do for you ?"

"I'll have one of those two euro bags of maize, if you please."

Wicker fetched one of the bags, placed it in a brown paper bag and handed it to Donovan, remarking as he did, "since

its your birthday Michael, that bag is on the house, okay?"
"Well that's right kind of you Wicker," replied Donovan,
"Thank you very much."

After further brief exchanges the old man bid farewell
and continued on the rest of his journey.

Arriving at the spot where the pigeons gather, including his favourite White Feather, he was surprised to see
there were none about. He looked up and down the street,
but none were to be seen. He did notice a clumped object,
however, a short distance from where he stood. He walked
forward to investigate. Horrified, he saw that it was his favourite pigeon, White Feather, lying dead on the road. He
bent down closer to investigate. What he beheld was the
frail corpse of his favourite pet bird mangled and crushed.
For several minutes he lay anchored to the roadway unable
to move. There before him was his best friend, dead to all
the world. He felt shattered. Suddenly a motor vehicle came
racing around the corner and screeched to a halt. The driver
wound down the window of his car and roared out, "Get off
the road you old fool! Do you want to be killed?"

The old man did not stir. The driver roared again.

Then, in graphic poise, Donovan lifted up the dead
pigeon in both hands, and, turning towards the vehicle
screamed at the driver, "Murderer, murderer! You killed
him, you killed him!"

The driver, taken by surprise at this sudden outburst
grumbled under his breath then quickly sped away. The old
man stood up, the dead pigeon in his hand. He walked into
a nearby newsagent shop where he secured a cardboard box
into which he placed it. He then walked around to Conways
pub for his glass of brandy; however, his whole demeanour
clearly showed that he was retreating into himself. Friends

whom he passed on the way were ignored; he walked like a man in a daze. He entered the pub, selected a quiet corner and seated himself down. He placed the cardboard box at one end of the table. He approached the bar, and in a low, almost inaudible voice ordered a glass of brandy. The barman, Paddy Murphy, called out, "God, on the brandy this week, Michael? Pray, what's the occasion?"

The old man did not answer. He paid for the drink and returned to his seat. Resting quietly he thought to himself how cruel the world was; death and destruction everywhere. Not even our little feathered friends were safe. So sad. He exchanged no words of conversation with any of the pub patrons sitting nearby; indeed in the days to follow some of them would remark how sad he had looked on that occasion. Like a man coming from a funeral, it was said.

He finished his brandy and rose from his seat. Clutching the cardboard box under his arm he walked towards the entrance. As he was just about to exit the barman, Murphy cried out "you're away then, Michael?"

Halfway out the door he paused, turned and stared back towards the bar. "What?" he cried, "Oh…yes…yes, I'm off to a funeral…to a funeral."

The barman retorted, "A funeral…and whose might that be?"

No reply was offered for the old man had exited on to the street. He now walked in the direction of Redmond Park. It was a place with which he was quite familiar. Before entering he stopped off at Courtneys hardware store and purchased a small hand trowel. Next he entered Dalys, a local florist. Here he purchased a single red rose. He entered the park, and, after discretely selecting a quiet corner he dug a small rectangular chamber in the ground. Into this he laid the cardboard box, on top of which he then laid the single red rose; he quietly uttered the following prayer:

"Go now my little friend to that new world far beyond, to soar and fly in the heavens, with all your pigeon friends; where death no longer reigns supreme, and the Sun it always shines, where no anguish nor anxiety will ever trouble your little mind. There you will fly and flap your wings in great happiness evermore, no unkind words ever pierce your heart, now, nor forever more."

He filled in the little grave, then rose up and left the park. He returned directly to his apartment. For the next two weeks he was not seen in public. He had failed to collect his pension, and friends began to be concerned as to his whereabouts. The police were called and receiving no answer the hall door was forced open. Mrs Reynolds, a neighbour assisted. There was no immediate sign of the old man; then, entering the bedroom they were horrified to see him stretched out on the bed, dead. His arms were folded crossways across his chest, and clasped between his joined hands was a crucifix and a long white feather. Beside him was a card which read "Happy 70th Birthday Mr Donovan." It was from Mrs Reynolds. Scribbled across it were the words "Murderers! Murderers!"

Presently an ambulance was called for and the body removed. As the police officer and Mrs Reynolds were leaving they stared at the white feather which had falling on to the floor. The guard bent down and picked it up, looked at Mrs Reynolds for several seconds without saying a word then, both bending their heads, left the apartment together in silence.

A Hearing For The Dead

"ABOUT TIME TOO," HE RASPED OUT indignantly, "Waiting nearly two hours, ridiculous."

"Its not our fault," cried the nurse, "We are very understaffed, you know."

But Sean Rafferty didn't know. He didn't want to understand. He had been waiting for two hours to see a doctor. His patience had run out. Suddenly the entrance doors were pushed open and two ambulance men entered with an injured man on a trolley, his shirt all soaked in blood.

"Road accident?" enquired the porter, as he held back the plastic doors.

"Murder, murder!" exclaimed the driver. "Desperate accident - absolute carnage! Two more on the way in - one dead. Terrible."

The crowd in the waiting room listened in silence. One lady was seen to turn pale at the sight of the blood; a young girl rose from her seat and quickly left the room. No one spoke. The accident victim was quickly ushered into the surgery area. As the inner plastic doors closed Sean noticed two doctors rush to assist the victim. Outside one of the waiting crowd spoke to Sean.

"Terrible business these car accidents. What does be the matter with them at all? Driving like lunatics; will they ever get sense?"

"Course it's the drink I blame. You wouldn't know who were the worst—the young people or the adults."

"It's all this so called prosperity we're experiencing," replied Sean, "It's gone to their heads. They don't have time to be caring about other people anymore: stiffer jail sentences—that's what's needed. Please God the poor devil won't be too bad."

Sean looked intently at the respondent. He was about thirty or thirty-five years old, of medium build, wore a polar-necked sweater and Wrangler jeans, and had two teeth missing from the right hand side of his upper jaw. This gave his face a somewhat distorted appearance.

"Let us hope you are right," replied Sean, "The poor devil looked in a bad way. It's the pressures people are under nowadays that is causing all these accidents, fuelled of course by heavy drinking. Some people will never learn that drinking and driving don't mix."

As he spoke he noticed a clergyman reading his breviary. He hoped that he would be saying a prayer for the latest victim that had just been wheeled in. Silence once more descended upon the room, and save for a quite whisper from a visitor checking in at the reception, no one spoke.

Sean rose from his seat, and taking some coins from his pocket walked over to the food-dispensing machine and bought a chocolate bar. As he resumed his seat the nurse returned and called in the next patient "Mr Collins please, Mr. Collins?"

A gentleman seated two rows behind rose quickly and followed the nurse into the surgery. A short while later the silence was broken by the arrival of a young man in his early to mid-twenties. He staggered somewhat as he approached the waiting room. He quickly occupied the seat previously vacated. He seemed out of sorts, uneasy in his movements, nervous like; he wore a shabby looking brown suit.

Sean, glancing in his direction, smiled. He hoped this gesture of friendship would put the man at ease. The young man took a bottle of vodka from inside his jacket. Others, noticed this and their disapproving looks immediately began to upset him. He grunted across at one individual in particular.

"Well, what are you looking at!" he roared out.

The other remained silent. Having drunk a mouthful of the liquid he turned his head downwards, and stared at the floor.

Just then the hospital porter, having observed that the man was drinking, crossed over the hall and ordered him to leave. He pretended not to hear. The porter renewed his call, "You have to move, sir; no drinking on hospital premises."

"I'm okay, okay, is…alright…don't worry," replied the stranger. These words he uttered without raising his head.

The porter persisted, "Come now, we must not hang about; good sir you must leave the premises, please. Drinking is not allowed."

"Can't go…can't leave…must rest," exclaimed the young man. He raised his head and looked straight at the porter. The lights on the ceiling reflected in greater detail the contours of his face. It was pale and haggard looking, as if suffering from exhaustion; his eyes were sunken into his head, while his hands were scarred and cut like as if he had been in a fight, or an accident. The porter turned away, not persisting with his request. The young man bent over and stared once more at the floor.

"Sad," cried Sean to the person sitting next to him, "sad how some people let themselves go, isn't it? And he only a young man. He can't be more than twenty-four years old."

"Course it's the demon drink again," remarked the other, "Kills many a person, the same booze."

With that the lad began singing. "Hello...hello to Shamus...sham O'Reilly, where are you...you, now. Dump, dum–dum, hey, hey, Waaas the matter?"

Everyone, except the reverend father on the right, turned their heads towards the singer, some with smiles of amusement on their faces; all could see he was drunk. One elderly lady seated slightly to the left of Sean continued to stare, her face expressing a look of sadness. Sean noticed a tear coming from her eyes.

The porter again approached the young man, "You will have to leave, sir; there is no singing allowed in the hospital: come now. You must leave."

"Oh leave him," shouted the old woman sitting on the left, "Can't you see he is not well in himself; he only wants to rest for a while."

"He is drunk, madam," roared the porter, "and singing is not allowed in the accident and emergency area, or anywhere in the hospital. He must either stay quiet, or leave."

The young man bowed his head in silence. The porter moved back towards the entrance, without saying another word. Then the woman who had spoken turned to the rest of the group. "The trouble is some people don't understand how life is for young people today. We are all afflicted by some difficulty or other." Looking over at the porter she continued: "if there were more understanding in the world, I suspect there might be fewer people sick."

Nobody spoke.

The old lady turned her head towards the window, and appeared to be weeping. Just then the nurse entered the waiting room.

"Mr Mulberry...Mr Mulberry please...Mulberry?"

"That's me," cried a voice from the rear of the room. The nurse retreated, followed by an elderly man with a slight limp, both quickly disappearing into the surgery.

Suddenly the young man began to sing again, "And, and...I know you will re...turn—return to me, the long lost love of my...m...y—Life, and then will come-come, my happiness to me—to me once mo...more, moo....Oree..."

Placing his head between his hands he ceased singing almost as quickly as he started. Putting one hand across his eyes he began to sob.

For Sean the silence was deafening. Turning towards the old lady on the left he noticed that she was still staring out the window. Just up from her the clergyman placed his head into the palms of his hands, then, turning the page of his breviary, continued on reading.

The porter approached the young man, and, taking him by the arm escorted him from the room.

"Leave off; leave off I say! I'm going. And I won't be back! I'm going back to my drunken friends...they're the only friends I have. You people don't understand how I feel. Don't think of me tonight when I'm sleeping rough in...in some back street or lane!" he roared

His eyes glowed fiercely. Sean was struck by their intensity. He stumbled against the wall, the dishevelled and worn-out condition of his clothes becoming more obvious to all in the room.

"I'm going...I'm going," he roared, "going to the only place where a man can get a hearing, or feel at home among friends; for it is there I'll be welcome; it's there I'll get a hearing: they know…they understand."

As he slowly departed through the plastic doors everyone was struck by the forlorn and melancholy expression on the strangers face. The clergyman in the front row suddenly stopped reading.

The old lady turned from looking out the window, and left the waiting room. As she did so she turned towards the porter, exclaiming "The young man is right; he's right to go back to his alcoholic friends, for it is only among the dead, is there a hearing for the dead!"

Just before passing out through the plastic doors she turned and looked scornfully towards those seated in the waiting room. The silence only interrupted by the entrance of the nurse, as she called for the next patient. "McCarty …Reverend McCarty, please."

The clergyman rose from his seat, folded shut his breviary, and with bowed head followed the nurse into the surgery.

A Child Called Star

This is the story of a child called Alakie, a small Star that appeared one night in the Heavens close to the Starry Plough. Alakie had been orphaned after Opas, the family of which he was part, were lost forever after entering the 'Black Hole', in the Heavens. With underdeveloped energy levels, Alakie, a junior Star, struggled to stay alive so that his mission to direct light upon the Earth could be satisfactorily fulfilled.

Eventually he succeeded in achieving his goal, thanks to the loving smiles radiated from Earth by thousands of children, and in particular one child called Robert.

Opas, the family of which he was part, had occupied a most favoured place in the heavens. It was much respected by all the heavenly bodies. Alakie was a child of the Opas constellation, which accompanied the family when it travelled in the universe, and particularly when it came to light up the sky. Alakie loved these trips, and though his energy levels were not fully developed, and the strength of his light limited, he was able to shine a little light upon Earth, which pleased him much.

All the heavenly bodies, including Opas enjoyed many

happy hours lighting up the Sky. Each Star had a particular job to do, and for thousands of years attended their tasks in a most satisfactory manner. That is until one night Opas, breaking the rules of the Cosmos, abandoned its designated route and entered the Black Hole, a place specifically forbidden to all Stars. Only once in the history of the Cosmos was a Star ever allowed to stray away from its appointed location, and that was when the Star, Hope, was allowed to appear in the sky over Bethlehem to announce the birth and arrival of the son of God.

When Opas entered the Black Hole, it was swept into the Outer Regions, an area where fire, brimstone, and death ruled continuously. Opas never returned. Alaki, a son of the constellation who was not with the family that night, was heartbroken. Suddenly he was alone, and frightened. He knew that his special mission was to shine down on Earth in the coming years. He struggled to come to terms with what had happened; still his immediate task was to concentrate on growing and developing. Thus it came to pass that one day the Creator, father of the whole Universe came to Alaki to tell him that he must travel across the Heavens towards the planet Earth. There he must lodge himself close to the Plough and Stars. His special job would be to shine down on all the children living there, and to take special note of any child that seemed sad or unhappy. Any such that he noticed were to be his special concern. Where he saw any child that looked sad or unhappy, he must beam down his special light upon him or her. This was his great responsibility; he must discharge this duty faithfully.

Thus the fateful night came and he set out on his long journey. This he did with some trepidation for his energy levels were not as strong as they should be. Fear stalked his soul as he went on his lonely way, sad that Opas, the family were not by his side. Eventually he reached the perimeter of the Starry Plough. The long journey had depleted his Light Force, and it was with great difficulty he began to carry out his task.

He remembered the stories his father had told him of all the Stars that had fallen to Earth. Each Star had represented a young child that had failed to come home. Other Stars had died because they had failed to keep up their energy and Light Force, sufficiently well enough to enable them to rescue those unhappy children from Earth. Even so he drew faith and encouragement from what the Star Hope had achieved over Bethlehem all those years ago.

As he rested from his long journey he looked with some jealousy at the great beams of light that emanated from each of the Stars of the Starry Plough. He longed to be back with Opas, the family, to be part of that great constellation of Stars that travelled throughout the Universe where he had been so happy; alas, they were far away—gone, lost forever. He feared that he would die. Suddenly one of the Stars spoke to him, "Do not look so sad my friend, for tonight you are in good company. We seven have been stationed here for many years and are very happy at our job of shining down our light upon planet Earth. Soon you to will feel the same so do not be sad. Focus your light upon the children of the Earth; communicate with them and they too will communicate back to you. For every child has his or her own special Star in the Heavens."

Alaki was much encouraged by what he heard. He looked upon the Starry Plough with great admiration, for they did glow greatly each giving off great light. He felt that one day he too, when fully grown up would have great energy—great light, which he could beam across the Universe and down on Earth, bringing great happiness to all the Humans—particularly the children. The nights passed quickly. He grew older, stronger, drawing hope and encouragement from his companions. He noticed too that his Light Levels, were getting brighter and stronger: he was most encouraged.

One night a strange thing happened. He was about his duty, as were all the Stars in the sky, when suddenly he heard a strange cry coming from a particular corner of the Earth. It was a cry of anguish and sorrow and so much did it penetrate into the heart of his being, he trembled with fright. He noticed too that all the other Stars began to twinkle much more than usual, for they too were disturbed by what they had heard. Alaki immediately concentrated his light beam on the spot from where the cry came. He discovered that it was a little boy huddled on a stairway balcony of a block of newly built apartments—tears flowing from his eyes. Alaki was deeply troubled by what he saw.

Now it had long been common knowledge among the Heavenly bodies scattered throughout the Universe, that Stars—through their beams of light—were powerful communicators, both to animate and inanimate objects; Alaki was particularly pleased about this and, this being his first chance to help, he went about it eagerly. Summoning all his available energy he immediately concentrated his light beam down upon the child, who at once raised his head and looked towards the sky. This was most pleasing to Alaki who, in his immediate sense of excitement, named him Little Star. He observed the boy wipe the tears—first from one eye, then the other. He then stood up and, looking skywards, appeared as if hypnotised by the beaming light; suddenly he spoke, "O beam of Starry light," he cried as again he wiped the tears from his eyes, "how happy and bright you look this night! Yet here am I —the product of an unhappy marriage, a father that drinks excessively and beats my mother—I am without brother and sister, cast out here into the darkness and oh of such unhappy heart:

> Will you spare a thought for me?
> O twinkling Star of the Heavenly skies?
> And will you find my guardian angel,
> And ask him to bring happiness to me,
> If not, soon my heart will break."

Alaki was deeply troubled. His energy level dropped. His light beam weakened. Its strength ebbing and flowing up and down for several minutes: he thought he too was going to die. Now it is well known throughout the Universe that it is only by maintaining an "inner strength" that all the Heavenly bodies are able to overcome evil and continue to do good; to hold their positions in space, and be an inspiration to the Creator, and a comfort to each other. He recalled what his father had said to him: "Always remember son that to defeat evil and promote the good it was essential that you focus your entire mind, your complete will, on the task before you. Further, that evil could only triumph when its strength becomes greater than that of 'good will,' hence the importance of retaining energy levels to their maximum at all times. Good will and love are the life forces that protect all. They are the driving forces that keep the peace; they have bonded together all the Heavenly bodies since the beginning of time."

Alaki, stirred by recalling his fathers' words was filled with renewed energy; he focussed his mind on the Good.

He beamed his light back to the boy on Earth. Again he recalled the many encouraging words of advice his father had given him, particularly those about happiness. He repeated in his mind what he had said, "always remember son that to bring happiness to all you must concentrate your thoughts, and your entire energy beam on placing happiness where it is most needed; for Will is the life force that triumphs over all adversity; Will is the son, the child that destroys all evil: the one thing that strengthens and unifies the Universe, keeping peace and harmony throughout."

He again focused his mind on the little boy on Earth. He beamed his light straight at his head. The effect was electrifying! The boy began to smile. Alaki was much pleased. "O how right my father was!" he exclaimed, "For now do I feel my energy, my inner strength rising within me; now do I see the way of the Good." He looked down at the Earth again and was pleased to see that the boy was still smiling. So intense became Little Star's smile that their two minds energised together: they now acted as one. Alaki had successively beamed down to Little Star the energy of life, the Good, the gift of the Creator. He was very pleased. He knew that his message was being received loud and clear. Wonderful!
Looking around the Heavens he noticed that the light from the Moon was stronger than usual. Also that the Stars of the Starry Plough shone brighter; all the Stars glowed so brightly it seemed that the whole Universe had become bright as day. His energy level continued to rise and he now felt that he was experiencing the dawn of manhood, of adult maturity: he now felt equal in stature to all the Stars in the Heavens. The feeling was good. Suddenly his moment of happiness was interrupted, for Little Star had stopped smiling. A great noise was heard of roaring, shouting, and screaming

as his parents entered on the balcony fighting and clawing at one another. Little Star became greatly upset. His spirit was shaken. He began to cry. Still his parents kept fighting, oblivious of the sorrow that disturbed and weakened their son's very soul. Suddenly, in the continuing tussle the boy's father pushed awkwardly against him, knocking him over the balcony; it was a tragic mistake for the boy fell fifty feet to his death. Both parents immediately stopped fighting, so horror-struck were they at what happened. They raced down the stairs to the bottom of the apartment block to find their son stretched out dead on the roadway. The anguish of both was uncontrollable. Neighbours and passers by quickly gathered around the boy. In the Heavens the light from millions of Stars began to flicker on and off; entire constellations were seen to shake. Some Stars fell dead from the night sky; a terrible calm suddenly gripped the skies; the Moon lost its brightness and became pale as death. The triumph of Evil over Good, over the death of innocence, shook the very foundations of the Universe: Alaki was shocked. His energy level and light beam weakened: sadness engulfed his soul. The energy levels and light beams of the Starry Plough also weakened, though they soon recovered. They moved quickly to help Alaki.

"Do not be distressed, Alaki," they cried in unison, "There are many such thoughtless and careless parents down on Earth; they don't understand the terrible hurt they visit upon their children. They are too selfish and uncaring to realise the damage they cause."

"Alas!" cried the Starry Plough, "that such things should happen; their selfish and endless fighting scars the whole Planet. Tonight Alaki you will fulfil your mission; this night you will bring home this little boy to take his place among the Stars. Each Star in the Heavens is that of a little boy who suffered badly on Earth, but the Creator took all of them up into the Heavens so that their innocence and love could be part of the Starry constellations that light up the Universe. This dead boy will be one of those Stars. This night you will place him there."

"This terrible happening has shaken me," cried Alaki, "My energy level is weakened; my strength has faded: surely the task is beyond me?"

"Never!" roared the Starry Plough, "A special place has been given to you here in the Universe, a place of honour, with an important job to do. This is why you were saved from the Black Hole. Tonight you begin to fulfil your mission; you must do as all Stars do when they come under emotional attack: you must concentrate your energy field, focus your whole mind on the Good, and beam down your field of light, upon this dead boy. You must call forth his spirit into the Heavens and there he will take his place with the rest of the Stars that light up the Universe. This is the beginning of your mission; focus, think—concentrate your mind: begin your great task, now."

Alaki looked at the Starry Plough. Their lights now beamed with a force and intensity that was a joy to behold. They were an inspiration to him: he was much encouraged. He looked around at all the other millions of Stars as they focused their Light Beams in his direction. Softly they whispered, "We await, Alaki, for our brother, Little Star, whom you bring home to us this night, and whose place among the constellations, reserved, shall be bright, ever bright."

Alaki thrilled to hear these soft voices as they travelled across the Heavens, and to see the many Stars that twinkled as they spoke.

He looked once more upon the dead body of Little Star. Again sorrow threatened to block out his Light Beam. He summoned forth with great intensity his energy field, the field of Good Will, and quickly gained strength. His Light Beam glowed stronger; his strength swelled up within him: now he felt ready for the task before him. He looked once more upon the sad spectacle on Earth. The distraught parents could not be consoled. They wept bitterly. Alaki focused his Light Beam down on the dead boy's body. Looking straight into his eyes he called again and again for him to rise up; however, Little Star did not stir. Alaki took fright and felt that his power was gone. He felt weak and the more he reflected on the fact that he was unable to bring Little Star home, the more frightened he became.

Just then a voice called out "Always remember son, that to defeat Evil and secure the Good it is essential that you concentrate your mind, your whole energy, on the task before you..."

It was the voice of his father, echoing and re-echoing in the inner consciousness of his mind what had been said to him in the past. His father's voice kept repeating the message, and, slowly Alaki began to feel his strength returning in ever increasing waves. His Light Beam grew brighter and stronger. The Stars of the Starry Plough smiled happily: it was time to bring Little Star home.

Alaki focused his Light Beam once more upon the boy. So concentrated was the light, and so bright it covered the entire corner where he lay. The small crowd that had gathered took fright at seeing this. No one could explain it; no one spoke. The boy's parents felt a strange presence about; the light too confused them.

Alaki spoke. His voice travelled along the Light Beam

that bore down from the Heavens. "Come home, Little Star, come home," he cried, "Take your place in the Heavens where your innocence and love will shine amid the Starry constellations that light up the sky."

A deadly silence fell upon those standing about; they all appeared like statues, as if in an hypnotic state. The Light Beam maintained its presence for several minutes, then slowly began to recede back into the sky. A strange, smiling expression appeared on the boy's face; a warm, contented look that was most pleasing to behold. Alaki was in direct communication with Little Star's spirit as it travelled up into the Heavens. The energy between them both radiated out magnetically. Soon he arrived close to Alaki and next to the Starry Plough. Immediately joy and happiness radiated throughout the Universe. The Stars of the Starry Plough danced in joy while millions of Stars twinkled and danced in an ecstacy of happiness; the spirit of Little Star—now turned Star, also began to twinkle and dance—just like all the other Stars.

Little Star was home.

As the nights passed he grew stronger and stronger, and soon his place was firmly fixed in the Starry constellation that lit up the Universe.

Now he too, just like Alaki, would shine down on Earth, paying particular attention to all the children, being ever watchful for any child that seemed sad or lonely. He was happy, very happy, yet he could not forget his mother and father. There were moments when he wished that he were back on Earth, sitting on his favourite chair beside them, for he loved them dearly.

He grieved for them for he knew that they were very unhappy. As the weeks passed he became more troubled at what he saw. He resolved to help them. Yet what could he do? He was not as strong as the Stars of the Starry Plough. His heart became sad. Alaki, observing this spoke to him, thus: "Be not unhappy, Little Star, over the troubled state of your parents down on Earth. Yes they grieve deeply as do many other Humans also. Many and varied are the foolish things they do; they cannot help it, for they are of flesh and blood. Millions of them choose unwisely the road they take in life, and they pay dearly for their mistakes; yet the Creator, who controls and directs the whole Universe, loves them. He does not condemn them, for he loves them dearly. I will ask the Starry Plough to increase the energy flow and intensity of your Light Beam, when they do you must begin at once to concentrate your thoughts on the spirits of both your parents; you must focus your mind on thoughts of Good Will, you must reach out to them in your mind: soon they will hear you and look to the skies in an effort to reach you. Then you must intensify your Light Beam on them both. You must energise it in a way that your mind and theirs shall become one. When this happens you will know that they have reached you: your love for them and their love for you will have connected. Harmony and peace will reign, not only for you here in the Heavens, but also for them on Earth."

Little Star listened to the wise thoughts of Alaki, and determined to act. Two nights later, on a bright Moonlit night, his parents were out walking along the local seashore; it was something they had become used to doing ever since the death of their son. It was peaceful here, the solitude lending comfort to the anguish of their troubled souls; they were still haunted by the tragic death of their son. Millions of Stars twinkled in the firmament of the Heavens this night. Little

Star was there holding his watching brief upon Earth as was his duty. He observed his father and mother walking along the strand. He felt the sorrow in their hearts. He was much troubled.

He immediately summoned up his innermost energy and concentrated his Light Beam on them with great intensity. As his Light Beam grow stronger and brighter he felt an inner power of great strength as he began to focus it down on Earth. Suddenly he heard a noise, or what he thought was a voice, or voices coming towards him in the Heavens. He wasn't sure. Were these the voices of his parents? He listened intently.

"See how the Stars twinkle in the Heavens tonight, my dear," cried his mother.

"Indeed," replied his father. "Isn't it wonderful how they brighten up the sky: they are a delight to watch."

Little Star's heart throbbed; they were indeed the voices of his parents. He grew excited. His father noted a look of sadness on his mother's face. He turned to comfort her, "Do not be sad my dear, for I know what you are thinking, it is about our Robert. I'm thinking of him too; he was our pride and joy."

She did not speak in reply. Instead she suddenly began to stare up at the Stars, and one Star in particular. She became very excited and drew her husband's attention to it. "Look, look!" she cried, "Out there—he's there—the one with the brightest beam: it's him. I know it is! It's our little Robert; he's up there with the Stars. Don't you hear his voice? See how bright he shines. Listen George: do you not hear his voice?"

By now her husband had thought she taken leave of her senses. He drew slightly away from her before speaking. He turned and looked up to the Heavens, and in particular to the Star she had referred to. To his surprise he too noticed that it shone more brightly than all the rest. He thought of their son Robert, of how he had died, and how he and his wife had been responsible for his death. His thoughts whirled round in his head as he tried to comfort his wife. He exclaimed to her, "Where, where my dear do you see our son?" as he put his arm around her shoulder to comfort her.

"There, there!" she cried, "The Star just to the right of the Starry Plough. See, my husband, how it beams down towards you and me; it's our Robert—I just know it is!"

Tears flowed from her eyes as she spoke. Slowly she gained control of herself. Her husband stared up at the Star as it shone brightly in the sky; he too noticed how it seemed to focus its light beam directly at them. With his arm firmly around his wife's shoulder, they paused, looked skywards, reflected.

Little Star knew that he had caught their attention. He spoke thus, "Do not fear for me, dear father and mother, for in the Heavens above you I rest, bright, shining—at peace. I am part of the constellation of Stars that light up the Universe; I am so happy here with the Creator. He controls and directs all life here: happiness reigns everywhere. Know that I pray every night for you both for I love you dearly. You are never more to be sad or lonely for I am truly happy here. When the Starry constellations are at work in the Heavens, you are always to look skywards for me, for I shall shine brightly always on you both. Do remember always that when I focus my light down upon you that I am your son, Robert. I have a new name now; now I am called Star—a child called Star. I shall be looking out for you both, always."

His parents received this message almost in a state of

trance; yet as they heard it, suddenly, sorrow left their souls; spiritual renewal embalmed their whole bodies: they knew they were forgiven their terrible mistake.

Against a background of rippling sea waves that raced ashore along the coastline, they continued their walk under a bright Moonlit sky. The Stars in the Heavens shone brightly that night, many twinkling on and off; yet for them one particular Star shone greater than all the rest; it was their son Robert. For them he was the brightest Star of all.

Daniel Murphy
King Of The Fairies

DANIEL MURPHY ROSE FROM BED at 3:30 PM on that particular afternoon. He felt refreshed, and was looking forward to his walk. Since moving to the country three years ago he took a regular walk on Tuesday afternoon of each week. He loved the open countryside. The various types of trees in all their variegated greenery gave the surrounding landscape an inspiring and picturesque appearance that he found uplifting. It was early summer and there was freshness in the air reflected in the plant life all around. The grass looked greener and fresher than usual; the hawthorn bushes were covered in white; the daisies fluttered gently in a slight breeze, and the singing of the birds in the hedgerows echoed a symphony of song, which he found a delight to his ear.

He thought of the famous composers, Bach, Mozart, and thought how they were rivalled in the wonder and beauty of these birds in song, and the rhythm of the blackbirds mating melody, and the skylarks enchanting song.

His walk took him down Courtland's lane, a short distance before he crossed a small field leading in the direction of the fairy mound—sometimes referred to as Leprechaun Hill. He was enchanted by this hill ever since the local villagers had told him about it. Some said it was the home of the "little people"—or Fairies—the spiritual home of the long passed Celtic tribe, the *Tuatha De Danaan*. He didn't take much notice of what they said, accept for old Garner; he was ninety-seven years old, and had a reputation as the local historian. He was very convincing in what he had to say. He encouraged Shaun to be circumspect about the hill, and in particular not to walk across it, instead he should walk around it, if at any time passing that way. "The fairies would be very put out," he cried, "if their privacy were disturbed." In deference to the old man's words Shaun made it a rule to respect his wishes. He set off at a steady pace. Arriving at the base he rested for a short time in the grass before going further.

He gazed upon the hill intensely before deciding to move on. Two choices faced him; if he went left of Leprechaun Hill he would find himself walking across McCormack's farm; he did not want to do that! McCormack was not partial to strangers walking on his land; he liked his privacy. His great-grandfather had been active in the Land League in the 1880's and had been jailed for agitating for land reform. Everyone knew how jealous he was of his few acres. Though it was the shorter route to his destination, he determined to go right instead. This would mean going the long way around to the Wad stream, but it could not be avoided. He would not cross McCormack's land.

He headed off at a cracking pace and soon reached the stream. This was his favourite place. Often he would come here to rest on the sloping green banks and watch the gentle waters flow past. It was midday and the sun shone brightly. He sat down, stretching out his long legs—the more to rest easy. Soon he was fast asleep and he began to dream. In his dream he heard voices calling "Come away Daniel Murphy, come to the fairy mound! Come away, come away where the land is fair and grand."

For several seconds the voices persisted. He suddenly opened his eyes and there before him stood three small fairies dancing and waving to him to follow them. He stared pointedly at them for several seconds, after which they slowly turned and beckoned him to follow, as they walked across McCormack's field. As he walked after them he continually heard their voices cry out:

"Come Daniel Murphy, pace yourself along,
For soon we must reach the fairy fort, before
The darkness comes along." "Before the darkness
Comes, before the darkness comes along!"

As they progressed on their way the three little fairies danced and sang to Murphy's amusement; occasionally one of them would look back to make sure he was keeping up. Soon they all reached the edge of the great big green mound, otherwise known as Leprechaun Hill. Suddenly one of the fairies turned and spoke to him.

Take the shoes off your feet and rest upon the grass,
For soon we three will enter here to see if you can pass;
And if the king is pleased after checking the history of
Your clan, then by God the door shall open and you may
follow on. But if the story is otherwise, then by
heaven he shall roar, and the earth shall open up - and
swallow you where you stand.

Murphy trembled with fright. Suddenly the three fairies

disappeared. He sat upon the grass and commenced to put on his shoes again. He was just about to lace up the first shoe when suddenly a voice roared out. "Off with that shoe, Murphy!" cried a fairy standing by, "prepare to meet your king! Enter now the fairy mound where the feast is about to begin. But first put on this coat of green, this green hat upon your head, for you must look like a fairy folk, if your not to be killed instead."

Murphy took off the shoe again and raised himself up. He quickly took off his own jacket and laid it on the ground, then, quickly put on the coat of green, and the green hat upon his head. Then, turning he saw to his amazement, ten fairies, all dancing, round and round.

"Come follow us immediately," cried they one and all, " You're invited to the fairy mound, and its wonderful banqueting hall." Just then to his amazement, as he stood and stared thereon, the roof of the fairy mound rose up before them all. "Come quickly now," cried the fairies, "let us go on in and join the fairy folk, who are now about to dance."

Murphy approached the entrance, swaggering forward in his green coat, he felt like king of the fairies, though he dare not start to boast. Soon he was upon the floor, a most strange sight to behold, as all the little fairies pulled his green coat— urging him to take the floor. He looked in the distance and there upon a throne, stood Amos, King of the Fairies, urging him on some more. Without further ado he placed his shoes back on, and in company of the fairies, they all roared, danced, and sang.

Then King Amos left his throne and joined Murphy on the floor, and together with the fairies they together danced some more. Amos spoke to Murphy, and this he had to say: "I knew your grandfather Murphy, long before he hit the clay!

We strolled and talked many a time down by McCormack's way, for he loved us wee folks always, forever and a day. Now pay careful attention to what I have to say, for it concerns your very future, and this mound of earthen clay; for hundreds of years past this hill has been our home but is shortly to be sold. At Reilly's auction in the town, set for this day next week, the farm and its possessions will there and then be sold. There'll be bids for Rafferty's farm, and our dear Leprechaun hill, which fills us all with fear, for which we now do seek your help."

Murphy listened with mixed curiosity to what the king of the fairies had to say, and was about to reply to his comments, when lo and behold the music struck up most loud. Soon the floor was filled with lots of fairy folk dancing to a host of Celtic airs, yet Murphy could not see any musicians anywhere!

"Ho, ho!" roared one fairy, "God bless Brian Boru!"

"Aye," roared another, "and the great Cuchulain too!"

"We want you to attend the auction," continued the King, "and buy the land; we'll give you the gold to do so. There is however one condition, and it is this: after you get the purchase deeds to the property you are to immediately insert a clause, duly witnessed, that this green mound, which we call Leprechaun Hill, must never—never under any circumstances be in any way disturbed, or sold. This is our ancestral home since long before the coming of St. Patrick; it is the entrance to the Kingdom of the Fairies; it is our little paradise; it's the place we call our home. Do you understand?"

"Perfectly, said Murphy. "It shall be done as you ask."

"Good!" cried the King, "In the meantime know this, that for your reward you will return to this fairy mound on the day after you receive the deeds. You will re-enter here—and you shall have as much gold as you like to take away. You will be a rich man Daniel Murphy! And in the human world you shall live like a lord of old. You shall be called Sir Daniel Murphy!"

Murphy's eyes lit up. "Gold, wealth, my own farm! I shall live like a king!" he thought. He could hardly contain his excitement.

"Come," cried the King, "to an inner chamber we'll go, there I'll feast your eyes on buckets of pure gold; with this you'll buy the farm, and save our fairy mound and by St. Patrick we'll retain our home from home, where future generations of fairy folk shall continue to dance around!"

Murphy and the King now danced their way into an inner chamber which was full of gold pieces; Murphy stared with amazement at the sight before his eyes: for several seconds he was speechless. He reached out to touch one of the bars, but the king quickly intervened: "Ah-ah!" cried the King, "You must not touch till first permission is granted."

They both looked at each other for several seconds, neither speaking. Over in one corner of the room Murphy had noticed a lone fairy busily mending shoes; he worked oblivious of their presence. Suddenly he stopped working, looked across at the King, raised the green cap from his head, and winked. "Now," exclaimed Amos, "now you may touch the gold."

Murphy did not speak; instead he reached out and touched one of the gold pieces. Immediately his body temperature rose, he sweated slightly, his imagination whirled in his head. His mind filled with thoughts of the future. King Amos put his hand on his shoulder. "Come," cried the King, "It's time for you to leave."

They both danced their way back into the main banqueting hall, where the King once more sat upon his throne. He cried out "Remember, Daniel Murphy! Two weeks from today you will come and stand on the east side of this fairy mound, after which you will be re-admitted herein; if you have the deeds with you shall have your reward; if not you shall be taken to that inner chamber where the glint of the gold shall deprive you of your sight. This land you shall never see again. Do you understand?"

The sight of the gold dazzled Murphy; he struggled to reply. "Yes, yes," he replied, "I understand. Two weeks from today on the east side of the fairy mound. It shall be as you ask."

"Good," replied the king, "This very day when you return home to your cottage you shall be met by Felim, keeper of the fairy mound. He will tell you where the gold is that you will use to buy the land. You will hide it away till the day of the auction. Mind that it is not stolen."

King Amos sat back in his throne. The music and dancing continued as all the fairies laughed and danced to their heart's content. The roof of the mound suddenly lifted. Murphy mounted the steps and climbed out.

After standing still for several minutes he finally commenced the walk home. As he went he reflected a curious sight. With his green coat and pointed green hat he was the subject of amusement by the several folks he passed. As he came within sight of his cottage he met Biddy Flanagan on her way to Town. She roared at him, "Daniel Murphy! Is it to the tailors you've been for a new coat and hat? Or to the fairy folk it seems!" She broke into hysterics of laughter. "You'll mind now they don't take you!" she roared. Murphy did not answer. Instead he confined his response to a short wave of the hand and hurried along. Soon he reached the front door of his cottage. He opened the door and entered.

Sitting on a log by the fireplace was the fairy known as "Felim, Keeper of the Fairy Mound." He quickly introduced himself, then instructed Daniel to follow him out to the garden. At the bottom of the garden, just behind a clump of bushes he showed Daniel a large pot of gold, which glittered intensely in the late afternoon sun. "Here," cried the fairy, "is the gold you are to have, to buy Tom Rafferty's farm and our mound of fair green land. See that you guard it and attend to our request; to save the home of the fairies—we know you'll do your best."

Murphy stared at the gold for several minutes, and then, turning to respond to the fairy, was shocked to see that he was gone. He looked here and there—up and down the garden—but the little fellow was gone, disappeared! He turned his eyes once more upon the bucket of gold pieces, and soon greedy thoughts began to enter his mind. They refused to go away. Still, he remained firm; he was an honourable man: he would fulfil his task. He would not disappoint King Amos. With the gold safely hidden away he once more retired indoors to rest for the night.

For the next few days he went about his business, and in his various visits back and forth to the town, because of his Leprechaun type dress, he was the source of much talk and speculation. Rafferty's farm was what occupied his mind, and his goal to secure it on the day of the auction. Eventually the day came and he promptly turned up at the appointed time. The auction commenced. Bids were quick and plenty.

He stood silent with his bag of gold on the ground beside him, as the bids continued. "£187,000!" roared one bidder.

This bid now out-bidding all others so far. There was silence for several seconds. No further bids were called. It was known for several weeks that several people were keen to acquire the farm; several anxious faces were to be seen about the room. The auctioneer was about to close; Murphy sensed this. He roared up, "£200,000…£200,000 I bid!"

Shocked murmured voices echoed around the room. Some asked questions about the bidder; some questioned if he had the money; others shouted in low voice, "It's the Leprechaun man: he's the bidder!" "How would he have such money and he only living in a cottage?" queried others.

However much was said there were no further bids for the farm to equal his, and so it went to him. In the ensuing few days much idle talk was heard about the town about Murphy; "And where in God's name would the likes of him get that kind of money?" quizzed one observer.

Speculation was rife, especially among the McCormacks. They were known to have had designs on securing the farm for themselves. No one could understand how he could have got the money; one old lady was heard to speculate that it was from the fairies that he had got it. Nobody took any notice. "Cracked," was how one commentator described her comment.

Murphy received his papers and returned home to his humble cottage. Soon he would make preparations to move into a new home and lands. For the present he forgot about the banqueting hall and King Amos; the fairies of Leprechaun Hill were the last things on his mind. Not having spent all the gold, the little remaining continued to dazzle his eyes each time he looked upon it. His mind was filled with thoughts of how he should spend it. In the coming weeks he sold the cottage and began to dress smartly. He then bought a new home. He sported a new car and began to frequent the town's hotels and more select pubs. He was generous with tips and in this way he soon overcame the animosity, which had previously been held against him for having acquired Rafferty's farm.

He carefully avoided giving any hint as to the source of his new-found wealth. None of the townspeople could wring the truth from him. Biddy Flanagan kept insisting that it was from the fairies that he had acquired the money; no one believed her: all felt she was cracked in the head. Murphy danced on. He soon became the dandy of the town.

The time appointed for his return to the fairy mound had passed, and though he had once or twice reflected on his failure to keep his promise, he did not trouble to go back. Then one night just after he had returned home, and as he was preparing to go to bed—a fierce rap was heard on the front door. He had been out drinking this evening; he was tired and the last thing he wanted—particularly at the late hour—were visitors.

With a sour, course expression on his face he thundered towards the front door, aggressively turned the handle and, pulling it open roared "Yes! What is it?"

There on the ground just on front of him was Felim, the Keeper of the Fairy Mound.

He cried out, "Daniel Murphy! You were to be back in the Fairy Mound to report upon your mission. You have failed to return! There is anger in the Kingdom of the Fairies; you are to return with me this very night to give an account of yourself. King Amos waits: you are to come with me immediately."

Murphy looked upon the fairy and, falling back against the hall door from shock, was speechless.

Fear gripped his whole body: he could not move.

"Come come, Daniel Murphy the very future of our home is at stake! The King waits! We have delayed our banquet till we know our fate!"

Murphy still did not speak. Then, in a flash of lightning, the fairy struck him with a wand. Murphy straightened up at once though now in a deep trance, appearing as one asleep. The fairy turned and walked away from the house, Murphy trailing behind. They both walked in the direction of the Fairy Mound. Soon they reached it. A humming noise was heard to come from inside. This was followed quickly by an eerie silence after which the roof of the mound opened up. Felim and Murphy entered. Hundreds of fairies were gathered about the banqueting hall, all looking sad: not a smiling face was to be seen. King Amos was seated in the centre of the floor. Then, touched by Felim's wand Murphy's eyes opened to look upon this august scene.

The king cried out, "Daniel Murphy the day has passed when you should have reported back, what now has come to pass! Did you buy this farm for us, together with this mound, that this our fairy homeland—be now safe and sound? Or have you took the other road and hoarded all our gold, that soon will see all us fairy folk—cast out upon the road! Give an account of yourself, and do it quickly now."

Murphy trembled where he stood. He could not find his voice. The king demanded the deeds from him; Murphy claimed they were lost. This angered the king greatly.

He jumped off his chair and roared, "Lost! You dare come here after the time you were instructed to return, and you say the deeds are lost! You are a liar sir! You do not even have your green coat and green hat. And where, sir, is our gold? We know that you only used half of it to buy the land: where is the other half? And look at your clothes? Last time you were here your garments were shabby; now you are dressed like a gentleman! We have seen our share of gentlemen, Mr Murphy; we saw them when they wore neat buckled shoes and the short waistcoat and high wigs; when they drove their coaches over the land—and the people—without any regard whatsoever. You have stolen our gold; you have behaved like a lord; you are not fit to be our friend. You will return immediately with the keeper of the mound to your house. There you will retrieve the deeds and return here at once!"

The king seated himself back down, and, with his left hand proceeded to adjust his crown. He did not speak. It was obvious his strong words had tired him. With a raised right hand he dismissed Murphy, crying, "Go! Immediately!"

In the company of Felim, they both left and began the walk back to Murphy's home. It was a moonlit night, calm and quiet. A fresh breeze was blowing. Travelling along they presented a curious sight; indeed in future days part of the gossip of the town would be this odd sighting of man and fairy marching across the Rafferty land! Soon they reached the house. Murphy, back in a trance, and following instructions from Felim, secured the deeds. They returned immediately to the mound. The King examined the title deeds. He was shocked to see that no clause had been inserted stating that whoever owned the land must never interfere with the mound. He called for pen and ink. He turned to Murphy. "Now sir," he cried, "you will write at the bottom of this document the following:

I, Daniel Murphy, being the owner of the lands outlined on these title deeds do hereby affirm that it is my solemn wish, both during the course of my lifetime, and that of my successors after my death, that the earthen hill, known as 'the fairy mound,' or, as it is called by some, 'the Leprechaun Hill', that this said hill—being the abode of the fairy folk—is not to be interfered with in any way, neither planted with trees nor flattened till at least 2000 years have passed. In pursuance of my wish I place these title deeds into the safe keeping of the town's public library, available always for public scrutiny.

Signed Daniel Murphy, gentleman."

Murphy did exactly as instructed by the King. The documents were then handed to Felim for lodgement into safe-keeping, after which they would be deposited in the library.

"And now," cried King Amos, as he sported an infectious smile on his face, "Now we will begin our banqueting dance! But first, our final words to you, Daniel Murphy. Because you sought to deceive us and steal our gold we place the following judgement upon your person: for 200 years you will disappear from off the face of the earth; you will wander about the heavens visiting one galaxy after another, and, to remind the townspeople about our wishes you will act—as directed by us from time to time, as guardian of this our home—appearing from time to time at our discretion by sitting on top of the mound wearing your green coat and green pointed hat. You will be the keeper of the mound; you will be the guardian of our home: This is our judgement for taking our gold. Now go."

Suddenly Murphy snapped out of his trance; he jerked himself upwards from the side banking flanking the Wad stream. He wiped his forehead for he was perspiring greatly. He rubbed both eyes profusely. As he made his way home that late afternoon he felt anything but well. He made himself a hot whiskey and went straight to bed. In the ensuing days some of the townspeople noticed that he was missing. On the odd occasion he would be seen wearing his green coat and pointed green hat. He would sometimes enter the bars and sit quietly alone, drinking. He never talked to anyone. Then one day some of the townspeople remarked that he was missing, for he had not been seen for some time. Then one night around ten o'clock Tim Jones, a local eccentric, burst into Fagan's bar: "Jesus, a whiskey quick Pat," he roared to the barman. As he struggled to the bar he tripped slightly and fell against a chair.

"What's the matter Jones?" replied Pat. "Are you ill," he asked as he quickly poured out a large whiskey.

"The Murphy lad...I seen him, I seen him sitting on the hill—the Fairy mound; Jesus I thought I was seeing a ghost!"

He reached out, lifted up the glass of whiskey and quickly swallowed a mouthful. "There, there he was, bold as brass— a big smile on his face and he sitting there in his big green coat and the pointed green hat, bang in the middle of the mound, his arms folded—smiling. I tell ye, the sight scared the daylights out of me. I'm not passing up that way again, no sir—never again."

As he finished speaking, three locals sitting nearby burst out laughing, much to Jones' annoyance.

"Give that man another double whiskey," one of them roared, as all three continued to laugh.

"Curses!" roared Jones, "is it taking me for a fool ye are? I tell ye I saw him there big as life, with that soft smile of his..."

"Was it a grin of despair?" asked one of those sitting close by.

"Or was it from taken with the drink that he smiled so, do you think?" asked another.

"Whatever it was it was very unpleasant to watch," cried Jones.

"All to do with the Rafferty land," cried Biddy Flanagan. "They wanted to hold on to it; didn't want the Fairy mound disturbed. The Murphy man was more the fool, she continued; he was the one that got the gold; he's the one the Fairies got. That hill will not be disturbed, for ill luck will visit any who interferes with it. You will not see him about this Town ever again, so ye won't, for the fairies have got him. He's keeper of the hill now and no-one dare go near it."

Those sitting close to her roared laughing; Jones, with a frightened look upon his face quickly finished his whiskey and left. Shortly afterwards Biddy Flanagan who had drank several drinks rose from her seat to leave. She cried out as she made for the exit, "To Daniel Murphy—King of the Fairies, king of the fairy mound. It's his new home and ye all better stay away…or ye all ill be taken, also!"

In the coming weeks Murphy failed to reappear about the town; then, at a meeting of the Town Council, the secretary read out a letter from him to the effect that he was going abroad for a time and could not affirm exactly when he would return. He further stated that it was his wish to leave the title deeds to the Rafferty land in the safe custody of the local librarian, and the said documents to be retained on the library premises

Till his return, he was never seen again in public. To this day it is locally recorded that from time to time a man wearing a green coat and a pointed green hat, smiling to himself, is to be seen sitting up on top of the fairy mound, otherwise known as, Leprechaun Hill, while a grey haired old woman—known locally by the name of Biddy Flanagan is occasionally heard chanting a toast as follows: "To Daniel Murphy, King of the Fairies, keeper of the fairy mound—our own Leprechaun Hill! Long may he reign!"

Judgement Of
The Three Chairs

THE STORY CENTRES AROUND A dream Richard Carey has, inspired by an appearance in the district court earlier in the day to watch the trial of his best friend's son, Brian Collins.

In the dream Carey reflects on the previous sixty years of his life, of the many good and bad things he perceives he has done, or not done. He is a very spiritually minded person; though only an infrequent churchgoer. He worries about dying before his time! He is really lacking in faith. He has recently turned sixty-five years of age.

Just before coming into the pub this evening he had a row with his wife. As he sits there drinking the incident plays on his mind. Added to this he is feeling a bit tired, and begins to doze off to sleep. In his sleep he has a dream. The story begins with a general discussion by some of the other drinkers sitting in the bar.

THE PUBLICAN. I see the Carey character is still here, Tim.

TIM MOONEY, *a barman.* Aye, there's no getting him out once he's had a row with the wife! Asleep again as usual.

CHARLIE RYAN. I still say it was a dangerous gamble to take 26,000 euros in Pack-link stocks was in my opinion an unwise move. For God's sake, man the Company has only been trading on the Exchange for just six months!

HUGH SPENCER. Yes Charles I know that, but just look at how well it has done in that short six month period, and moreover, its general performance since the Company was set up just three years ago.

CHARLIE RYAN. All very well! But what guarantee is there that its rapid rise will continue into the future? Trading conditions are getting tight on the world markets just now; plastics are not having an easy run. I think you are making a mistake on this one, Hugh.

Richard Carey was suitably positioned in the bar to be able to hear this and other conversations being carried on by the pub's patrons; he did not deliberately listen to what was being said, but given the size of his ears, and their range of hearing, hearing what was being said was not in the least difficult. However on this occasion what momentarily caught his imagination was the three chairs placed at the west wall of the bar; he likened them to three judge's chairs, the centre one about sixteen inches higher than the other two; made of a good, solid oak-like timber, they were well carved, and the more he looked at them, the more he felt they had a royal touch. They looked authoritarian; they reflected a sense of command, and coupled with the seating benches facing north and south, one could easily be forgiven for thinking one were sitting in the courtroom where he had been earlier in the day!

Richard Carey had a little too much to drink; and before leaving home that morning he had a row with his wife. He was tired and felt sleepy. Slowly he began to doze off. All around him conversation on various topics continued among the patrons. Soon he was comfortably adjusted in his seat, and fast asleep. Suddenly a strange voice beckoned to him.

"Richard Carey! Stand up at once and face the court. Clerk, read out the indictment."

The clerk, a neatly dressed court officer was clad in a two-piece outfit reminiscent of that worn by royal courtiers from way back in the seventeenth century. Carey stood up, looking very confused. The clerk read from several parchments of paper.

"Richard Carey, you stand accused before the honourable justices, here presiding, viz. Faith, Hope & Charity, of a multiplicity of criminal offences of a varied and diverse nature extending over sixty years, as follows:

1. That while attending junior school you acted the part of a school bully.

2. That you "jilted" one Catherine Ryan, leaving her standing at the altar, pregnant with child.

3. That all your life you were mean with money, refusing charity to those less fortunate than yourself.

4. That you ignored your wife was mean towards her and treated her poorly never once taking her on a decent holiday.

5. And various other sundry crimes that shall be entered in the court record."

"How do you plead?" asked the three judges.

A shaken and stunned Carey took several seconds to reply. "This is terrible," he cried. "What am I doing here?"

"How do you plead?" roared the clerk of the court. "Your answer, sir—at once."

"Not...not guilty," replied Carey. As he uttered these

words he slumped down in his chair and a cry was heard from the public gallery.

"Not guilty! Not guilty—rubbish!" roared a bald-headed man.

An elderly lady was seen to rise up in the gallery and wave her walking stick in Carey's direction; as she did so she cried out, "Felon, felon! I lived beside him all my life your worships, and a meaner man you never did meet!"

"Silence!" roared the three judges, together. "Clerk of the court would you kindly read out the details of the first deposition."

"Your Honour, I have here a sworn statement from one Horace Murphy, retired stockbroker of 66 Place Avenue, New York City, who outlines how the defendant, one Richard Carey, a former classmate, did bully and intimidate Mr. Murphy on numerous occasions when they both attended St. Thomas's primary school in the city of Dublin:

```
Horace Murphy Esq.,
66 Place Avenue, New York City
United States of America
To whom it may concern.


Dear Sirs,


Between 1947 and 1956 I attended St.
Thomas' Primary school in Dublin City. In
the class I attended was a fellow pupil,
Richard Carey, a boisterous, talkative,
greedy, and selfish and intimidating fellow
as ever you might meet in a day's walk! We
were the best of pals, and, as I seemed to
```

possess more of the goodies of life—which in our schooldays were usually bars of chocolate, sweets and the odd lollipop, I shared generously all of these with him never expecting anything in return. One day, while returning to school in his company, he asked me for a bar of chocolate; as I had none to give on this particular occasion he got quite angry and proceeded to slap me several times in the face. Needless to say I protested most strongly, but was immediately threatened that if I did not bring him a bar of chocolate by lunchtime on the following day, I would be severely trounced.

I was too scared to tell my parents, and to ensure that I did have the chocolate bar the next day I stole the money to purchase it from my sister's coat pocket.

Having succumbed to Mr. Carey's bullying and intimidation on this occasion the matter did not stop there; indeed it continued for several weeks and was reflected in some of the most embarrassing experiences in front of the other pupils that I had to endure.

Eventually I had to leave the school as my health was being affected...

"The plaintiff your honour goes on to detail some of the more embarrassing incidents referred too, and they are many and varied. Shall I read them out your worship?"

"Refrain for the present, Mr. Thaw," replied Judge Hope. "Prisoner at the bar, how say you to these charges?"

"Lies, all lies!" roared Carey, "I never once in my life interfered with him. It was he who asked me for sweets; why his father was a company director, and they were a well-off family—well-off but mean; and that's the truth of it. Didn't he have to leave the country when he was eighteen for getting Celia Jackson into trouble? Flee the country from the Jackson's—otherwise they were going to throw him into the river Liffey."

Townley, the state prosecutor interjected, "And what about the incident on the way home from school on May 23rd when, before several of his classmates, you deliberately pulled off Mr. Murphy's trousers and hung them high up on the blackthorn bush in Cooley's lane? Or the day you boxed the poor lad about the ears because he would not sing the song *Danny Boy*?"

"Your honour," continued the clerk of the court, "we have three further depositions from former classmates of Mr. Murphy's, setting out further incidents of a gross and disgusting nature; moreover, we submit documentary evidence from these classmates who cannot be present today as they are abroad in Australia, but who specifically request in writing that their testimony be admitted against the defendant as they too suffered at his hands."

The state prosecutor handed the depositions to the other judges, viz., Faith and Charity. They perused the documents for several moments, after which they handed them down to the Clerk of the court, who immediately began to read them out.

"Your Honour I will now read the next deposition which

comes from an elderly pensioner, one Thomas Neary, of 66 Rile Street, Manchester, England:

Dear Sirs,

I am delighted to have this opportunity to testify before this court upon the terrible suffering visited upon my daughter thirty years ago by that notorious man Carey, who because of his heartlessness turned the golden hair upon her head, to snowy-white and left her with a broken heart which has never mended even to this day!

In 1978, when my Catharine was in the prime of her youth, when the dazzling beauty of her eyes rivalled the sun, while the warmness of her engaging smile won hearts all around, this man Carey—who by deceits and lies burrowed his way into her affections, engaged her to marry, and then your worships—horror of horrors!—having made her pregnant promised to take her to the isle to marry, but on the day appointed—never turned up for the wedding! Jilted, left to fade in her bloom! From which she has never recovered! Sadness, sadness, your worships - it sent her poor mother to an early grave!

Oh can the court not feel the horrendous depths of loneliness and sadness to which her very soul was plunged after the execution of such a dastardly deed? There she stood—the very flower of womanhood in her wedding dress of satin white; a smile upon her face that would melt the coldest of hearts, and a love flowing from her bosom that warmed up the very chapel in which we all stood, waiting, waiting...Until at last she was finally abandoned on the steps of the holy altar and from which she continues to pine away to this very day. It is my fervent hope that righteous judgement will be visited upon this heartless miscreant for the cold and callous way in which my daughter was treated. Thank you your worships for patiently listening to my complaint.

Signed, Thomas Neary.
Manchester, England.

The three judges, Faith, Hope, and Charity, exclaimed forcefully upon hearing this tale.

"Dastardly!" roared Faith.

"Inhuman!" roared Hope.

"Murder most foul!" roared Charity. "A child abandoned—horrible."

Looking at the prisoner all three exclaimed together, "How say you to this deposition, Richard Carey? how do you plead?"

"Not guilty, not guilty!" roared Carey. "I was forced to the altar —forced I was. She knew I did not love her. I told her so many times: I told her I was not the marrying kind that I could only be her friend. It was her brother's fault. They swore to kidnap me and force me to marry her, so I had to flee the country. I'm innocent, innocent I say! I did not get her with child! That was that guy Moran; he did the deed; it was the year Kerry won the all-Ireland football final, so it was."

"Innocent!" roared judge Faith. "Impossible! You killed the lady's faith; you murdered a loving heart."

"A dastardly deed," cried Hope. "You killed the hope that lived in her heart, you did it without remorse; brutal like the daggers that sank into Caesar! Can this courtroom, or any of the jury recollect from the whole realm of human history a greater crime, a more foul deed, a more heartless act—than the crime of a "love" that was murdered?"

"Heinous act!" roared Charity. "How terrible. Trodden on like a flower in the springtime of its youth; without mercy, without hope, without charity. A terrible deed. Alas the babe!"

"Clerk of the court, read out the next charge," cried justice Faith.

By now Carey began to sweat profusely. He shuffled uneasily in his seat; with his right hand he was noticed to continue wiping his brow with a white hanker-chief. He mumbled quietly to himself, so much so that some of the other patrons in the lounge began to take notice. Intermittently, he began to roar out to himself, "I'm innocent, innocent I say!" This greatly amused the other pub patrons sitting close by.

The clerk rose from his seat and began to shuffle nervously some papers he was holding.

For several seconds he glanced around the courtroom; he bowed his head several times and his face was seen to assume a look of forlorn sadness: indeed his colleagues began to look in his direction wondering what was the delay in his reading out the indictment. Then he raised his head promptly, looked straight at the bench, particularly judge Hope, and immediately began to read as follows:

"Your worships, it is with great sadness that I read before you the final charge brought today against the defendant, for in truth, as you will shortly hear, this charge puts in the shade, so to speak, the previous misdemeanours already read before the court, and shows conclusively the hardheartedness of the defendant and the callous manner for over thirty years in which he has treated his wife. But first let us hear of the level of meanness that the defendant so practiced."

"The defendant, your honour, never once in his life took his esteemed wife, Mary Claire Carey on a holiday! Thirty years they were together—thirty long, mean years, and the only place they ever went out to was a bus trip to Bray Head!"

"Despite having an illustrious career in the public service, and a commensurate salary that allowed the family to live comfortably, such a tight hold was retained on the purse strings, your honour by the defendant—that we have it on good authority that Mrs Carey was only allowed a new dress every three years—aye, and on some occasions that was extended to five years!

Moreover, we also have it on good authority that on the 23rd of October 1945, while the good lady was returning home from 10 o'clock mass her dress ripped down the side due to wear and tear, and to retain herself decently covered she had to borrow her neighbours overcoat to cover herself, or otherwise walk home half naked exposed to the gaze of everyone she passed!"

Roars of condemnation echoed from the gallery upon hearing this.

"Disgraceful! Miser! Bray Head indeed!"

"Tis not true," roared Carey. "I was not mean. I supported a family of six children, it was the war years, food was scarce; money was tight—I was never mean! Never I say."

"Silence!" roared judge Charity. "Continue the reading, Mr Conway."

"Thank you your honour," replied the clerk.

"The defendant, your honour, mentions six children. Ah, how sad were their lives! There was young Timothy, nine years old, dressed poorly, the laughing stock of his contemporaries because of the hand-me-down clothes he was always dressed in, while the defendant, your honour found time to catch a plane to Newmarket racecourse in England! There he lost hundreds of pounds backing horses that never won! And as for drinking, why the defendant had an unlimited capacity. We have testimony from independent witnesses, your honour that have confirmed every word we state. A most shameful record."

By this time Carey was in a most deplorable state. He began to shuffle a good deal in his chair, and in one instance—despite being still asleep, straightened himself up, extended his right arm out directly towards the judge's chairs, and began to roar wildly. Just then the door of the lounge suddenly swung open and in entered Mrs Carey. She had a distinctly angry look on her face; she headed straight for her husband.

She cried out, "Drinking again is it you are! Is there no end to it at all? Home. Home I say; you're a disgrace to yourself!"

As she uttered these words she began to batter him over

the head and shoulders with her handbag; the blows were so fierce Carey immediately wakened from his sleep, crying out as he did, "What...what's going on...Kathleen. It's you! What are you doing here? My dinner, what about my dinner? The judges, Faith, Hope and Charity. Where are they gone?"

"Judges, what judges?" she replied.

By now the patrons of the pub were in convulsions of laughter at the antics—not only of Carey, but also of his wife as well.

"Ten years in jail!" roared one of the punters.

"The full sentence to be served!" roared another. "No remission."

All present roared with laughter as Carey was hauled out of the pub by his wife. As he passed through the door he was heard to cry out, "I'm innocent—innocent I say! I was never unkind to anyone your worships."

Romance Among The Flowers

Miriam Esker stood before the GPO, in O'Connell Street, Dublin. It was 7:30PM on a bright, cool, summer evening. She looked pensive, almost forlorn as she stared at the bowls of flowers lining the centre of the street. Her holiday in Ireland was finished in two day's time. Early on a Sunday morning she would board the 9:30AM flight at Dublin Airport, and fly back to Derbyshire, England.

She thrilled at how lovely the flowers looked. Set in round metal bowls, they gave the street a picturesque colour and reminded her of the flowers back home in her mother's front garden. These would be in full blossom just now. She thought of the tender loving care her mother would lavish upon them. Yet the loveliness of the flowers did little to ease the sadness she felt in her heart. Her romance with Stan Penfield had ended four weeks ago; to make matters worse, today was her twenty-ninth birthday.

Penfield was Irish, and though they had been together for two years, she discovered he did not love her. The affair was over. On impulse she had flown across to Ireland for a short holiday. No one could say what impelled her to do so; indeed she wasn't quite sure herself. Yet something had drawn to Dublin. Perhaps it had something to do with the fact that her great grandfather had come from Ireland. County Meath, to be exact.

Staring across at the GPO her thoughts wandered back over the many stories and tales about Ireland told by her former boyfriend. He had fired her imagination, aroused her curiosity about all the beautiful places to be seen in Ireland. They agreed that one day they would come over together to see them all: alas, it was not to be. She stood alone, staring at the famous Cuchulain statue in the window of the GPO. Tears flowed from her eyes, as her soft womanly heart ached and pined for her lost love. This was not to be a happy birthday, she thought.

She turned her head slightly so that the people passing would not see the tears of sadness roll down her face. Looking at the statue, she thought of the epic struggle of this great warrior, of how he had fought so valiantly, and triumphed—even in death! She too would triumph. She too would overcome her sadness, her broken heart. Looking down O'Connell street she felt a new surge of hope blossom in her breast; it energised her whole body. Penfield had never loved her. She would put him out of her mind, forever. She would look to the future. Move on.

The sun was sinking slowly in the western sky. A slight wind began to blow. It was a cold wind, getting stronger by the minute. The flowers started to sway backwards and forwards, as if dancing to the soft musical echoes that burst forth from the breeze. She decided to return to her hotel. She arrived back at 8:00PM, went straight to the restaurant and ordered tea and toast. Mrs. Tinkler, another resident with whom she had recently become acquainted, joined her. She was over from London for a few day's holiday. She reminded

Miriam of her mother; they were so alike, she thought. She was glad of her company, even though she knew it would not be for long. Mrs Tinkler had a deep interest in Art and had come to Dublin to visit the Art Galleries, and in particular to see the Francis Bacon Studio in the Hugh Lane Art Gallery, Parnell Square. But she was a very fussy person, always on the move. She immediately began to engage Miriam in conversation.

"I hope you are enjoying yourself my dear," cried Mrs Tinkler.

"Yes, very much," replied Miriam, as she struggled to be convincing.

"And have you been to see any interesting places today, then?"

"Indeed, Mrs Tinkler," replied Miriam. "I went to see the Botanical Gardens in Glasnevin, most interesting. I saw many exotic plants. You should go there before you return to London. I think you would enjoy it."

"No my dear," replied Mrs Tinkler. "Much as I would like to I wouldn't have the time. I'm going to an Art exhibition just up the Town; would you like to come?"

Miriam declined. She really had no interest in Art.

"Thank you, Mrs Tinkler, but no. "I'm going to have an early night. A little tired after a long day: you don't mind?"

"Of course not," replied Mrs Tinkler. "You're quite right to retire early. Dublin can tire one out so easily. I don't know whether it's from the weather, or the people! There is so much hustle and bustle going on; it can be quite exhausting."

They both laughed.

"So tell me, Mrs Tinkler about your love of painting; how long has this been your favourite pastime?"

"Ever since I was a teenager," she replied. "My uncle in

America was a great painter; well I think he was. Though like so many painters he got little recognition for his work. It was he that aroused my interest, and when he would come to exhibitions in London, we would meet and talk for hours about his work and all the great painters of the world, Goya, Rembrandt. He even wanted me to take up painting as a career, but I declined."

"Over the years I developed an interest in Irish painting. You know this country has produced some great artists. I came across a book some years ago entitled, *Irish Impressionists of the 19th century*. Filled with information about Irish painters that lived and worked in France and Belgium. It was a most interesting book. The pictures illustrated were fascinating. Anyway, there am I going on and on as usual: once I get started I forget to stop! It's time I was off. Are you sure you won't come to the Exhibition? I'd be delighted with your company."

Miriam paused before replying, "No thanks. I appreciate your inviting me, but not this time."

"As you wish then," replied Mrs Tinkler. As she rose from the table Miriam smiled at her. She was so like her mother. She had a warm infectious smile, just like her. She could have hugged her on the spot! It was hard to refuse her invitation.

"You go and enjoy yourself," cried Miriam. "I shall see you later."

Miriam watched her as she walked out of the restaurant. After this brief encounter with this most charming person, she was left with a warm feeling that did much to lift some of the unhappiness from her heart. For this she was grateful. She finished her tea and biscuits and returned to her room to sleep for a few hours. It was ten o'clock when she awoke.

She dressed quickly and went down to the hotel lounge. A traditional Irish music group were performing before a full house. She found the music soothing, and having ordered a drink, sat down.

Suddenly the lead singer called for song requests. Several were handed up. Then the following announcement was made: "Now, ladies and gentlemen, our next song is entitled *She moves through the fair*, and is requested by the gentleman to my right for the young lady in red over in the far corner."

Pointing at Miriam, he continued, "Yes lass, I think you have stolen young Mr. Wallace's heart away!"

The audience laughed, as he commenced to sing. Miriam blushed. Loud applause followed the singing of this most beautiful Irish air; Miriam, quite taken that it had been re-quested for her, smiled, as strong emotional feelings surged through her body. During the singing her admirer gave a number of glances in her direction—anxious to catch her attention. Indeed an elderly lady-sitting close by remarked on this. Miriam smiled at her as she tried to conceal the deep feeling of inner excitement she felt at this sudden attention by this unknown admirer.

A short while later Patrick Wallace, for such was his name, while passing through the lounge turned suddenly and spoke to Miriam. "Well lass, did you like the song? I sung it espe-cially for you."

"Well thank you," replied Miriam, half smiling. "That was thoughtful of you."

"Are you Irish then?" asked Wallace.

"English," retorted Miriam, "from Derbyshire. Though I do have some Irish blood."

Patrick Wallace was by now leaning forward, both hands-gripping an unoccupied chair at the table where Miriam was sitting. He continued "I should not be surprised if you had, for you've got the good Celtic look about you, or my name is not Patrick Wallace, by the way."

"Cheeky," retorted Miriam.

Suddenly an elderly lady sitting at the next table intervened. "Do ask the gentleman to sit down my dear; and such a handsome young man, too."

Miriam, blushing slightly, invited him to sit down.

"Could I get you something to drink?" Wallace enquired.

"Just a glass of ale," cried Miriam, "Any ale will do."

Wallace called the waiter and ordered two drinks.

"So, you're from Derbyshire, England then. Tell me all about it. Is it a big town, a city; does it have a large population? And what brings you to Ireland?"

For a few seconds Miriam stared intently at him. She thought how fast he was; and so many questions! Cheeky bugger. Yet, her heart was in a flutter. She was excited by the attention. He was handsome, tall, and sported a cocky air about himself. She smiled warmly at him before replying. He was in casual dress, wore a brown, open-necked shirt and matching slacks. He was of thin build, sallow complexion and had nice blue eyes. They rang bells in her heart! She was also struck by the restless look in his eyes—calm, but with all the potential of an explosive volcano. He was forward too, but it was a forwardness she liked. And after the collapse of her recent relationship, she was enjoying the attention.

They chatted and laughed as she told him about her hometown of Buxton in Derbyshire. About the Peak district with its five hundred and fifty mile national park; the valleys, hills and dales and the great natural beauty to be seen; she spoke about the Irish poet Thomas Moore who was inspired in his writings by the natural beauty of the area, particularly Upper Mayfield in the town of Ashbourne. She urged him to come on a visit; he would not be disappointed. Eventually they retired for the night. They agreed to meet the following evening at 7:30PM at the flower bowls opposite the GPO in O'Connell street.

In her hotel bedroom Miriam thought no more of her collapsed romance with Penfield; with Patrick Wallace's face appearing constantly in her mind she could sleep very little. Having enjoyed his company for most of the evening, she felt in love again. Eventually she fell into a deep sleep. The following morning Mrs Tinkler joined her at the breakfast table.

"Well my dear did you have a good rest last night?" she asked.

"Well, yes and no," retorted Miriam. "I came down to the lounge and nearly got drunk!"

"You didn't!" exclaimed Mrs Tinkler. "Drunk! I don't believe it."

"Well, not quite," cried Miriam. "But Mrs Tinkler I met this really nice man, Patrick Wallace! We spent most of the evening together; he was so nice: it was wonderful. He is an Irishman. Lives here in Dublin. We are to meet again this evening at 7:30PM. I'm so looking forward to it."

"Why that is wonderful, my dear! I'm delighted for you. I cannot think of a nicer person I would like to see in a romantic relationship, or get drunk, for that matter! Ah, romance, courtship, wedding bells, the best days in a woman's life; I do wish you all the luck in the world. It's wonderful news, wonderful! I'm so happy for you."

"Thank you very much, you're so kind. Tell me, the Art exhibition, was it good?" asked Miriam.

"It was great, just great. There was a large attendance and I met some lovely people. An exhibition in oils, you know, and the artists—well, we can have every confidence in Ireland's artistic future. There was a Miss Louisa Broderick, one of the most up and coming painters; and Miss Bracken, just turned twenty-three, a most gifted artist. Oh, I wish you had been there to see her work! Fantastic. And of course there was the Francis Bacon studio, a truly great painter: overall a most delightful evening. But enough about me and my old exhibition. Tell me all about this young man you met last night. Is he handsome, rich? Has he a pleasant personality?"

"Well I only just met him," cried Miriam. "I cannot say whether he is rich or not. Handsome, yes, pleasant—absolutely. As I said we are meeting again this evening. We will see how it goes."

Miriam leaned back in her chair and looked intently at Mrs Tinkler for some moments. Her thoughts roamed. "Good God!" she thought to herself, "If I'm not careful she'll have me married off next!" She smiled and thanked her for the nice thoughts. She was quite taken by Patrick, enjoyed his company, and hoped that they would have an enjoyable evening together. After further brief exchanges Mrs Tinkler finished her breakfast and went into town. Miriam left a short while later to do some shopping, and, to get her hair set. She had an important date to keep.

That evening she met Patrick as arranged. They both expressed pleasant smiles in a deep and engaging way. Standing beside the flower bowls she felt her heart beat faster and faster as they talked. For the rest of the evening they strolled around the town.

Patrick talked about the fine eighteenth-century houses in Parnell Square, and how Dublin had developed over the years. He talked about the famous Irish writers, Shaw, Joyce, Moore, and O'Casey. As she walked by his side she felt swallowed up in the happiness of his company. He spoke with an air of authority; had a confident and resolute manner; she felt safe in his company. Time seemed never-ending: her happiness was complete. Learning that it was her birthday the previous day they returned to the hotel restaurant where they had a fine meal and several glasses of red Burgundy wine.

Eventually they parted for the night, Patrick promising to take her to the airport next morning. Miriam returned to her room in a state of exhilaration. Patrick Wallace was filling a void in her life. His whole personality and conversation had overwhelmed her. She felt she had been to the top of a large mountain; a dark cloud—the unhappy memory of Stan Penfield, had been lifted from her heart. Lying down on the bed Patrick Wallace's face was continually before her eyes; tired, her last thought before she went asleep was of love. Patrick Wallace and Dublin town had captured her heart. The next morning he drove her to the airport. As she prepared to board her plane they both agreed to write to each other, and meet again as soon as possible. Settled on board Miriam reflected on her holiday in Dublin; coinciding with her twenty-ninth birthday, it had turned out to be a very happy occasion. Having left England with a broken heart and a lost lover, she now left Ireland having met a man whom she felt really loved her—and with whom she was very much in love. She chuckled to herself. With these thoughts in mind she soon fell fast sleep.

At home among the flowerbeds in her mother's front garden, romantic thoughts filled her head. She plucked a red rose. She smelt its sweet aroma; as she did so she turned her head towards the western sky. The sun was setting. She thought of O'Connell street in Dublin town, of the flower bowls and the petals of the flowers swaying before the whirl of the early autumn winds; she thought of the GPO, of Cuchulian—that great ancient Irish warrior—and Patrick Wallace—her hero, who had held her hand in a spirit of true romance. She sighed as she bent down to pluck a second rose. Holding them both between her two hands she exclaimed: "Yes!" Love had returned, thanks to her wonderful holiday, and romance among the flowers in Dublin town.

A Soul For Heaven

WILLIE BRADLEY WAS A GOOD FRIEND OF MINE. I use the past tense because I may not see him again. I hope I will, but when I saw him last week I wasn't very hopeful. It was while walking through the shopping centre that we last met. Looking in Murphy's window I was hoping to spot a bargain sale for socks; no such luck I'm afraid. As he was about to pass me, he remarked, "A nice morning Gerry," in a somewhat stuttered voice. "Aye it is to be sure Willie," I replied. "You're keeping well I hope?" "As good as I can," he responded, as he shuffled his dishevelled looking body from side to side.

He did not look at all well. He had grown a beard, a mixture of grey and black hair that clung to his face in an untidy manner. It was as if he just carelessly stopped shaving and let it grow wild. His clothes were untidy and one shoelace was undone. His face looked unwashed and there was a forlorn look in his eyes that gave off an appearance of deep sadness. I had seen him on previous occasions walking through the shopping centre, but never as disorientated as this. I was filled with a deep sense of sorrow at the appearance of my friend; I struggled hard not to show it.

"And God be with the days when you use to play the

football," I cried, "Aye, and the day you scored the winning goal for the home county and sent 40,000 Connacht voices screaming to the high heavens! By God Willie you were the man then, so you were!"

Willie was momentarily staring into the distance. He turned to look at me, his eyes brightening up. The cheeks of his face moved slightly as if preparing for the delivery of a major speech. He replied, "You know Gerry, I remember that day well. Two minutes of play left, that's all; and that Cavan referee, why, he practically done us out of the game. The Derry lads got away with murder, and that half-back, what's this his name was? Yes, Canavan, he'd been givin' me a hard time the whole afternoon and I was determined to contain him before the final whistle..."

"And by god you did surely," returned Gerry, "Why, when Thompson sent that high ball across, your climb to the skies that day and score was magic: pure magic I say. A great goal, so it was."

Willie smiled. He raised his right hand and with clenched fist shot it at a seventy-degree angle into the sky. There was fire in his eyes and I declare that for a few seconds it was as if his whole body were back on Croke Park about to repeat the performance! I was delighted to see this new fire and enthusiasm emanating from him.

"And the welcome back to Galway," I continued, "Now wasn't that something to remember?" He resumed his relaxed poise, but looked at me somewhat sadly.

"Aye it was a great welcome home indeed. Thousands turned out to watch us bring old Sam back. The bonfires blazed for miles around! Sadly the poor mother died the following morning; we were all shattered."

"Yes I remember that. A terrible sad happening Willie,

terrible sad," returned Gerry, "Unfortunately such is life. We know neither the day nor the hour that the good Lord calls us home. But it's to a better life she's gone, I'm sure."

Willie looked at little sad. I tried to cheer him up.

"So any other news at all?" I asked. "That son of yours, Richard, is he still in Africa? By the way lets go into the café. I'll buy you a coffee."

Willie was reluctant, but bowed to Gerry's persuasion. His face brightened up somewhat at the mention of his son's name. He shuffled about uneasily putting one hand in his pocket. "He is to be sure," he replied. "Married now. Two kids the last time he wrote home. Mind you I can never understand what the hell he's doing in Africa; couldn't he be as easily back here in his own country instead of out there thousands of miles away among a load of foreigners."

"It's the times, Willie, it's the times. They're forever changing. Look at Dublin now with it's bell-ringing trams, and that spike in O'Connell Street! That gateway to heaven! Yes the times they are a-changing alright: whether it's for the better, well now that's another matter my friend."

Willie began to fidget uneasily; he looked here and there, as if he were lost; I didn't know which way to respond. I think our small talk was beginning to upset him. I had watched him for weeks on end wandering around the community, going nowhere. I believe he did not know himself just where he was heading at any one time. I was sorrowful for him. He was a man without a future it would appear. And yet in truth his future was before him; did he realize it? That was the question. I knew what I had to say to cheer him up. I could talk a lot of nostalgic nonsense about life; I could attempt to cheer him up by reflecting again on old memories; but the time for half-truths was past. Looking back was no longer an option. He would die soon; this I instinctively knew. I must re-animate his faith, somehow; must give him that belief and confidence, that sense of expectation of looking forward to a great event, rekindle that fire, energy, and directness of purpose that drove him skywards on that great day back in 1967 when, with pure magic, he drove that ball into the back of the Derry net. I pondered on my approach. I thought for a few seconds. Tomorrow was St. Anthony's feast day. I consulted. I was about to speak when Willie cried out "I don't think I'll be long for this world Gerry. The head doesn't feel the best lately; there's no future for me anymore—except six feet under." As he uttered these words he grew very sad. I was sure he was going to weep.

I moved quickly to raise his spirits.

"Six feet under! Not at all!" I cried, "Forget about the six feet under. Who knows when any of us is going to die, and whether we do know or not what difference does it make? It's not the dying Willie that we should be concerned about—it's when we are reborn again, that's what our minds should focus on. Life after death, not death before life. Always keep in mind that man is made up of both body and spirit; the body grows old and there is damn all we can do about it; but the spirit—now that's another story. The spirit is alive and eternal. I'm not depressing you now Willie?" I asked.

"No but you're beginning to sound like Father Thompson from over yonder!" cried Willie, "Seriously, is there such a place as heaven when we die? I mean, are we reborn again to a new life, that's what I'd like to know." All I see around me is chaos and confusion. No one has come back to tell us if there is a heaven or a hell, so what the hell are we to believe?"

"Willie," replied Gerry, "thousands of people die every

day around the world. The spirits of those poor souls take flight out into the universe; their bodies are committed to the earth. In due time, as the good book says, they will all turn to dust, but their spirits will not turn to dust! They will enter a world I believe is a beautiful place. A world where there is no fighting, no wars; where the aroma of perpetual love will be the all-embracing force. In that world mothers will be re-united with their sons and daughters, husbands with wives, brothers, uncles, nephews. There will be no sorrow, no tears. It will be a world where each of us will be re-born again! All we need is faith and belief."

Willie looked hard at Gerry for a couple of seconds before replying.

"You know Gerry, I think you missed your vocation; I think you should be doing Father Thompson's job. I don't believe that nonsense about heaven and a life hereafter; when you die you die, and that's all there is to it. You're no more— kaput, gone. As you said yourself, dust—nothing more. It's the end."

"But that's just the point Willie," replied Gerry, "It's not the end. Death is only the beginning. Look, let me explain it to you this way: It's like a mathematical equation. Listen.

Phase one—(a)=Birth. (b)=Life (four score years and ten) (c)=Death. You have lived out your allotted time, you now go to sleep; you die.

Phase two. The spirit (d) rises to meet the creator, God. The flesh goes six feet under and turns to dust. Man ceases to exist as a material human being. He now claims his place in the universe. We are the heirs of the Kingdom of Heaven. No more pain; no more suffering; the whole human race, in spirit, is at one with God."

"By God Gerry this is all very heavy stuff. If it is as true as you say, then why doesn't this God of whom you speak reveal himself and tell us if what you say is in fact true; why doesn't he show us this new kingdom of which you speak? Will you tell me that," cried Willie. Gerry noticed that Willie was getting a little agitated, not in an overtly aggressive way, but his general attitude became different. He could see that his brain was becoming more active; his curiosity was aroused; this was good he thought.

"I cannot explain why the creator does not reveal himself. I expect he has his own reasons. Perhaps he is revealing himself in ways we do not see; ways we do not understand. To figure that out you'll have to read the prophets. Certainly you could start with the Bible. It's really not for me to say. But this I will say, that all those big planets suspended out there in the universe, Jupiter, Saturn Mars etc., well they just didn't appear out of nowhere, somebody put them there, and by God he must be some powerful guy whoever he is! It's really down to faith; and more important—faith in the God above."

"So you firmly believe that there is a life hereafter, Gerry? That some life-force is out there in space calling the shots?" cried Willie.

"I haven't the slightest doubt in the world about it," cried Gerry. Somebody out there has created this wonderful universe. I believe we were put on this earth to enjoy ourselves, not to worry nor be overburdened with care, but to enjoy the simple things that the creator has put at our disposal. Far too many of us worry about dying, about gathering up excessive wealth, when in truth we should be carefree and happy while living. We must learn to recognise the beauty all around us; to appreciate the great bounty that God has put at our disposal; to understand and appreciate it. That's what life should be all about. If death is to be thought about at all, then in my humble opinion it is something we should not be over-concerned about: we should see death as the gateway to life; the shedding off, as Shakespeare says, 'of this mortal coil' which has burdened us all the days of our lives. Moreover, we must always remember what Christ said about the hereafter: *In my father's house there are many mansions; where I am going you cannot come, but you will follow me hereafter, for I go to prepare a place for you.*"

"You know Gerry this is heavy stuff; I only came down to buy a loaf of bread and by heaven your giving me a theological talk about life and death!"

"About life Willie—yes," retorted Gerry, "But life after death. I don't mean to bore you. You're my friend, and the last thing I want to see is any friend of mine walking around as if there is no tomorrow. The future, Willie, belongs to the dead—not the living. Oh yes, the living now have their future, a material future; what I'm talking about is their spiritual future; that great age that comes after we pass on. That, my good friend, is where the future lies. In that great big universe. The real future of man only begins after he dies, not before.

Never lose sight of that fact. Lead the good life. Faith will lead you confidently on to the next. Keep in mind what I say, that we are made up of two elements: material body, and spiritual soul; grasp the significance of this statement and you'll become a new man overnight. You will think no more of the sorrows of this world, but the fact that these will all pass away.

Each day, week, month, year and one hundred years, will appear as nothing but a minor inconvenience; the great encouraging truth you will quickly recognise is the all-pervading truth that our real future lies before us, not behind us. For this has been foreshadowed by God himself. In the meantime you keep yourself busy. Read a book, take long walks, and bring the dog with you. Dogs make ideal companions—they are loyal, loving and carefree creatures. If you haven't got one, then go to the nearest dogs and cats home and get one."

"Well I better go and get that loaf of bread or if I don't I'll end up in the dogs and cats home myself!" cried Willie, "But Gerry you're getting old yourself, surely you must be worried about dying. Like you are going to die like the rest of us—doesn't that worry you?"

"Not in the least, Willie" replied Gerry, "A material death is inevitable. A spiritual death is not. It's faith in life after death, that gives us the strength to endure the many difficulties and inconveniences that burden us from the cradle to the grave. We worry unduly about the most petty things in life, like having a car—two cars in some cases; a big house, lots of money, plenty of holidays, etc., sure when you look around at the way world is going, I can't understand why so many people are sick, distressed and worried about dying, when in truth they should be more worried about staying alive! The human race needs to tidy up it's sense of values; they need to be setting some markers on their behaviour; redefining their sense of values, if they are to live peaceful and happy lives. If we are to look to the future with confidence, then we need to be asking ourselves some serious questions, like what life should really be all about. Wouldn't you agree?"

Willie paused before replying. His facial expression assumed a thoughtful pose; I had obviously given him something to think about. He replied, "I don't think about such things anymore. I haven't the energy. Mind you, your comments about the distinction between body and spirit, well I hadn't given them much thought. As you say there are two sides to Man—the spiritual and the material. Now I understand why that arthritis keeps giving my left knee such a hard time! As you say it's the human condition, and there is little we can do about it. But as regards the spiritual…"

"Yes, interjected Gerry," somewhat quickly, "The human body is a great machine—if machine you can call it; but it has its weaknesses. It is not perfect; it has a short life span; it is the temple, so too speak, for our spirit, that is all. Its time span is limited. Not so the time span for the spirit. And so Willie, you and I we have our spiritual side: we are spiritual beings and the future belongs to us! And by God, when you think about all those huge Planets out in space, why the Creator must have a mighty great future planned for all of us, that is what I say. And what a future it must be!"

Willie finished drinking his coffee. I observed his facial expression—especially his eyes. They had a sparkle in them that wasn't there before we entered the café. His body became more erect; he looked about at the other customers in the café. He even nodded to an old neighbour of his, a Mrs Branigan, whom we both knew well. He had an air of excited confidence, certainly of less hopelessness than when I first encountered him in the shopping centre. I was pleased with this. He turned and spoke to me, "Well now Gerry I think it is time I got that loaf of bread and headed home Can't keep herself waiting. So thanks for the coffee—and incidentally, your theological talk on life and death! Interesting, very interesting."

"More common sense really, Willie," returned Gerry, "More common sense, I say—and less theological. As I said our guides to the real home truths of life are all around us, if only we had the good sense to see them. You take care now, okay. We'll talk again."

"We will surely, Gerry. We will surely," replied Willie.

I finished my coffee and left the café. As I did so I watched him as he walked down the shopping centre. He displayed a confident air in his stride. I noticed him salute other shoppers. He looked more the man I knew several years earlier; he had a strong, confident, well-meaning air about his person: I was glad to see this. My words had raised his spirit; I was glad that I convinced him that life really only begins after death; that faith in the future is the sustaining force of life: that which liberates us from death in life—taking us forward into, life after death. Turning away I headed home pleased with this day's encounter.

Three weeks later I was in the shopping centre when I met his wife, Mary. I had just returned from a holiday in France.

"Well Mary nice to see you again," I cried. "And tell me how is that husband of yours? Well I take it?"

For several seconds there was no reply. Something was wrong. Mary looked anything but well. Paler than usual, there was also sadness in her eyes, something I had been slow to notice. She greeted me almost inaudibly, "Ah, Mr. Cavanaugh, sure Willie passed away two weeks ago, tomorrow. Died peacefully in his sleep, so he did."

"I am terrible sorry Mrs Bradley to hear this news," cried Gerry, "I had no idea. Carmel and I only got back from holidays yesterday morning; I'm really very sorry to hear this news, please accept my deepest sympathy."

"Thank you Mr Cavanaugh. I did miss you at the funeral for you and him was always good friends. Strange, for three or four days before he died, it is almost as if he knew he was going to die, he kept asking me to make sure the messenger was at the graveside when he was being buried. I think he was raving, Mr Cavanaugh. I kept asking him, 'What messenger?' But all he did was smile in reply. Then, the night before he died, he turned to me in the bed and said, 'Mary, Mary, everything, is fine; there's no need to tell the messenger to come. I understand now what he was talking about!' Kept crying out, 'He was right, he was right! Life only begins after death! All you need is faith, just faith.' He was so excited Mr Kavanagh, I couldn't make head nor tail of it. Whoever this messenger was he must have told poor Willie something very important, for I declare to God I never in my life seen such a peaceful look on a dead man's face as I seen on his that night. Most strange it was, most strange."

"Well if he had the look of peace on his face like you said Mary, now wasn't that a great comfort? I mean to know that he died peaceably and happy, and in his own bed—sure what more could a man ask for? As regards this messenger he was speaking of, well, who knows who that was. If that person raised his spirits, lifted and renewed his faith, then isn't that all that matters? After all to have faith in this life is a great thing; to have the faith and vision to see life immortal in the next, now isn't that the most wonderful thing of all? Willie was a very fortunate man, Mary; very lucky to have grasped this truth before he died. I feel happy for him now, for it's certain he's in paradise this day."

Of Pleasant Days Of Old

It was 9:55AM. Exactly when Peter Murphy arrived at Rawlins café. He had come in just in time to avoid the early morning rush-hour crowd that soon would be storming the café for their morning coffee break. He ordered tea and biscuits, then, settled down to read the morning newspaper. This he had to defer, for his thoughts called him back to his recent return visit to Birmingham City, England.

It was a warm, sunny morning, and his appointment to meet a good friend at 12 o'clock was on schedule; he had lots of time to spare. He reflected on the outcome of his recent visit to Birmingham, England, a place he last visited thirty years before. Having just returned from that city nine days earlier, he recalled with mixed feelings his arrival at Birmingham railway station on the previous Sunday afternoon; he recalled the many red-bricked buildings he had seen there, all of which seemed to swallow up both train and station; a cold eeriness exuded out of each red-brick wall, focusing his thoughts more pointedly on this great industrial city.

He thought of the thousands of her sons and daughters that had died in the two great wars, and of the thousands more who had worked in factory and mines to build up the nation's great industrial strength.

He felt the calm, the quiet, as the train slowly rolled into the station terminal, infusing a little sadness into his soul. He felt admiration, yet sadness for all her people, and for all the suffering they had endured. Two world wars, and a great depression. Sad.

Staring out of the train window he remembered the short prayer he had once uttered to himself when he had been here before: "Lord bless the sons and daughters of this great city, and remember always her dead sons and daughters; Lord bless this City, always." Soon the train stopped and he stepped out on to the platform. He recalled surrendering his ticket to the gate porter and heading out on to the public streets for the first time in over thirty years. It felt strange—very strange. By now the rain had stopped and the sun had come out; as he was in no hurry he walked about the town to once again re-acquaint himself with her city streets. Birmingham had changed. But he had changed: he too was older now.

One of the first places he went to was the City of Birmingham Public Library. Ah, how pleasant was his earlier memory of this! Such a huge library; and so many books! In the summer months, as a young lad, he had visited it so many times reading almost every book on Irish history that he could lay his hands on; and the library staff, so helpful and courteous: what pleasant memories. He thought of the suburbs of Sparkhill and Sparkbrook, where he lodged, and of the big, strong, farmer's son from Skibbereen, Ireland over working to earn some money to support the farm and family at home. And Wolverhampton, where he had played soccer for Solihull United, and that marvellous goal he had scored from a corner in his very first match! He still could hear the cheers of the English lads as they roared "Great goal, Paddy! Well done, Paddy, great goal." He had been the hero of the hour that day; there was neither Irish nor English—only the team, and they won!

He recalled the great Perry Barr stadium, its wonderful racetrack where for several weeks he had trained on a Tuesday and Thursday nights. He recalled all the English lads with their nice tracksuits and fine blazer crests. He was only twenty years old then; he had no crest on his tracksuit of green: He would soon fix that! Sitting there in the changing rooms of the stadium he thought of the O'Neills and the O'Donnells, the O'Connors, aye, and the Burkes of Clanrickard! The O'Briens of Thomond and the O'Malleys of Mayo. By Jesus, he cried, I'll give them crests, crests they will never have seen—and when seen they will never forget. Inchiquin and Mountjoy marching through Munster, Spenser, *The Faery Queen*, we don't forget.

He recalled writing home to his mother, the following letter: "Dear Mother, I am well over here in Birmingham, have a job, and my digs are okay. The landlady is from Cork, and apart from being a little tight with the food, is alright. A fellow county man of hers, tall, of strong muscular build, and with an appetite like a horse, finds that he cannot survive on the rations of food the landlady doles out: we have reached agreement to share some food that we will buy together. He is a fine strapping strong lad who has come to Birmingham to earn some extra money to support the farm and family back home; I am quite fond of him. He is a perfect example of the rural folk from the heart of our country. Hopefully the landlady won't catch us eating the food we bring in!"

"My purpose in writing to you is to ask you to go into

town and see if you can buy me a crest badge (linen) of the four provinces of Ireland? If you are successful will you send it to me as soon as possible? I am enclosing a postal order for £1.50; I wish I could make it more, but wages are not great over here and it is all I can afford.

Write soon.

Peter."

Just over one week later he received a reply. His mother and all were well and she had enclosed a linen crest showing the insignias of the four provinces of Ireland. He was delighted! It was a Friday morning when the letter came; he would sew the crest on to his green tracksuit, and by Jesus next Tuesday night in the changing rooms of Perry Barr stadium the English boys would see a real crest!

The following Tuesday he arrived at around 7:00PM for his usual training stint. It was a fine early autumn evening. The changing rooms were fairly packed. As he undressed and donned his tracksuit one of the English lads noticed the crest. "Hey Paddy," he exclaimed, "what's the crest about? Is it a north county emblem, eh?" "It looks like something worn by the Royalists in the days of Charles 1st!" roared his mate.

They both laughed.

Roger Tompkins, an athlete with whom he had made friends, then interjected and asked Peter what did the crest actually stand for.

"The crest is representative of the four provinces of Ireland, Ulster, Munster, Connacht, & Leinster, these four provinces go to make up the Nation of Ireland for nigh on 3000 years. Known as the Celts, our ancestors originally hailed from Greece, and comprised bands of tribes known as the Miliseans, Firbolg, Tuatha De Danaan, Parthelonians, each of whom colonised the island at one time or another, until we eventually won our national freedom."

Peter recalled finishing his comments at that; he did not want to drift into a history lecture, particularly with the sons and daughters of the nation who colonised Ireland for 700 years! He proceeded out onto the track. It was a cool, mild evening. Not a cloud in the sky; dry, and ideal for running. He felt very fit. He recalled that it was well made, the ashes firmly bedded down and the white lines clearly marked out. He limbered up for some minutes before starting his run. As he did so his thoughts roamed over many things. "Worn by the Royalists, indeed!" "Where do they think they're coming from?" "Stupid people!" Ho…ho…ho….He breathed in and out slowly, carefully, while proceeding at a steady pace. "Poor Charles. They didn't show him much mercy; cut off his head in 1649; no mercy—without any compassion: fools!"

Two thirds away down the track he increased his pace—moving faster, ever faster. Then he stopped for a rest. Suddenly, out of the blue a javelin landed quite close to his feet. "Good Christ!" he exclaimed. "The bastards are trying to kill me!" He moved away quickly from where the javelin had dropped. He became scared. He paced slowly around the rest of the track, and only remained training there for a further half hour. He retired to the dressing room, changed, and went home.

Three nights later he decided to go to a local dance club not far from his digs. It was a small dance hall, with about twenty-five people in attendance. He engaged in a couple of dances and in doing so became acquainted with the beautiful Miss Berle Hartford. She lived out near Aston Villa's football club, in the Sutton Coalfield area; she was handsome, friendly, and chatty. They left the club together and he decided to take her home. As they stepped outside she enquired where was the car? Car? What car? He didn't have a car. He hailed down a cab and soon they were on their way.

He remembered arriving at a housing estate where she lived, and in a nearby lane they stopped to have a chat. He was fascinated by her English accent. They talked at some length. She enquired, as it was late October, if he would be going home to Ireland for Christmas. He replied that he had not made up his mind yet. Shortly they parted company, yet not before they had agreed to meet again two nights later.

As he roamed home to his digs that night he thought to himself how handsome she was, and so friendly; she had a lovely figure, and he really loved her English accent!

He felt a little sorry for her about her experiences with the Irishman from Fairview. This gentleman had courted her for nearly two years, and then ran off and left her. He thought of his job, and decided that it was time to look for another; the place where he was working did not pay well, so he would look around.

About a week later he saw a notice in the local evening paper of a firm that were looking for general operatives; he decided he would apply. Having arranged an interview he called to the company at the appointed time. As he entered the reception he noticed some scribbles on the wall, which read "This firm pays lousy wages, not worth working here." The writing was in small print. He trembled as he stood there. What if he was offered a job? What would he do? Dilemma! Can't walk out now. Reception knows.

The boss called him into the office. After a brief introduction he told Mr. Penrose, for this was the gentleman's name, that he had secured another position closer to home, and that he was no longer available to take up an offer of work. The manager was quite surprised to hear this. Meantime Peter sat there almost trembling in his trousers, for he was not used to telling lies: he was a good Irish catholic, and telling fibs was not part of his make-up. The manager expressed his thanks to him for having come all the way in to tell him he had got work elsewhere, and, shaking hands they parted. With a strong sense of relief Peter left the office and made for home.

Two weeks later, and as a result of answering an advertisement in one of the evening papers he secured a job working for the Birmingham telephone service; job title was trainee linesman. He was delighted to get this start, as money was getting thin on the ground. The job involved going around Birmingham city as part of a four-man crew, repairing and installing telephone lines. This involved climbing wooden telephone poles and renewing the overhead wires, installing new wires, and carrying out routine maintenance.

There were teams of four to each truck. He recalled the characters that were on his team. There was Stanley Penfield; he wore glasses—a reserved, quiet, pleasant, person. A gentleman, and a committed worker: the type that would inspire you to take him into your confidence if you wished to discuss anything personal. He liked Penfield. Then there was the big man, he forgot his name; yet he particularly recalled that he had a very brusque manner; kept asking him about the IRA, and had a most annoying habit of chewing raw onions! "Great for your health," he would roar, "raw onions. You can't beat them." And then he would shout at Peter, "What about this IRA, eh Paddy?" Peter would ignore him: he would say nothing.

One day he came into work and the big fellow was missing; he enquired where he was.

"Oh, he is gone into hospital. Something wrong with his stomach," was the reply.

"So much for onions!" chuckled Peter—to himself, of course; he didn't want the others to see that he was laughing at the big feller's misfortune. That would never do!

He thought of Finley, the other member of the crew, and what a character! Occasionally they both would have to climb a pole to undertake some repair work. Peter would tremble in his trousers. For when Finley would reach the top of the pole he would hustle and shuffle back and forth—shaking the pole into the bargain, nearly giving Peter a nervous breakdown, and not holding still until such time as he was fully secured and quite comfortable. And then he would roar down at the ladies passing on the footpath, "Hey ladies! There's an Irishman up here wants to make your acquaintance."

Peter would be mortified. But he was a great character: a bit mad. Peter liked him.

As he sat there drinking his coffee his thoughts were suddenly interrupted. "A penny for your thoughts Peter," cried the stranger. "Terence Murphy. Hope I am not too late?"

"Terence! My old friend," cried Peter. "Delighted you could make it. I've been just reminiscing on my recent trip to Birmingham; you remember we spoke about it three weeks ago?"

Sitting down beside his friend, Terence replied, "Aye, I thought with that look upon your face that you were reminiscing about something important. Still I bet you're glad to be back in old Dublin—right?"

"Undoubtedly, Terence. But I have to confess that there is always something magical about one's former experiences. It is never easy to put out of your mind the memories of 'pleasant days of old' no—never."

"Or the girl you left behind!" exclaimed his friend.

Peter nodded and smiled. "You'll have a coffee Terence?" asked Peter. "Of course," replied Terence. Immediately the two friends got down to work on their projected business idea.

The Window

NOTHING EXCITING EVER HAPPENED at the select cluster of red-bricked houses, located just off the main road leading eastwards out of Dublin. All the neighbours were agreed that Apple Way was a quiet, select, and picturesque location in which to live.

It comprised eighteen two-storey dwellings built over a hundred years ago. They were of uniform design throughout, and the fine bay windows gave them a distinctive character that was quick to catch the eye. Moreover, with the current state of the housing market, any one of them would fetch a high price if offered for sale on the open market.

None of the Apple Way residents however, showed any inclination for selling; a close knit and happy community they had their own bridge club, Residents Association and an active secretary, Mrs Reynolds, who organised frequent social outings. Life was good here, that is until suddenly one morning the MacKay family left without saying a word to anyone. The neighbours were very disappointed. Their sudden departure was a mystery. Mrs MacKay was very popular at the weekly bridge club meetings, yet it had been noticeable for some time that she was very irritable of late, snapping at club members for no apparent reason. Their sudden departure was a shock to everyone.

For several weeks the house lay derelict. Then early one morning a building contractor arrived and began erecting scaffolding in front of the house. Renovation work was quickly begun, inside and out; however, what excited the neighbours most was when the old bay windows were removed and "straight" windows installed in their place. This drew a gasp of horror from all. "Monstrous!" cried Mrs Placket, otherwise known generally as Countess Placket because of some historical link with English nobility. The new windows installed stood quite out of line with the windows on the adjacent houses; they did not blend in at all. When the work was completed the house was put up for sale.

For several weeks it lay unoccupied. Eventually a new owner moved in, or so it seemed. All the neighbours were keen to find out who the new owner was. Yet, apart from a change of curtains on the windows, the new occupants were not to be seen, either day or night. After much consideration it was decided to write to the planning authority and demand that the windows on the front of the house be replaced with new bay style windows "in keeping with the architectural layout of the windows in all other seventeen houses in Apple Way," as Mrs Reynolds, secretary to the residents association, put it. In the meantime continuous efforts would be made to contact the new owners. It was decided to make a house call.

On a Thursday afternoon at exactly 3:00PM a delegation of three ladies from the Association knocked at number 7 Apple Way. All waited for the occupants to emerge. No one did. Mrs Placket knocked again: still no answer. Drawing back from the hall door they surveyed the whole front of the house to see if they could notice anybody inside. No one seemed to be stirring within.

After a brief discussion they decided to leave and return another day. The secretary, Mrs Reynolds paused for a moment; she remarked on the strange quietness of the afternoon; not a bird was heard in song. She called the attention of her colleagues to the odd colour of the curtains on the upper floor windows; these were pulled across—almost closed. She was experiencing a cold feeling coming over her, and urged her colleagues to hurry along home. For the next couple of nights Mrs Reynolds was a troubled woman. She could not sleep. She kept seeing the large windows with the curtains half closed, and in the days that followed she experienced sleepless nights for reasons she could not explain. Her husband decided to call in the local doctor. However, the matter was diagnosed as not serious; medication was prescribed and she was advised to rest and generally take things easy for a week. She began to sleep better at night. In the meantime no contact had been made with the new owner of number 7 Apple Way.

At their weekly bridge club meetings the same question always came up. Was there anyone living there at all Mrs Placket would ask? The neighbours were at a loss to figure the whole thing out. Meantime it was learned that no planning application had been filed with the local authority for renovations to the house. It all seemed so strange.

As the neighbours continued to watch nobody was seen either entering or leaving the house. Then one cold and windy evening, just at the beginning of Autumn as the ladies were going to a resident's meeting, suddenly they observed a hooded figure emerge from the house and bolt towards a waiting taxi. Mrs Placket cried out, "Good lord, have you ladies seen that?" Gobstopped, the ladies stared in silence. The mystery person boarded the waiting taxi, which quickly sped away. At the resident's meeting the topic of conversation was very much about who the hooded person was; Mrs Placket was intrigued and could focus her mind on little else. Mrs Reynolds was equally out of sorts and urged the ladies to finish the meeting early, in order to avoid travelling home in the dark. All concurred. Two more weeks passed without incident; then one night the affair took a new turn. Mrs Reynolds was coming home after visiting her sister in Renalagh, when she noticed a light in the upstairs window of the MacKay house. Her curiosity aroused, she moved closer, pausing in the shade of an elm tree in front of the house. It was now 11:33PM and there was an eerie stillness about the night. Staring up at the window she noticed the curtains pulled across one of the windows. A figure dressed in white holding a lighted candle passed back and forth across the room. Every couple of seconds it would stop and stare out into the night. Half paralysed with fear, Mrs Reynolds fled the scene towards her home. Arriving she knocked loudly at the hall door. As the door opened she surged forward, collapsing into the arms of her husband, Mark.

It was several minutes before she could speak. She described to her husband what she had seen. "A ghost, a ghost!" she yelled. "I saw it, upstairs, standing in the room…walking backwards and forward, candle in hand." With these few words she fell into a swoon. Her husband fetched a glass of brandy and, carrying her into the sitting room, he placed her beside the warm fire. She took a large drink of the brandy and revived sufficiently to be able to talk. She explained in more detail what she had seen. He listened with patience to what she had to say, but found it difficult to believe. He could see that she was overwrought; for the present he focused his attention on helping her to relax. After comforting her for some time—they both retired to bed.

The next day Mrs Reynolds was still uneasy. She repeated to her husband what she had seen the night before. Apprehension and fear still gripped her. She refused to leave the house. In the coming days some ladies from the bridge club called to see her; listening intently to her story, which very soon became a major talking point in Apple Way. For the next fortnight the area was very quiet, then, one night as the ladies—including Mrs Reynolds—were coming home from their mid-week bingo they noticed a lone figure standing in the shade of the large trees that fronted the house. It was a young man. He stood there, motionless, staring up at the window. In the pale moonlight his figure silhouetted across the green lawn, given added mystery to his presence. The ladies watched with intrigued interest. Suddenly he hastened away, quickly disappearing from out of sight. This strange happening was much discussed, yet less understood: all were agreed that only time would reveal what strange happenings were going on in the McKay household.

Four nights later a loud knock was heard on the hall door of Mrs Reynolds house. Opening the door Mrs Reynolds was surprised to see young Robert McKay standing there. She invited him in. Young Robert explained the reason for the sudden departure of the family. The cause arose from the collapse of Mr McKay's business and the family were forced to sell off many assets—including the family home; it had caused great distress. The matter was made worse by the disappearance of his mother, which was a source of great tragedy to him, personally. As he related his story, tears rolled from his eyes. Mrs Reynolds was visibly distressed at witnessing this scene; she insisted that he stay with her, at least till his mother returned. As the days rolled on nothing new or unusual occurred in the area: Apple Way remained quiet. Young Robert McKay remained with the Reynolds family; he seemed happy enough. Yet on occasions he would be noticed, late in the evening, standing under the elm tree in the front garden staring at the upper bedroom window of his former parents home.

He never discussed why he did this to anyone, not even to Mrs Reynolds, whose kindness was always dear to his heart. Then one day he left the house early one afternoon and did not return. Worried and concerned, Mrs Reynolds reported the matter to the police; despite an extensive search no trace of the lad could be found. Then one night Mrs Reynolds and several of the ladies were returning home from their usual bingo outing. They noticed a light in the upstairs window of number 7.

Approaching closer they saw a female figure dressed in white standing at the centre of the window, pointing in the direction of the elm tree. It began beckoning to someone, or something to come forward. Suddenly a hooded figure emerged and walked straight towards the front door of the house. The Apple Way ladies were awestruck, as they watched. "What's happening?" cried Mrs Placket. "Who is it—can anyone tell?" No-one answered. Slowly the crouched figure moved forward, occasionally glancing at the upstairs window as the lady in white continued to beckon. Then the hall door opened and the hooded person entered.

Intrigued with curiosity the ladies moved forward. After what seemed an eternity the hall door opened, and a male figure emerged carrying a female all dressed in white. The ladies drew back with fright. Behind, walked young Robert

Mackay, head bowed low. Mrs Placket cried aloud, "My God what's happening?" Suddenly, a slight darkness set over the scene as dark clouds temporarily obscured the bright evening moonlight. Three of the ladies took fright and fled, shouting loudly as they did so: Help! Help! Help! Several neighbours heard the commotion and soon a small crowd had gathered. Meanwhile the male figure carrying the lady in white, paused and laid the body on the lawn. Young Robert Mackay, drawing close to him, put his hand on his shoulder as both wept profusely. The ladies were stunned to notice that the man was Mr Mackay himself, while the lady on the ground was his dead wife, Patricia. An ambulance was quickly called for and all three were taken to hospital. As they were leaving a newspaper fell from Mr MacKay's pocket; Mrs Placket picked it up. It was dated August 14th, just over two months ago. The following notice, circled with a pencil mark, was listed:

London Chronicle, August 14th, 2002. Body of dead woman found in London flat.

 Last night the body of a blond middle aged woman was discovered dead in a flat at 66 Ely close, off the Harrington road. Believed to be from Ireland, she was dead for some days. The police say that foul play is not suspected. The body has been removed to the morgue for post-mortem examination, while efforts are being made to trace her relatives.

Over the next week there was much speculation among the ladies of Apple Way as to what was the cause of Mrs MacKay's death. Some said a broken heart brought on by the sale of the family home; others speculated differently. One mystery which engaged all their attentions, was, how

Mrs MacKay's body, reported dead in London on August 14th could turn up in her former home in Apple Way on September 16th. The last word was left to Mrs Placket, who, upon receiving a present from her brother in London, wrapped in an old copy of the London Chronicle newspaper, noticed the following report:

London chronicle, August 17th, 2002

Woman's body disappears from morgue. Police are appealing to anyone who can help them discover the whereabouts of a female body, which disappeared from the morgue sometime in the last twenty-four hours. She was a blond, middle-aged lady, five foot ten inches in height and believed to be Irish. If anyone has any information or can assist in any way, would they please get in touch with inspector Raddle at Ely Road police station, telephone 7764. Or with any local station."

Looking at the other ladies, Mrs Placket remarked, "Such, ladies, are the strange encounters that can sometimes occur in all our lives."

The Cupbearer

"Spare a copper mister, spare a copper, please!" Thus cried the hunched figure of a man on the pavement, back against the wall. Dishevelled looking and unshaven, eyes somewhat bloated, Sean Cody—for such was his name, was someone seen about the streets of Dublin town trying to keep body and soul together, begging for alms.

It was 7:30PM, of a summer evening as Tom Harkins and Peter Hanley walked past. "Bloody nuisance these characters," cried Harkins. "The law should ban them from the streets. They are everywhere these days."

Hanley did not reply. Looking back, he remarked, "He looks a fit individual; you'd think he would get himself a job instead of sitting out on the street begging. Sad."

"These guys don't want to work, Peter," continued Harkins. "They have it made doing what they are doing. Probably drawing the dole and spending several days week bumming money off the tourists. I heard they could knock down close on eighty to one hundred euro a week—all tax-free! Sure why would they work? They have it too handy."

"They would make that much in a week, you reckon?"

quizzed Hanley. "It's what I have been told," cried Harkins, "eighty to one hundred euro a week. So why should they look for work?" Hanley remained silent.

Arriving at Murphy's pub they entered the lounge to await the arrival of their wives. It was the Harkins' wedding anniversary and, as they were neighbours and good friends, they had decided to have a night out together. Dinner had been arranged around at the Avarsi restaurant for 9:30PM later in the evening. Both were in good spirits, and looked forward to an enjoyable evening.

"Do you know," cried Hanley, "that over two hundred people a week sleep rough in Dublin? Just think of it—two hundred souls sleeping in cardboard boxes, in doorways, some with barely a rag on their backs; sure if it wasn't for the charitable organisations working around the town at night, these people would be in a pretty bad way."

"That guy we just passed on the street outside did not seem too badly off!" exclaimed Harkins. "No sir—he looked fit and well. He's probably one of the cleverer types; probably nothing wrong with him at all. I would never give these guys any money. They should be made to work, instead of living off the rest of us. Wouldn't you agree?"

"Well I always like to keep an open mind about those I see begging in the street; you know the old saying, Tom, 'There but for the grace of God go I'. We don't know the personal circumstances of these people, do we? Perhaps they suffer from some illness?"

The conversation was abruptly stopped by the arrival of both their wives. A round of drinks were ordered. Peter proposed a toast and hearty congratulations to Tom Harkins and his wife on the occasion of their wedding anniversary. After having several drinks and much conversation, they left for the restaurant at 9:15PM. Once again they walked past where the beggar was sitting. His body was tilted forward facing the roadway. He cried out, "A copper, spare a...copper, mister...A copper for...for a cup of tea, please?" They ignored his plea. Mrs Harkins turned her head and looking back glanced straight at him. The beggar raised his head and looked at her; there was a look of emptiness in his bloated eyes. Mrs Harkins noticing this, her face exhibited a pitiful expression.

They soon reached the restaurant. The next two hours were spent in celebration and song. They made new friends with three other couples who were also celebrating anniversaries. In a warm and friendly atmosphere all enjoyed the excellent cuisine on offer. After enjoying a most pleasant night they headed back to collect their cars from the local car park.

Passing down the street they were surprised to notice that the beggar was still there. He seemed to be asleep. Mrs Harkins remarked how busy the street was, lots of people coming and going. The situation of the beggar troubled her. He did not move or gesture. Mrs Harkins bent down quickly dropping a small parcel of food at his feet. Moving on they collected their cars, and went home. The next morning Tom Harkins was sitting down to breakfast with his wife. It had just gone eight o'clock. The morning news was being read out. The voice on the radio was quite low. Mrs Harkins remarked, "Rise up the radio, dear. You know I like to hear the news first thing in the morning." Her husband, not feeling the best from the previous night's outing, grunted—but obliged. The following came over the air:

"At 4:00AM this morning the body of a man believed to be in his forties was discovered in a doorway in Princess

Street; he had been dead for some time. It is understood he was frequently seen begging around the city. The body was removed to the city Morgue for further examination and identification."

Mrs Harkins was about to eat a piece of toast; she paused after hearing this. She looked at her husband, exclaiming "Tom, surely that can't be the man we passed last night after we left the restaurant. Could it? Good Lord," she continued, "found dead—how tragic!"

Her husband, conscious of the sensitivity of his wife on such matters, replied, "I don't think that was the same person. The guy we passed was further up the street. Like a good woman eat your toast."

"But I'm sure it was," she continued. "The very same."

"How can you be sure it was the very same," he blurted out, somewhat angrily. "Sure we hardly looked at the guy we passed. Finish your breakfast, woman, and leave it. I have to be off shortly."

Mrs Harkins remained silent. Harkins finished his breakfast and left for work. Mrs Harkins was troubled by what she had heard. She was sure it was the same man. She recalled the small parcel of food she had dropped at his feet the night before. "Surely the poor devil is not dead," she thought. She could not get him out of her mind. Was he the beggar they had passed? Or was it someone else: her mind was on fire with curiosity. Unable to contain the suspense any longer she resolved to go straight to the city morgue and see for herself.

When she arrived she was shown into the mortuary room where the body was laid out. The attendant, after enquiring if she would be all right, withdrew. She felt a strange loneliness about the place; the silence was deafening: she trembled slightly. She felt very much alone. As she approached the corpse, she made the sign of the Cross. Yes, it was he.

He was fully clothed. His face was drawn and haggard looking, eyes bloated out. "My God!" she cried. "How terrible." Tears flowed from her eyes. Unable to look any longer, nor bear the deafening silence of the room, she said a short prayer and left.

That evening Tom Harkins dropped into his local pub for a drink. He would meet his neighbour, Peter Hanley for a couple of pints. It was customary each week for them to do so. He arrived at seven o'clock. Peter was sitting at the bar; there was two pints of Guinness on the counter.

"And the top of the evening to you Peter," cried Harkins. "I see you've arranged the usual." Lifting one of the pints, he exclaimed, "Your health, Peter!"

"And to you, Tom," returned Hanley. "A good night last night?"

"Indeed," replied Hanley. "Kathleen enjoyed herself greatly. Sheila said to me this morning that we must do the same again."

"Aye," replied Harkins, "I fully agree. But that beggar bumming money, I think that upset Kathleen. It should be outlawed. Don't you agree?"

Hanley lifted his pint, sipping it slowly. He replied, "Oh, by the way, Tom, you might like to read this in the Herald."

He handed him the newspaper.

Harkins began to read, "At 3:00AM this morning a man in his late thirties was found dead in a doorway in Princess Street. He has been identified as a Mr. Sean Cody, a well-known Dublin beggar frequently seen around the city. Mr Cody had been in and out of psychiatric hospitals for many years. A spokesperson from the local Health Board described Mr. Cody's death as sad. With a little more understanding this man could be alive today. It is a tragedy which affects us all."

Harkins handed the paper to Peter. He took a large gulp of Guinness. "Well, perhaps he was one of the more genuine beggars," he cried. "But I still think most of them are gamming on."

Hanley gave Harkins a cautious look. "Gamming on?" he cried. "Perhaps in some cases; however, I think it is always best, Tom, to keep an open mind; after all how can we know what is going on in another man's head: what sorrows he or she is carrying. Sad, very sad I think."

For a while there was silence as neither spoke. Shortly after they both finished up their drinks and headed home.

Three days later the Rising Star newspaper ran an article on the plight of the homeless in Dublin. Peter Hanley was at work. Sitting down to his morning tea break a colleague remarked, "Terrible sad all these homeless people with nowhere to live, Peter. Look at this, some poor soul being buried in the paupers' graveyard...Tragic." Peter took the paper from his colleague. He was surprised to see that of the two mourners present—one was Tom Harkins wife, Kathleen. "Why I know this woman," cried Hanley. "Oh?" returned his colleague. "Someone of importance is she?" "Very important," replied Hanley. "A woman of wide sympathies and understanding, I believe, not only for the living, but also for the dead. The homeless of Ireland need more people like her today."

The Auction

The clock struck 8:00AM as Paddy Rafferty sat down to a breakfast of eggs, rashers, tea and toast. He had a wry smile on his pale sallow face. The early morning sunshine beamed through the kitchen window. He reached forward to the radio and turned on the early morning news. Today was auction-day at Buckley's auctioneers, and as usual he would be in attendance. Having previewed the catalogue he was elated to see listed a William IV rectangular mahogany table, an item that held his special interest. As he neatly dissected his rashers into smaller pieces, he was determined to secure this particular item, no matter what the cost.

He had a passion for antiques in general, and in particular for items of household furniture from the seventeenth and eighteenth centuries. He was looking forward with more than ordinary interest to this auction. Thoughts entered his mind that he might not be successful in his quest; two of his ablest opponents, Richard Garry and the "flyer Burke" would be there also. Both were always on the lookout for items of "period" furniture. He anticipated another interesting contest!

He carefully calculated his financial budget. "Let me see,"

he thought. "What is it likely to realise? Would it be £800? £1000 maybe, or even £1,500?" He moved towards a drawer in the kitchen press. He opened it and drew out a small notebook. This contained details of a number of entries about items sold at previous auctions, including prices paid. He opened the book. "Lets see, yes, a George III inlaid mahogany corner display cabinet…Sold for £2,600…way out of my league I'm afraid." He examined several other figures, which gave some indication of how the auction price might go for the William IV table; after carefully reassessing available money to spend, he felt he was in with a good chance of securing it.

He finished his breakfast and retired to his sitting room. This was his favourite room in the house. Approximately twenty-two feet by eighteen, it was colourfully decorated and amply furnished. He sat back in an easy chair, itself of old style craftsmanship. He gazed at the numerous items of furniture, some from the nineteenth century, others of the early twentieth, which he had acquired at past auctions. In a beautiful glass cabinet he gazed upon his late nineteenth century silver cutlery set, which he had secured at a recent auction. His thoughts roamed, to acquire the William IV table would make a valuable complement to his present collection. With the auction commencing at ten he delayed no further. He finished breakfast and left immediately. He arrived there at 9:40AM to be greeted by Tommy Cole, the auctioneer in charge for the day. Tommy was an old friend from way back.

"Top of the morning to you, Paddy!" cried Cole. "You're ready for another day of action, no doubt?"

"As ready as ever I'll be," exclaimed Rafferty. Leaning close to his friend's ear he whispered, "Are you ready for the

Burke and Garry combination, Tommy, that's what I'd like to know? That William IV table on your list, should raise a bit of excitement, I should think."

The auctioneer looked at Rafferty, smiling cautiously.

"But never fear, Tom, I'll give them a run for their money, rest assured of that!"

"Indeed, they'll be so busy trying to outdo each other they're sure to fall between two stools—as you and I have so often seen happen to them in the past."

They both chuckled with laughter. "Anyway," rejoined the auctioneer, "the best of luck to you Paddy. I know you've been after a piece like that for quite some time; I hope it works out for you today." As Rafferty nodded his head in appreciation the auctioneer passed on into the main office to prepare for the day.

Rafferty entered the auction room and sat himself down. He recognised several familiar faces, but there was no sign of Garry or Burke. He hoped they would not turn up. He noticed some latecomers enter and casually inspect some of the items on display. Just then his two main rivals entered the hall and sat down directly across to his left. By now the hall was fairly full of interested bidders. Some had anxious expressions on their faces; some smiled: some grim-faced. A little tension pervaded the air. Rafferty watched as each item was auctioned off. He noted the efficiency with which Tommy despatched his business. There was keenness among bidders—a keenness he had not seen before. He noticed Mulligan, a keen observer of all that went on; he did not bid much—this was mainly because his particular interest was old paintings: today there were few on offer. When he did make a bid for an item it was with a coldness and emotional detachment that was little pleasant to watch. Statue-like, he merely nodded when bidding: Rafferty always watched him more out of a deep sense of the way he bid. Eventually item number 146, the William IV table was declared. The auctioneer called for bids. From the centre of the hall a bid of 300 euro was called. Successive bids quickly followed, with Burke, Garry and Rafferty hotly competing against each other, until eventually the sum offered reached 2,400 euro. Rafferty looked about the hall; there was a picture of resignation among many of the bidders; he could see that securing of the table would rest between himself, Burke and Garry. He gritted his teeth as he looked up at the auctioneer; he was determined to have this item—no matter what the cost.

"Two thousand six hundred I am bid," roared the auctioneer, as his words echoed across the hall. "Do I have any advance on 2,600? Come now gentlemen, a fine William IV table in immaculate condition...Yes, is that a bid, sir? No? Do I have 2,650? Yes, thank you sir."

And so the bidding continued till the offer reached 3,100 euro—from Garry. Rafferty was devastated, the bid ruling was already two hundred over his budgeted figure; it looked like his arch rival would secure the table.

The auctioneer prepared to close. Rafferty gritted his teeth. What could he do? He tossed the idea back and forth in his mind, struggling to decide. As the seconds passed the tension mounted. Looking across the hall at Garry he could see a grinding sneer on his face, a smile of triumph that quickly infuriated him. Suddenly the auctioneer prepared to close—"I have 3,100. Are there any further bids?"—He quickly glanced at Garry and Rafferty, then around the hall. None were forthcoming. He raised his hammer to strike. "Going once, going twice." "Three thousand three hun-

dred!" roared Rafferty. "Thank you sir," cried the auctioneer. "I have 3,300, who'll give me 3,500?"

There was a short silent pause, and with no further bids
offered, he roared, "Sold to the gentleman at the end of
the hall!"

Rafferty glanced around the room, in particular at Burke
and Garry; both were silent. Garry had a sombre look upon
his face. Burke was smiling. Having come to a satisfactory
payment arrangement with the auctioneer, he retired to a
nearby café for a well-earned cup of coffee. Here two old
friends joined him, a Mr & Mrs John Corrigan, both of
whom had been at the auction.

"A good days work for you, Paddy," remarked Corrigan.
"You sent the other two packing again I see."

"Aye," replied Rafferty, smiling gleefully. "They looked
none too happy to be sure! I was determined to get that
table, John, no matter what it cost; beating them gave me
great satisfaction, so it did."

After conversing for a short while Rafferty excused himself and went to arrange for the delivery of the table. Driving
home late that afternoon he noticed lots of activity around
the estate where he lived. It was Halloween that night and
the kids were out in large numbers knocking at doors looking for apples and nuts. He felt a sense of excitement, of gai-
ety. As he passed Parkview Common, a giant bonfire stack
was at an advanced state of preparation; he too felt excited,
uplifted: soon his William the IV table would be arriving
home. Entering his house he was greeted by his wife, who
was quick to remark upon the smile of satisfaction on his face.
"I see you've had a good day at the auction," she quipped.
"As always," replied Rafferty. "Routed the other pair."

"So you got the table then?"

"I did," replied her husband. "But enough of this idle chatter woman; away with you now and make me a nice cup of tea. You'll see the table later on when it's delivered."

Mrs Rafferty did not comment further, retiring to the kitchen as instructed. Her husband, sat down to warm tea and toast, and a read of the evening paper. At 8:30PM that evening a knock was heard at the hall door; it was the deliveryman. Rafferty quickly opened the door and accompanied the driver to the van; however, when it was opened the mahogany table was nowhere to be seen! The driver was gobstopped; Rafferty was furious. In a high pitched voice he demanded to know where his table was. The driver could offer no explanation. He definitely loaded it on to the van earlier in the afternoon. He could not understand where it had gone. Rafferty demanded that he immediately revisit the previous delivery addresses to determine if it had been offloaded by mistake. He insisted on going with him. After about an hour and a half's drive, and after calling to all previous dropoff points, the table had not been found. Rafferty's anger became more apparent in the forceful exchanges between himself and the driver as they drove back to his home.

On the way they passed along Parkview Common. Here the massive bonfire was now blazing furiously. Dozens of young children and youths—many dressed up in typical Halloween costumes—were gaily dancing and singing around the fire. Rafferty looked in their direction. Suddenly he gasped out in horror: "Stop! Stop! I see it—I'm sure it is. My beautiful table! They're burning it!"

The driver quickly pulled over to the side of the road. Rafferty jumped out of the van and raced towards the fire. He roared aloud: "Stop! Stop, I say! My table, my beautiful table, you're burning it!" All the children stopped dancing around the fire and stared at Rafferty, as he made frantic efforts to retrieve it but the flames were too high and the heat too intense; he was forced to withdraw further and further back from the fire. After some further shouts of abuse at the youths and children, he turned and, muttering to himself, walked back towards the van. "My beautiful table… William the fourth's reign…what would they know? Value? Nothing."

He paused before getting back into the van; he turned and looked across at the bonfire, staring as if in a trance. Suddenly his eyes opened wide in some amazement, for there among the onlookers he was horrified to see Garry, standing among the crowd, smiling. He waved in Rafferty's direction. As Rafferty climbed into the van, he placed his head in his hands, sobbed slightly, lamenting the fact that he had been outsmarted at this day's auction after all.

Rover's Happy Return

Michael Aster was up bright and early on that summer morning back in 1997. For the previous twenty-four hours the thought of following up on the latest lead where their favourite dog, Rover, was had dominated his mind. Rover was the family pet for over twelve years, but had recently strayed. Michael and his wife, Fiona, were both very upset. Practically every avenue had been explored in an effort to locate him, but without success. These included talking with the postman, insurance man, even the milk delivery rounds man, all to no avail. With all the children grown up and gone away, the house was lonely during the day; Rover had been good company for Fiona: she particularly missed him at present.

At breakfast she would recall those early morning walks they would take together strolling down Checker Street, passing the local library, up Penitent's avenue, around by Rafters roundabout, and head straight down Oakland Street into Oakland Park. There she would let him off his lead and they both would enjoy an hour of fun and enjoyment. She missed her favourite pet so much, and those walks together in the park, that Michael became worried her health might be affected. Something must be done to find Rover, and quickly.

On this particular morning they were both delighted to receive a letter indicating that a dog answering Rover's description had been picked up ten miles away in an area known as O'Connors Glen; this was a half mile from the picturesque village of Haven Wood, an area they both knew well. The correspondent, a Mrs Sheerer, had written to say she had seen Michael's notice in the Wayside Chronicle newspaper, regarding Rover. She had recently taken a stray dog into her home matching his description. She invited them to call to her whenever was convenient to see if in fact the dog was really theirs.

Fiona and Michael read over this letter with avid excitement. It contained a phone number: Fiona rang immediately. Mrs Sheerer was delighted to hear from Fiona, and told of how she came to have Rover. She spoke of how friendly he was, and they should come and collect him whenever was convenient. When Fiona was finished on the phone she turned to Michael, exclaiming, "I'm so excited, Rover found at last!" Putting her arms around Michael, she hugged him warmly, thanking him for keeping up the search for their favourite pet. Michael said nothing, just quietly smiled. That afternoon they drove out to O'Connor's Glen. It was a place not unfamiliar to them. On many occasions before they had driven past it on the way to the town of Cracker-Wood, some eleven miles further on. Fiona was from the country, and Michael often took her on a Sunday afternoon drive to see, "the lovely Irish countryside." As they headed off Michael noticed that she had a particular glow on her face; she was looking forward to the trip and to seeing the beautiful fields of ripening wheat, and the white blossoming hawthorn bushes now in full bloom along the roadside embankments. "Who knows," she thought, "perhaps they might have time to stop and gather some cowslips?"

Michael was a most careful driver. He drove slowly to ensure that his wife had ample opportunity to enjoy the scenic countryside. Fiona's thoughts now centred on the beauty all around her; with the birds singing and the summer wheat almost ready for cutting, how divine it all looked. She thought how wonderful it would be to stroll through the fields, bask in the summer sunshine, and never have to leave these most pleasant scenes! But for now it was Rover, her favourite pet dog, which dominated her thoughts. She hoped he would be well, and that Mrs Sheerer would have given him enough food to eat. Rover always had a good appetite. She wondered too if he would have missed her and Michael, and the daily walks they would have taken to Oakwood Park. She knew he loved those walks and when in the mornings she would reach up to the kitchen dresser for the lead, he would get very excited.

Approaching the park he would bark loudly and upon release from his lead would race off around the green in a frenzy of excitement. Once there Fiona would sit on the park bench, stretch out her legs, and enjoy the warm sunshine; she would enjoy the smell of the park flowers, just now coming into season—making those walks with Rover a memorable experience.

These were her thoughts as they drove along in the direction of O'Connors Glen. Her thoughts again focused on Rover; how would he react when he saw her and Michael? Would he rush up to her and lick her face, as he had so many times in the past?

Michael, noticing the pensive expression on her face, interjected, "Now dear, don't you be fretting about Rover, you know what Mrs Sheerer said, he is in good health, is being looked after, and soon we will be collecting him and bringing him home."

Fiona looked at Michael; encouraged by his words she leaned across and gave him a kiss on the cheek, replying, "Yes dear, but I will feel better when we arrive and see him for myself. It has been going on three weeks now since he strayed, and I'm sure he must be fretting. What I don't understand is why he strayed in the first place!"

"Well he is not a young dog," cried Michael. "At twelve years of age he will require closer watching when we bring him back."

"Perhaps you're right, dear; we will have to do that when we get him back."

For the rest of the journey they both sat back in silence. The day seemed much brighter, now, and with the warm sunshine about there was a great summer feeling in the air; a type of day you just wanted to laze about and soak up the sun. Fiona sat back in her seat, stretched out her feet and tried to relax.

Arriving at O'Connors Glen, they were soon in sight of the picturesque village of Haven-Wood. Within minutes they were there. It comprised a cluster of eighteen lovely cottages, a small shop, while some yards beyond, a bowling alley. Michael and Fiona were struck by the peace and calm of the area; so engaging —almost spiritual in a way: they both felt quite at ease here.

They stopped a local villager and enquired where Mrs Sheerer lived. "Oh," the stranger replied, "that would be the old lady living out the road a few hundred yards from here. Turn around and head back they way you came in. You can't miss it; it is the last cottage on the right: can't mistake it. You'll see and old dog sitting at the front gate. Okay?"

Thanking him, they drove back at once. Approaching the cottage they noticed Rover sitting outside. Fiona was thrilled at the sight of her favourite pet.

She jumped from the car, waved both arms in the air, crying out "Rover, Rover! Come here boy. Come here!"

Rover quickly recognised his beloved mistress and barking profusely he raced forward to meet her, bowing his head, almost apologetically because of his absence from home. Fiona embraced him warmly, while Rover, continuing to bark loudly, licked her face several times. As this happy encounter was proceeding Michael noticed an elderly lady standing at the entrance to the cottage.

Conjecturing that this was Mrs Sheerer, he approached her, "Good afternoon! Would you be a Mrs Sheerer, by any chance?"

"To be sure I am," she replied. They both shook hands.

"We're delighted to make your acquaintance; this is my wife, Fiona, you spoke to her on the phone. We would like to thank you for contacting us about our dog; we really missed the old pet."

Mrs Sheerer invited them both into the cottage for a cup of tea and biscuits, and for an hour they chatted. She explained to them how she had come to befriend Rover, and how they both had been getting on so well these past weeks. As Michael listened he could see that she had grown quite attached to Rover, and that they had been good company for each other. Finally, after what was an enjoyable meeting Michael and Fiona bade farewell to Mrs Sheerer. With Rover safely retrieved, they all headed for home. Discussing the matter on the way they both agreed that she had looked after Rover very well and was deserving of some reward; she had refused to accept money for taking care of their favourite pet, yet they felt they had to reward her some way. Michael recalled that he had been approached by one of his friends, a Mrs Cassidy; she was seeking a good home for a young collie pup. Michael mentioned this to Fiona. They both looked at each other, exclaiming together "Yes! We know just the person—Mrs Sheerer!"

Having acquired the collie they drove back to the cottage the following week. Mrs Sheerer was surprised to see them again. She invited them in, after which they presented her with the young collie. She was delighted. "I shall name him, Rover!" she exclaimed. "Aye," replied Michael and Fiona together, "it's a double celebration of Rover's happy return!"

They all burst out laughing at this most happy outcome, yet none happier, in every way, than Michael and Fiona as they drove home later that day.

The Coming Of Age Of Miss Louise Maguire

It was five o'clock exactly when Christine Maguire arrived at the Swain Hotel. She expected that all the preparations for her younger sister's birthday would be in place. It was Lisa's twenty-first today. This evening she was having her birthday party. Christine was filled with excitement for her. No special surprises were expected. All the guests were invited, including a host of her young friends. Lisa was a very bubbly, extrovert teenager, full of life, and with a strong independent manner. She loved nice clothes, was always dressed well, and was regarded as a very outspoken person for her age. She spoke German fluently, and on occasion, and particularly to cause a stir, she would deliberately interject some German phrases in conversation which would not be understood by those listening. This made her unpopular with some, and excited jealousy among others. Lisa was not bothered. Good humoured and full of life, she had much going for herself; to all her friends she was the "rising sun of youth" on the Dublin social scene.

John Corcoran, the manager, greeted Christine as she entered the hotel. They spoke about Lisa's birthday party arrangements; he invited her to inspect the room where the event would take place. All was as expected. As they looked about the room the musicians engaged for the evening arrived and prepared to set up their equipment. After thanking him she then adjourned to the resident's lounge and ordered a gin and tonic.

This evening she was in a reflective mood; she thought of her teenage years and how unhappily her life had turned out: at thirty-three years of age she was a divorcee, without children—alone. She was resolved that her kid sister would never end up as she did, and that her birthday party would be a success. She was determined that Lisa would never endure the suffering and humiliation that she had experienced. She glanced at her watch. It was 5.35 PM exactly. She finished her drink and went out to Clancy's department store to collect that present she had ordered for her friend, Kay Harahan, who had recently had a new baby boy. When she returned twenty minutes later she was delighted to see that some of their country relations had arrived for the occasion. Several were gathered at the bar. There was Mark, her brother in law, a practicing solicitor now living with his family in Meath. Tommy, her brother—the ever laughing comedian! He lived out in north county Dublin and always made her laugh; indeed he was her favourite brother and had been a great comfort to her, particularly at the time of her divorce. By 7:15PM the crowd began to swell; several aunts, uncles, and many of Lisa's friends had arrived.

The atmosphere was engaging and merry. However, Christine noticed that Lisa seemed noticeably uneasy, almost sad looking; she approached her and took her to one side enquiring what was wrong. Lisa was not forthcoming with any explanation, and no amount of probing by her sister could discover the cause of her present strange mood. Christine did not press further for an explanation; for the moment the matter was dropped.

At 7:45PM, a little later than expected, Lisa's boyfriend, Robert O'Connor arrived. Neatly dressed, and displaying all the signs of having had a few drinks, he was in most affable form, smiled at everyone, walked straight to Lisa and embraced her warmly. This brought a smile to her face; she began to look more cheerful. Christine, observing this, was most pleased. She looked at them both, remarking, "That's better! Can't have my little sister looking off colour on her 21st birthday now can we?" Robert looked curiously at Christine, yet resisted the temptation to ask her what prompted this particular remark; he just smiled at her.

The musicians now began to play, opening with a delightful chorus of traditional Irish melodies; these soon had the audience swirling about the dance floor. *The Fields of Athenry*, *The West's Awake*, *Sweet Sixteen*, and many other songs besides soon filled the air. Even the hotel manager couldn't resist a swirl as he crossed the dance floor to speak to a colleague. Midway through the evening a large birthday cake in the shape of a castle was wheeled into the centre of the room. Graced with twenty-one brightly shining candles, it presented a heart-warming scene. Lisa and Robert were called forward, Lisa to do the honours ably supported by Robert. As they both blew out the candles cameras flashed from all directions as lots of photographs were taken. Lisa and Robert together cut the cake. Someone shouted, "a toast to Lisa and Robert!" With that Mrs Maguire stepped forward, right arm raised calling for silence. She spoke as follows:

"I would first of all welcome you all here for this memorable occasion—my daughter's 21st birthday. Both my husband and I are particularly proud of Lisa, who has always been an exemplary daughter, well behaved, considerate and thoughtful of others; we rejoice to see this day, this coming of age and are very pleased, too, with young Robert who has proved himself a thorough gentleman—the type of young man we are glad to see dating our daughter. That's as much as I am going to say ladies and gentlemen, unaccustomed as I am to long speeches! Can I ask you all to join me now in a very special toast—to Lisa on her 21st birthday, and to Lisa and Robert for their future happiness together."

All raised their glasses as Mrs Maguire called out "To Lisa—happy birthday dear daughter!" All raised their glasses, crying aloud "Happy birthday Lisa!" "And again," cried Lisa's mother, "to the future happiness of Lisa and Robert!"

The responding acclamation from the crowd echoed to the ceiling, as the band played happy birthday. The cake was now distributed to all the guests. Once more the floor was filled with dancers, as the band played ever more bouncy tunes. As more drink was consumed some individuals broke out into song, while others gave impromptu speeches of congratulations to the happy couple. Yet nothing electrified the atmosphere as much as the sudden speech of young Robert. With more alcohol taken than usual he approached Lisa's parents and began thus: "Mr and Mrs Maguire...I...I am particularly glad to be here this evening and to know you both, for I...love Lisa very much." Suddenly he turned and stood up on a chair nearby, crying out as he did, "I am delighted to meet you both here this evening, and...and, to welcome everyone! When our son is born we're, we're going to name him...Roderick Maguire O'Connor after that great king that ruled in Ireland in the sixth century! He was a great king Mrs Maguire, a great king."

He stepped down from the chair, and, crossing the floor

slumped down into an armchair. Most of the dancers had stopped dancing to listen to his speech, and now that it had concluded they just stood there a little confused as to its content. Those relations close to Mr and Mrs Maguire were stunned by what had been said; Mrs Maguire was seen to turn pale in the face. Lisa's sister, Christine shuffled quickly across the floor and confronted her sister, thus: "Did he say a new baby?" she asked Lisa. "Pregnant—you're pregnant! My God what has come over you both. Expecting a baby —on your 21st birthday, are you crazy?" Lisa blushed but did not reply to her sister. She stared across the room at her parents who were in deep conversation; turning, she lunged at her sister, "Yes, pregnant—what of it? It has happened sooner than we wished but by God Robert and I are delighted!"

Christine was stunned by the intensity of Lisa's retort. She did not reply, instead it was noticeable that tears flowed from her eyes as she turned to look away. Suddenly she turned back and threw her arms around her sister hugging her warmly crying out "My little sister, my little sister—expecting a baby!" They both embraced warmly for several seconds.

As the music and dancing continued a hastily convened family conference took place. Lisa's parents were not slow to comment on Robert's speech, particularly by the manner in which he had blurted it out. However, what was done was done and both were reconciled to the news and wished them well. Robert for his part considered it wise to maintain a respectable distance from Lisa's parents for the rest of the evening. As the evening was coming to a close the last word was left to Lisa's friend, Caroline Daly, who, at a little after midnight, suddenly jumped up on one of the chairs and in a loud voice burst into song singing that great Irish air *She moved through the fair*. She was quickly joined by a chorus of voices as everybody else joined in. As she concluded the song, and with glass of beer in hand, she finally roared out in fine voice, "To the coming of age of Miss Louise Maguire! Well done Lisa!"

The Postman And The Dog

HACKER THOMPSON, POSTMAN, rolled out of bed at 7:00AM on what was to be the beginning of an ordinary day of mail deliveries, or so he thought. Ordinarily he would be looking forward to his days work. He was the "outdoor type." He liked to be out and about among the people. He enjoyed the fresh air, and he thoroughly enjoyed his work. He had no regrets at having given up his job as a long distance driver, seven years ago, and joining the postal service. However, recently the company had introduced new work practices, which involved switching routes where postal staff worked. This week he was working in the Hillside estate to the west of the city. This would be his fourth week to deliver mail here.

He became friendly with some of the residents, like Mrs Crane at number 6, or the old age pensioner, and ex-army corporal, Mr. Walker, in 32—nice people; the type that would keep you talking all day! But then there was the Hamilton family; all out of work, and, according to local intelligence, not known to be early risers, except of course their pet dog—known locally as Dasher. Now Dasher was a mongrel, alert as a fox scouting for his dinner on a late summer evening. Dasher didn't miss a trick He hated strangers.

Twice in the past four weeks he had almost taken a lump out of Hacker Thompson's leg; he was not impressed.

Sipping his tea, his thoughts rambled over how he could avoid being attacked again. Should he bring along a piece of poisoned meat to…No. Bring his grandfather's walking stick to beat him with? No. The stick was too valuable. He would have to find some way of getting past him, he would have to! Particularly if he had some mail for the house! After all, there was no guarantee that this dog would be tied up or locked away The Hamiltons were not known for their diligence in attending to such matters.

Running his hand across his unshaven chin he pondered deeply on the matter. Agnes, the wife was a terrible nagger; she was continually at him for no reason at all. He decided to finish his breakfast quickly and be away before she got up. He felt near breaking point, and if she didn't stop he would up and leave. He thought deeply about what he could do about Dasher. He thought about the layout of the area, about the central green on front of Hamilton's house; he normally approached the green starting at the south end at number one, proceeding to number ten, then crossing over to number eleven on the west side of the square, eventually finishing off at the north end. This section covered numbers twenty to twenty-nine. Dasher normally stood guard at the gate entrance to the Hamilton house, and from the moment Hacker would enter the square Dasher would begin grinding his teeth sharpening them in preparation for a kill. He must formulate a plan otherwise he ran the risk of losing a portion of his good trousers—or worse still, a portion of his leg!

He decided to do the following. He would bring a short length of stick complete with a four to eight foot length of narrow rope—looped at one end; and as Dasher came running towards him he would swing forward the looped end over the dog's head and pull tightly. Then he would tie the rope to one of the nearby trees, before continuing with his deliveries. Whoopee! He quietly chuckled to himself. That will fix him!

Having finished his breakfast he gathered the materials he needed and left for work. At precisely 10:45 AM Hacker Thompson entered Hillside Estate, complete with mailbag, short length of stick—with rope attached. As anticipated, Dasher the mongrel was sitting outside the front gate of the Hamilton household, head erect, and surveying the area. Spotting Hacker he began a slow, steady growl, interspersed occasionally by a robust bark. Hacker was about to begin his mail drop with a letter for number four; he paused at the gate before doing so; he stared over at Dasher. His facial expression reflected grim determination; his lips contorted: anger swelled up in his breast. He dug his feet into the soft earth upon which he stood. He felt like dropping his mailbag, racing across the green and grabbing Dasher by the throat, and choking the living daylights out of him. He restrained himself. He had his plan; he was confident it would work. He delivered his two letters, one to number four, and further letters to numbers seven and nine.

Now the moment had arrived. He paused outside number 10 for he had mail for numbers 11, 14, and yes, Hamilton's house—number 16! He checked that all was in readiness, then with a firmness of pace he walked across to number 11, opened the gate, walked up to the letter box, paused, looked over his right shoulder. Safe? Yes. He deposited the mail. Then whirling around he headed out the gate. He paused again. He stared down at Dasher. The mongrel stared straight back at him. Here was a meeting of minds! A clash of the Titans. Man verses dog: Hacker gritted his teeth in preparation for the coming encounter. His blood began to boil: he was seething with anger.

He took the stick complete with rope from under his arm. To divert Dasher's angry look he suddenly raised his left arm in the air, and started whirling it about. This seemed to infuriate the dog for he began howling like mad. Hacker moved forward, slowly; man and dog stared defiantly at each other. In the poise and disposition of each it was clear there would be no surrender; a fight to the death would now take place. Suddenly, Dasher, with hair on his back firmly standing up, made a fierce charge towards Hacker. With the speed of an athlete Hacker cast the looped rope straight at Dasher's head; it was a direct hit. Hacker gave a fierce pull. The rope immediately tightened around the dog's neck—stopping him in his tracks. The dog yelped and struggled for all he was worth; but he could not get loose. A smile came over Hacker's face. "Got you my fine friend!" he exclaimed. He pulled the dog across the green and quickly wrapped the rope around one of the trees. He stood there for a few moments grinning at the dog, and then carried on delivering the mail.

As he slowly walked on he quietly chuckled to himself. Ah, the peace of it! That little bastard totally immobilised! How refreshing, how pleasant! As he walked up the pathway of number 16, the Hamilton household, he paused, turned back and walked right to the gate. Stopping, he looked across at Dasher tied to the tree; he smiled, cursed the dog under his breath, and to annoy him further he even waved at him! Dasher rolled and twisted, howled, barked and tried everything to break loose, but all to no avail: this just wasn't his day.

Checking the contents of his mailbag, Hacker, very pleased

with himself, carried on. As he walked down the pathway he gave a few intermittent hops and skips, rather like a man dancing; his plan had worked out perfectly. Just before he left the green he turned and looked back at Dasher, who, now was quite subdued. As he finished delivering the last few letters one of the residents, noticing his good humour, remarked, "In pleasant good fettle this morning, Hacker!" "Aye, retorted the latter. "Got some loose ends tied up this morning," adding, as he looked back at Dasher, "Quite remarkably too, I'm glad to say!"

Day Of The Crow

Peter Cassidy struggled out of bed at 7:30 that morning. His head felt like concrete. A banging noise kept echoing inside it. He felt terrible. He rushed downstairs, put on the kettle to make a mug of black coffee. He slumped into his favourite chair as he waited for the kettle to boil. With his head thumping away he cursed the night before and the heavy drinking bout he had engaged in. He couldn't blame the Brady fella, for he was as bad a drinker as himself; the fact is they both made pigs of themselves, and that was that!

He pondered over how much money he had spent. He put his hand in his pocket and took out a bundle of coins plus a note, and placed all on the kitchen table. Twenty, fifty, one hundred, two, three, five, ten—plus a ten euro note, in all sixteen Euro was all he had left. He had blown quite a lot the night before...he couldn't bring himself to say it. He leaned forward and put both elbows on the table, covered his head with both hands moaning of what fools we all are—blowing and wasting our hard-earned money—drinking to excess with nothing to show for it all except a thumping great headache! Madness, madness.

"We should never have joined those Liverpool fans," he

groaned. The kettle boiled. Cassidy made his coffee. It tasted nice, at least it eased the pain in his head, somewhat.

He sat there sipping away at his coffee. There was an unusual silence in the house. His wife, Kathleen was upstairs sound asleep; he could hear her snoring. Looking around the kitchen he focussed his attention on each of the objects that were there: the kitchen table, the cooker, the delf on the shelves—even the floor tiles, cold and colourful though they were. And the round table, silent, lifeless. All the objects were lifeless; all were dead, except himself. He was alive; he had feeling—and a bloody great big headache to boot! He thought about the universe, the planets, Saturn, Jupiter, Mars, Uranus, all suspended in space—nobody holding them up, just positioned there in that great cosmos we call space. Amazing. Who put them there? God only knows. Who keeps them there? God only knows.

A thumping pain went through his head; putting his hand across his forehead he gave a suppressed cry of pain. He felt the agony of the silence; he felt cold. "Cursed drink!" he cried out. He chuckled to himself. "I swear I will give it up!" He ran his hand across his brow, slowly, in an effort to ease the pain. Sixteen euro left. He felt ashamed; he felt so foolish, wasting all his money. Suddenly the cawing of a crow broke the silence of the morning. It sounded like it was coming from the hall, or the sitting room.

"Blast it, it's that bloody crow on the chimney pot, again! *Caw…caw…caw…*on it went cackling for all it was worth: probably waiting for me to light the fire. Bloody thing stands on the top of the chimney pot every day warming itself from the heat of the fire. You'd think it was human."

After a couple of minutes it stopped. Peter Cassidy felt the pain in his head more acutely; the sound of the silence in the house was much stronger; it began to get on his nerves. He thought of putting on the radio, but did not do so. It would only wake up the rest of the family. He did not want that.

Caw, caw…caw, caw

"Blast it! There it goes again," he screamed. "I'll bloody kill it." And then it stopped. Peter again felt the terrible emptiness of the silence. He sipped his coffee. Kathleen's snoring sounded louder; he stared at all the dead inanimate objects all around him. The pain in his head was going. It was cold in the kitchen; he decided to turn on the gas cooker. Still the silence.

He stood up and went out into the backyard. There was a cold chill in the morning air. Looking up at the roof he could see that the crow was still sitting on the chimney pot, still shuffling its wings hoping for a little heat to come up. He stood there watching. Crows, strange birds, very strange. He waved his arms about profusely to try and scare him off, but the bird just stared down at him. Again he waved his arms; still the bird did not stir. He picked up the sweeping brush that was standing over by the wall and hurled it vertically into the air; that did the trick: the crow quickly flew away. He returned into the house, cleaned out the grate, and lit the fire. Then, after turning on the radio he stretched out his feet to relax and listen to the early morning news. "Thank God that headache has eased," he chuckled. It was eight o'clock. Another day begins. "The day of the crow," he cried as he stretched out in his armchair and slowly sipped the rest of his coffee.

The Glove

"Ah! To be or not to be—that is the question," exclaimed Brown. Pointing to a glove that lay on the pavement, he gestured to his colleagues, "Gentlemen, observe. You see before you one neat clean looking glove. To whom does it belong? Nobody knows. Shall I pick it up? Yes? No? How say you, Parker? Or you Thompson?" Silence.

Brown paused momentarily after making this short speech. He had just emerged with his three colleagues, Parker, the tax official, Jones, the architect, "flunker," Thompson, a dealer in stocks and shares, and Murphy, a general office clerk. They had been having their usual end of week drink in Midigans pub in Dublin's O'Connell street. It was 4:15PM on a Friday afternoon. All were in jubilant mood, and looking forward to the long Easter bank holiday weekend.

They stopped to observe the glove; it was a gentleman's, left-handed, with grey leather exterior, expensive looking, its loss sure to be regretted.

"Well gentlemen," continued Brown. "We have just spent the last hour and a half discussing luck; the fortune and misfortunes of life, and how you, Flunker in particular, love to dabble and try your luck in the stock markets. Who, therefore, will pick up this expensive looking single glove?" For several seconds no one spoke.

"Not me!" remarked Jones.

"Spoken with firmness and resolution!" roared Brown. "And what about you, Parker? Will you try your luck?"

Parker grimaced, but declined, "No thank you! It's bad luck to pick up a glove from the ground. You pick it up."

"Who says it's bad luck!" exclaimed Murphy. "That's a load of nonsense. Right Brown?"

"If you say so, Bob," retorted the latter. "But then my aunt was a very superstitious woman, she thought it was bad luck to pick up a glove that had fallen to the ground. She had no time, for fortune tellers, or those card readers, a lot of bonkers, she called it; lived to the ripe old age of ninety-seven years. Who knows?"

For the next few minutes these exchanges went back and forth as to whether the glove should remain on the ground, or whether one of them should pick it up. Brown kept pushing the issue, and went so far as to nearly cause a falling out between himself and Parker. Argument continued, fuelled by the Guinness consumption that had occurred a little earlier. By now the four friends were causing a nuisance by obstructing pedestrians coming and going, along the pavement. It was noticeable, too, that a police officer walking down the centre of the street was staring in their direction. The matter must be resolved, soon.

Suddenly, a ragged looking, poorly dressed man was seen to approach in their direction. Aged about forty, of stout build and unshaven, he had all the appearance of a beggar. He wore a single brown leather glove on his right hand. His appearance caused a momentary pause in their discussion. Coming closer to them he looked straight at the glove on the pavement. He stopped, turned right and stared in a shop window. Almost as quickly he turned back to the centre of the pavement, stooped down quickly, picked up the glove and carried on up the street.

"Well," cried Brown, "what about that, Eh? No worries or concerns about bad luck there! There he goes, one glove richer—and a quality glove by the looks of it. You could have had that, Bob, or you, Parker."

All laughed, except Murphy.

"By the looks of him he could do with a bit of luck," replied Parker "Sure the man hardly has a rag on his back; he won't gain much comfort from an extra glove. Mind you he might get more notice: whether he will want that is another matter. He'll be seen now wearing odd coloured gloves; maybe it will bring him some luck!"

"Most amusing," cried Brown.

As he walked up the town in the direction of the Parnell monument, one of the friends noticed him take something from inside the glove; this he quickly lodged in his over-coat pocket.

The following week the four friends met as usual in Midigan's pub. After an hour and a half, as per usual, they left and headed up towards the Parnell monument. On the way Parker stopped to buy an evening paper. Flicking through the pages he suddenly exclaimed, "Good lord, Jones, listen to this: Lotto jackpot of 1.77 million euro won by a Dublin beggar." Brown, Thompson, and Jones stopped in their tracks: all cried out together, "What!" Jones grabbed the paper from Parker. All turned their eyes on the article, which Jones read as follows:

" A Dublin beggar has today become the proud owner of last Wednesday's Lotto jackpot of 1.77 million euro. At the

Lotto office this morning to collect his cheque, he was accompanied by a group of friends—all beggars! They cheered loudly as he collected his winnings. Interviewed by our reporter, Rose Hammond, he declared his good fortune was, "due entirely to his new, neat fitting glove just recently acquired. This contained hidden warmth, which exceeded his every expectation; moreover, he declared that the arthritis in his left hand was now considerably reduced, for which he thanked the good Lord above. Quizzed as to what he would do with the money, he declared—to the cheers of all his friends—that this very night he intended to hold the biggest beggar's party ever to be seen in Dublin town! All beggars were invited, neat dress not essential! "Bring your own mug," declared the lucky winner. The gathering roared with laughter.

Pulling back from the paper the four friends looked at one another, some grinding their teeth in derision.

"It can't be!" exclaimed Parker.

"Impossible!" roared Jones.

"The lucky dog!" cried Brown.

Murphy remained silent.

Passing the Grisham hotel they noticed the ragged old beggar standing on the steps of the hotel entrance. He was clean-shaven, smoking a cigar, and had a big smile on his face. One of his more notable features, remarked upon by some passers by, was the odd glove—one grey, one brown, which he wore. He paused for a few moments; then, turning he retreated back into the hotel.

The last word was left to Brown. "So, Parker, it's bad luck to pick a single glove from the ground, eh?" Grim-faced, he turned away without uttering a word. As they walked towards the Parnell monument no further words passed between any of them. Reaching the monument all except Murphy turned and went their separate ways. Reflecting on the beggar's good fortune, he chuckled to himself, "the lucky beggar, 1.77 million Euro...picked up the glove: a man of vision, a man of enterprise! And you, Thompson, the dabbler in stocks and shares! Where was your enterprise, your intuition?" Looking up at the Parnell statue he started to read the epitaph—"No man has the right to set the boundaries…" He gave the uncrowned king of Ireland a firm salute, chuckling to himself just before heading towards Gardiner Street, yes, a lucky beggar; a man of vision; he deserved to win—Even if it was somebody else's luck!

Far Cry From The Hills

JAMES TINMAN O'NEILL, an overweight, six foot three inches tall American, had just arrived in town; it was showdown time and the long wait of trigger-happy Cassidy, locally described as the 'loud-mouth from Ireland,' was about to end. It was the year 1866. The ending of the American civil war had left its legacy of social disorder in many towns in both Union and Confederate states. Longhorn, South Dakota, was one such town.

Tinman was a federal marshal called in by the local town council to clean up Longhorn, and with a record of over 100 convictions to his credit from six other States, Cassidy had good reason to be worried. O'Neill's arrest and conviction record to date was as follows: 46 hangings for pre-meditated murders, 34 life sentences for aggravated assault, and the balance comprised of jail terms from 3 to 17 years. Tinman was a force to be reckoned with: his parents, were the O'Neills who had come to America sixty years earlier from Ireland.

Cassidy, an avid student of Irish history, particularly since he had come to America, kept thinking of Benburb, 1646 when the O'Neills led the Irish to victory in battle against the old enemy. He leaned across the bar sipping his whiskey, thinking to himself: was today to be his *Benburb*? The O'Neills were well known for their prowess as fighters; placing his left hand on the holster that held his gun, he felt real cause for concern. Marshall 'Tinman' O'Neill had arrived in town at sun-up this morning, and was expected at Jefferson's bar at any moment. Cassidy was filled with worrying premonitions.

He took two whiskeys to steady his nerves. However, this did little to help. He snapped at the bartender demanding to know what he was staring at. The barman immediately apologised assuring him that no offence was intended. Cassidy looked around at the other customers in the bar. Several were playing cards. He took out his six-shooter, twirled it around his right index finger then, without warning fired up at the ceiling. There was immediate silence as everyone looked in his direction. No one spoke. All returned to what they were doing. Yet this was not to be the end of the matter. He fired a second shot up at the ceiling; this time several customers stood up and quickly left the bar. Tension was rising, as Jefferson Bar became a place of fear. Cassidy grew angrier by the minute. He reminded himself of what his mother had always said about whiskey drinking: "stay off the whiskey son, for it's only a madman's drink." But he did not heed her advice. He began to get boisterous; he roared at everyone: "Well, what the hell are you all looking at? Haven't you ever heard a shot fired before? Go back to your drinking and gambling before I shoot the lot of you! I'm a Cassidy—a Cassidy from the Emerald Isle, and I'm afraid of no one. Understand?"

Nobody spoke. He called for another whiskey.

"Would you not leave it at that Mr Cassidy!" cried the

barman. "Maybe go home and sleep it off; you'll feel better then."

"Go home and sleep it off!" roared Cassidy. "Why I ought to blow your head off for a remark like that. Another whiskey and be quick about it! Or it's your mother in heaven you'll be serving whiskies too before the sun sets this day. Are you hearing me?"

"Of course Mr Cassidy, of course. Right away sir. One large whiskey coming up," cried the bartender.

Nervously, he poured the whiskey into Cassidy's glass, filling it to the top so as not to upset him.

"That's better," cried Cassidy. "Now leave the bottle, and don't disturb me again—understand?"

"Of course Mr Cassidy, of course," answered the barman. Cassidy put his gun back into his holster, but not before he gave an intense glance at all the customers seated, his facial expression suggesting that if he were bothered once more he would wreck the place. Just then Winkler, the resident pianist started to play the piano. The musical notes reverberated from wall to wall; Cassidy was annoyed. He stormed across the bar floor and demanded Winkler play an Irish song.

"What would you like, Mr...Mr Cassidy?" asked Winkler.

"D'ya know Danny boy?" roared Cassidy.

"Yes...yes. I think I remember that one," cried Winkler.

"Then play man, play—and be quick about it," roared Cassidy. "That's what this country needs more of—Irish songs. There aren't enough of them played. It's why the confederate South lost the war—not enough Irish songs from the ranks. I declare if they had played Danny boy instead of Dixie, Robert E. Lee. would have ended up in the White House. So play man—and good and loud while you're at it!"

"Yes sir," cried Wrnkler. Right away Mr Cassidy. Cassidy walked slowly back to the bar. Nobody stirred or spoke. He leaned once more on the bar counter. As the music played tears were seen coming from his eyes. He swallowed another mouthful of whiskey. Some of the card players stopped what they were doing, sat back in their seats and began to look a bit sad. Cassidy noticed this. He cried out: "Now there's a song to raise the spirits of the dead!" He roared. "If there are any among you with the smallest drop of Irish blood in your veins, sing! Sing up, I say!"

A few people did start singing. This went on for several minutes without interruption; then, suddenly a tall, gaunt figure entered the bar. The singing ceased at once, but was immediately continued by the stranger. Gasps of surprise echoed from everyone, for the stranger was none other than, Marshal James Tinman O'Neill! Those drinking scattered in all directions; some jumped through the windows to escape; others raced for the front doors; still others dived under tables. An explosive tension filled the bar.

O'Neill walked over to the piano player. He paused, then, turned towards Cassidy just a few yards away. He declared: "Cassidy, my name is marshal James O'Neill and I'm arresting you for disturbing the peace of Longhorn, and for continuously harassing the good people resident here; hand over your gun and come with me."

Cassidy turned and stared at the marshal for several seconds but did not reply. He lifted his glass and took another drink of whiskey; then, leaning forward he placed the glass on the counter. He thought of the great general Owen Roe O'Neill who led the Irish to victory at Benburb in 1646; perhaps the marshal was a descendant of the great O'Neill himself? His hand shook as he filled his glass with whiskey again. A terrible premonition came over him. Was today to be his Benburb? Was he to die if he engaged in battle? The thought haunted him; his fears increased. He straightened himself up. He looked straight at O'Neill.

"Tell me marshal, what is your date of birth," he asked.

O'Neill looked hard at Cassidy before replying "June 5th, 1819," as he adjusted his jacket to give freer access to his gun holster.

Hearing this Cassidy went pale as death. This was the date, June 5th, 1646 which gave O'Neill his great victory at Benburb. Cassidy now knew that he would surely die; the omens were not good. He must surrender his pistol and return with the marshal, or face certain death. He took a further drink of whiskey, his hand shaking a little more than it did the last time.

It was decision time: either fight or submit. The marshal called: "I say again I'm placing you under arrest; surrender your gun and come with me."

Cassidy turned and faced the marshal. "Can't do that, marshal. This here is my town; you have no jurisdiction here. I think you should go about your business."

Marshal Tinman drew six paces back. He prepared to draw. The atmosphere was very tense. Both men stood staring at each other; for Cassidy the battle of Benburb was about to be re-enacted.

Loud gunshots rang out as both men drew and fired their weapons. The marshal was hit. He staggered sideways along the counter then fell to the ground. Cassidy fell backwards and collapsed: he had been mortally wounded. The marshal had only sustained a flesh wound to his right arm. Struggling to his feet he approached Cassidy. He stood down on one knee; he cried out: "Why, why did you have to draw!" "This matter could have been settled better between us."

Cassidy beckoned him closer, then, with one last gasp cried out: "Benburb, Benburb.should have known…should…"

The marshal stood up and walked towards the exit. He approached Winkler. "Benburb…what did he mean?" Winkler looked at the marshal, and replied: "That name was one of his most cherished memories from the old country. He was forever talking about it; some battle fought by the Irish against the English in 1646: he was forever ranting about some general called Owen Roe O'Neill and his great victory."

The marshal turned from Winkler after hearing this; he looked around the bar. He cried out: "Victory! When is death ever a great victory for anyone?" He stormed out on to the street. As Cassidy's body was being removed, the rest of the bar patrons returned to their seats. Winkler sat down and began to play, *Danny Boy*. Soon everyone present joined in the singing, some with tears flowing from their eyes.

IV

AUTOBIOGRAPHY OF A DOG

1

Birth and early memories
I move to a new home
My first visit to the Vet
Adventures in the Park

MY FIRST ENTRANCE INTO THE WORLD WAS pleasant enough, so far as I can remember. I was born somewhere on the south side of Dublin Town; precisely where I cannot tell. I had two brothers and one sister—both very furry like myself. I was removed from home shortly after I was born, and my recollections of family relations and home surroundings are necessarily scanty. However, one distinct memory I have is that of a foul smell coming from four-legged creatures with small curly tails! I noticed, too, that they had large noses, and grunted all the time. At the rear of the house where I was born there were quite a few of them, and they seemed to have never ending appetites! I called them pigs.

I recall on one occasion, just after I had arrived into the world, that three or four of them were about to devour me for a meal. I was saved from near death by the diligent attention and prompt action of my mother; from this experience I was very frightened and clung close to her in the early weeks after I was born. Despite my initial fright I was looking forward to a happy life in my home surroundings. My furry coat kept me free from cold and, being the winter I had great fun with my brothers and sister bouncing and sliding around in the snow in our back garden. The future looked bright, or so I thought.

Though I could not speak, my sight was good, I had excellent hearing, and I could not help noticing that I was not quite the same as my mother—in outward appearance, in particular. This I believe was because I was of the Labrador race, whereas my mother was a pure bred Alsation—one of the better classes of our species, as I subsequently learned. As the weeks passed and I grew and developed, I quickly became familiar with the different types of animals from around our area. One day, while learning to chew a piece of meat, I overheard a family member of my master's household remark that I would shortly be going to a new home; I became real concerned, and barked several times to demonstrate my anxiety.

Shortly afterwards I found myself bundled into a shoebox and taken in the mistress' car for a drive. This was all very frightening, as we drove through new and unfamiliar surroundings; eventually we arrived at our destination. I was now handed over—box and all, to a complete stranger; my mistress, with what looked like water coming from her eyes, gave me a warm hug before departing away.

I was quickly ushered into my new home still in my shoebox, placed on the floor in the sitting room, and became the subject of an excited inspection by all members of this family. I observed that some of them were tall and fat; some were small—all nosey, and curious to learn all about me. They began pulling my nose and ears, lifting me up and down—in a most discomforting manner: I was hungry and wished they would dispense with their examinations till later—and for the present dish up some grub! One of the smaller ones cried out, "Daddy! Daddy! what name will we call him?" To this the mistress of the house promptly replied, "Don't worry about that for the present dear, we will attend to that after tea, okay?" I was now given a bowl of warm milk to drink, which I quickly devoured and, feeling exhausted from the days events, soon lapsed into a sound sleep.

When I awoke much later I found myself again in the midst of a family gathering, with a lively discussion going on; moreover, having been blessed from birth with the ability to interpret and understand the talk and actions of the humans, I quickly understood that the topic of conversation was none other than what name I was to be given. At length it was decided that I was to be called Prince. With that the younger members of the family began to pat and cuddle me in a most warm and affectionate manner; I became very excited, and felt that I was going to be very happy here in the years to come. Plans were immediately set in motion to make a new kennel; also I was to get a new dog collar and lead. The collar was to include a silver disk with my name on it. I soon became familiar with all members of my master's family, including Roger the Turtle, and Alice and Jack, the two rabbits—whose hutch I learned would be close to my new kennel. One day I was quite chuffed to overhear the mistress of the house say that they would be planting a tree in my honour, and which was to be called "Prince's Tree." This I felt was most heartening, and pleased me much.

Though I was of the mongrel breed, and would not be

perceived as a better class of dog, I nevertheless felt great pride in myself; indeed, in the weeks that followed, and what with the good looking after I was receiving from my master and mistress—together with the love and affection lavished upon me by them both—I was made to feel very much part of the family.

In due course I had to go on a visit to the local Vet, for a check-up. It was an occasion I shall never forget. As the Vet in question was not too far from home I could be walked there. Imagine my feeling on that bright spring morning as my mistress led me out in my new collar and lead, not to mention my new silver disk that sparkled in the sun. I was the pride of the dog world. Moreover, conscious of the affluent community surroundings in which my new home was located, I deliberately refrained from attending upon the calls of nature, either on the pavements or hedges, until we reached our destination.

In due course we arrived at Oakwood Veterinary Services, under the directorship of Dr. Jeremiah Scone, Vet. Having been ushered into a waiting room and the preliminary registration procedures completed, we settled down to wait our turn to be called. The surroundings were quite pleasant and there were about twelve other dogs of different sizes and shapes waiting to be called. One particular dog, a bulldog, I believe, was particularly ugly; he stared at me quite intensely: in my youthful exuberance I was not sure whether to laugh at his physical disposition and appearance, or weep with sorrow. Before I could make up my mind, suddenly, he leaned forwards toward me and let out an unmerciful snarl that almost ended my life. I quickly ducked for cover under a nearby chair, and did not come out for some time.

Later I emerged and, anxious to make my presence felt,

I immediately urinated on the floor, to the horror and consternation of the other masters and mistresses, all of whom
gave my mistress a stern look of disapproval. My own personal thoughts were that in our world a dog must do what
a dog has to do; my fellow creatures were impressed and all
strained at their leads to cross the floor—anxious to make
my acquaintance. I was overjoyed. Presently a lady in a white
coat appeared with a mop and bucket and quickly removed
the offending pool; I meanwhile, having ducked out of sight
again, until things settled down.

A short while later I was brought in for examination; I
had no idea what to expect. The room was large, and had
two examination tables placed close to each other. I was immediately placed upon one of these, and subjected to a most
horrifying experience! I was hardly certain whether I was
to live or die; moreover, the discomfiture of my position
was compounded by the screams and protests of another dog
who, immediately was about to be prodded by a long needle!
His mistress was in tears at having to witness—aye, even assist in the agonising treatment being applied to her affectionate pet. I trembled at what fate awaited me when my turn
came! Sitting there on the table I thought to myself, "well
I know that I am only a Mongrel dog and not to be compared to a better class of my species, such as the Poodle across
on the table opposite; however, as I do have feelings, hold
nothing but good will towards all dogs of whatever class or
breed—including humans—I shall place my hope and faith
in mankind and hope that I will be treated kindly on this
occasion."

A discussion ensued as to my general well-being and, after
some exchanges between my mistress and the Vet, I found
myself being lifted up, turned over—and, moreover, my ears

poked, my teeth examined, together with other parts of my person—all probed and examined in a most unfeeling manner; it was all most undignified, even for a dog. Suddenly the lady assistant appeared with a long needle: I was to get an injection! I glanced across at the Poodle on the other table; he had a grin on his face, almost as if he knew what was going to happen, and was laughing at me. I gave him a stern look to reflect my disapproval. In a matter of minutes it was all over. I received my injection and we were quickly on our way. As we passed through the waiting room I gave a confident bark and glanced around at all the other dogs—except of course that nasty Bulldog that had so ungraciously snarled at me shortly after our arrival. Soon we were back home.

Later that evening and after having a satisfactory meal I retired to my kennel in the backyard and fell fast asleep. I did not wake till 10:00 AM the following morning. As I was about to rise and stretch my legs I noticed this round, brown object curled up in the kennel beside me! I took fright at this—particularly when it suddenly moved. However it turned out to be Roger the Turtle whom, by way of a practical joke, one of my master's children had placed in the kennel. I was not amused. Later that morning I overheard from a family conversation in the kitchen that I was to be taken to the local park for a visit. I became very excited about this.

The following morning around midday the mistress and I walked there together. It was a fresh, spring morning and the sun was shining brightly; presently we arrived at the park. The grass was well trimmed, and there were numerous seats upon which to sit. There was also a large pond in which were numerous variety of birds, including ducks, all swimming about. It was a most picturesque scene. We both sat down to rest. However, under the warmth of the midday sun my mistress soon fell asleep—but not before she had unbuckled my lead so that I could play about. I observed the general scene with some caution and did not immediately begin rushing about, much as I would have liked to. As these scenes were quite new to me I was reluctant to move away from my mistress; however, my lack of patience and youthful exuberance were not to be contained: I had to explore these new surroundings. Jumping down from the seat and in a manner calculated not to disturb my mistress, she by now had begun to snore! I strolled across the grass towards the pond, paused near the edge and observed the various wild birds in all their various colours and sizes that were swimming there. I had not long been engaged here when suddenly a frightening drama began to unfold. A four legged creature—called I believe a cat—was running rapidly towards me, pursued by a small dog with great determination. This cat was in a most distressed state, as it raced for its life. It was being pursued by a large human, like my mistress, who appeared equally distressed and was roaring out in a loud voice "stop the cat, stop that cat!"

Those humans who were about the park viewed this scene with a mixed curiosity, and only limited interest; indeed some of them appeared highly amused. For my part I had to jump out of the way, else I should have been trampled on or, worse still, pushed into the pond and drowned.

Still I was frightened out of my wits and instinctively ran across the park to a cluster of trees to hide. Peering out from my safe retreat I rested for a while till all the excitement died down. Later I emerged and debated to myself what I should do next. Feeling energetic and full of curiosity I decided to venture forth and explore the Park further. Strolling though the area I was impressed by a little bridge which extended over the pond and also by the many different coloured flower beds to be seen. There was a great aroma and freshness here that I found most enjoyable. I had not travelled far when I noticed the following sign:

ALL DOGS ENTERING THE PARK MUST BE ACCOMPANIED
BY THEIR OWNERS, AND MUST BE ON LEADS.

T. Murphy,
Parks Superintendent.

Reading this sent a tremor through my body; I looked nervously about, pondering what I should do next. Just then I heard this barking noise in the distance. I whirled about and looked in the direction from which it came. Racing towards me was this medium sized dog who, very quickly, came right up close to me sniffing and smelling every aspect of my person. He panted, smiled, and gave every indication that he was delighted to make my acquaintance.

I was glad to know him, too; indeed in our sudden encounter he informed me that, being a mongrel dog the same as myself, it was pleasure to meet me. He told me that he was lost: he had been returning home from the country on his masters open-backed lorry when he had fallen off. As we exchanged opinions about our individual life experiences we set off to explore the park, and to see what new adventures might engage our attention. We had not travelled far when a most interesting sight appeared; four of the strangest creatures emerged from a nearby cluster of bushes. One of them—all brown and with a keen, motherly look—eyed us cautiously; another had a strange looking comb on the top of its head: it was what I believe the humans call a rooster

or domestic cock. It had a fearsome look in its eye and strut-
ted about with the air of a king. With my newfound friend,
Boxer (for that was the name I had given him) we paused
awhile to observe this scene. Boxer spoke, providing the following information: "Now Prince, my friend, here we have
some very interesting scenes; indeed, we, and you in particular—given that you are at a very young age—will need
to take account of all the new creatures of the world that you
see about you. This collection of feathered objects you see
before you are called, 'Hens,' except of course the one with
the comb on his head: he is called a rooster; he tends to be
very jealous of those brown coloured hens which he likes
to call his own. We in the dog world fraternity regard ourselves as superior to all hens and roosters: whereas they are
only good for cackling and laying eggs, and being eaten by
the humans, we, thanks to the great Benefactor are regarded
with special care; he continually looks to our welfare.

Prince was intrigued with his new found friend's stimu-
lating conversation as he focused his eyes alternatively on
the rooster and his companion. As these feathered creatures moved on, Prince and Boxer began a game of chasing
around the Park, which amused greatly those humans who
were strolling about. Suddenly Boxer roared out "My God…
quick! Into the bushes—it's the dog catcher, and he has seen
us!" "Dog catcher—what's that?" cried Prince. "No time to
explain now," said Boxer and with that they both scurried
across the park and hid under a clump of bushes. They remained there till it was safe to come out. Prince pressed the
matter further, asking Boxer to explain what a dog catcher
is. "Ah," replied Boxer, "the dog catchers have an unpleasant
job to do, Prince. They sneak up on you and suddenly throw

a net over your head and whisk you away in a van to the dog pound. There you stay until some kind human comes along and offers to give you a kind home."

"Do there be many dogs in the pound," asked Prince. "Dozens," replied Boxer, "I was in there once myself for a week. My heart was pained greatly at what I seen there; to be fair the food was not bad, and the attendants—those few that were there were very nice: real humans, Prince, ones that loved our kind. But it was a sad experience; sad in the sense that it broke my heart to hear the other dogs screaming and barking the whole night through; aye, and crying too! I saw dogs big and small with tears flowing from their eyes; I tell you it would have melted the hardest of hearts. So my friend we must be careful or we too might lose our freedom, as has happened to many of our kind in the past. I was fortunate in that a kind person took me out of the place and gave me a nice home."

As I listened to Boxer I observed him closely; he was, I reckoned, an experienced dog of the world; he was reasonably groomed, though appeared to be not well fed; his teeth were bad: indeed, some were missing. Still, he struck me as one who had a good understanding of life: I was glad to have him as a friend. I noticed too that in speaking of the Pound he had a slight look of sadness on his face. I resolved to cheer him up. "Come on Boxer!" I cried, "race you to the pond." In my enthusiasm to get there first, and to my utter consternation, I overran the distance and, upon reaching the edge of the pool, slipped over the edge and fell in. All the wildlife in the pond stopped immediately what they were doing, and, with raised heads, looked in my direction.

I kicked and splashed for all I was worth in my struggle to get out of the water; indeed, I was in a most distressed state. Meanwhile all the Ducks, Swans, and water hens swam quickly towards me and, seeing the state I was in, cackled and chirped in one chorus of concern to draw attention to my plight. With that, in jumps Boxer to my aid, a friend faithful and true. Swimming quickly towards me he grabbed me by the neck and brought me out of the water. I immediately collapsed on the ground—exhausted.

I was so grateful to Boxer for rescuing me I just about summoned up enough energy and gave a little whimper of appreciation and thanks, while continuing to recover my strength. Meanwhile the incident drew the attention of some onlookers, who began to praise Boxer for his brave act in pulling me out of the water. Boxer, with becoming modesty, raised his head to acknowledge this; furthermore, and not to be undone, all the wild life in the pond approached the waters edge and in one unified chorus chirped, sang, quacked and flapped their wings in praise of what he had done in acknowledgement of his brave deed. It was a moment I shall never forget. I quickly recovered my strength, and Boxer and I continued on with our walk. As we moved away from the pool I turned and in the loudest voice I could muster barked my heartfelt thanks to the feathered friends who had alerted everyone to my plight.

As we went on our way I thought of my mistress whom I had left sleeping on the park seat; I felt sure she may have awakened and might be wondering where I had gone: I felt that I should really be getting back to her soon. Meanwhile we continued our rambles, exploring all the different sights around this most pleasant place. It had become quite a hot day so we decided to lie down close to some bushes and rest awhile. We were but a short while there when suddenly this long pole with a net on one end was cast over Boxer. It was the dogcatcher!

Poor Boxer wriggled and struggled fiercely to get free. He barked and screamed out for all he was worth, but all to no avail: he was entangled in the net and there was no escape.

"Run prince!" he roared, "run fast as you can and don't let them catch you!"

I was in a state of shock, so much my legs could hardly hold me up; yet I somehow gathered up enough strength and ran fast as I could out across the park. My escape was a success. Alas! Poor Boxer, my friend—would I ever see him again? As I turned in the direction where my mistress was sleeping, I could not restrain the tears that flowed from my eyes. I noticed that she was now on her feet staring around the park to see where I had gone. I immediately barked to catch her attention. She saw me and cried out "Prince, Prince, come here boy at once." She put on my lead and collar and without further delay we made our way home.

As we approached the park exit one of those noisy motor vans drove slowly past us; it was the dogcatcher! I shivered nervously. Stealing a slight glance at it I was shocked to see inside my friend Boxer; he was scraping at the wire mesh on the doors trying desperately to escape. My heart was sad, as I could not help him. I barked furiously for several minutes to say that I would never forget him and hoping that someday soon we would meet again. Within a few minutes the van had disappeared out the park gate. My heart sank as the mistress and I walked home that day; I felt in a truly dejected state.

2

A very strange dream
A visit to the dog pound
I am reunited with my friend

THE EVENING SAW LITTLE IMPROVEMENT or change in how I had felt about Boxer; I ate very little food and could not help thinking about him and how he might be suffering now. The day's events had taken their toll on me: I was exhausted and very quickly fell into a deep sleep.

During my sleep I had a dream. I dreamed that the great Benefactor came down from Heaven and stood directly in front of my kennel; he came in the shape of a Mongrel dog just like me, except much larger. Suddenly he reached in to my kennel with one of his large paws and tapped me on the shoulder.

"Wake up Prince," he barked, "and come with me. Wake immediately for we are to go on a long journey to the Kingdom of the Dogs."

I stood up slowly, like in a trance, and climbed onto the Benefactors back.

"Hold on now," he cried as slowly we ascended into the

Heavens. As we went along what sights I beheld! A massive expanse of space with thousands of little lights in the sky, Stars, I believe the humans call them; and how they lit up the firmament: it was wonderful!

Passing though Space we passed huge balls suspended in the Heavens. "What are they?" I asked the Benefactor, to which he replied, "My name is not Mr. Benefactor. I am the Benefactor's chief appointed representative throughout the Universe. I am called 'Toby of the Brave Heart'. One of my jobs is to supervise the Kingdom of the Dogs for him who is the great benefactor of the entire animal world, and in particular to see that all dogs are happy—both in the Kingdom, and down on Earth. Those large objects we are passing are called Planets. Jupiter, Mars, and Venus; that bright one we passed earlier on, that was the Moon: a very special planet for all life on Earth, particularly the humans."

We passed by one particular planet, which gave off a lot of heat; we heard dogs howling and barking: it was all most frightening. Prince shook with fright upon hearing these, and nearly fell off Toby's back.

"My God," cried Prince, "what's that noise?"

"That," cried Toby, "is the outer planet called 'Far from Home'. It is a very sad place; hundreds of dogs are lodged there, disobedient dogs of all shapes, breeds, and sizes. There they must stay for hundreds of years to atone for the terrible things they did while on Earth."

"What things?" asked Prince.

"Some were cast there for killing sheep, others for savaging cats and committing other misdemeanours of a varied kind. They angered the great Benefactor by refusing to obey the laws of nature—written on the hearts of all animal kinds; there they must stay to atone for their misdeeds until the Benefactor decides to bring them home."

As they travelled further on their journey, Toby and Prince seen many more wonderful sights; eventually they came across, 'Paradise Valley'. This was the final resting place for those humans who had done well while on Earth. They paused to have a closer look.

"This is the Valley of Universal Light," cried Toby, "Here there is no hunger or thirst, no wars or fighting of any kind; all is peace and harmony. There are lush green valleys, smooth flowing streams—and most of all, nobody ever grows old: nobody ever gets tired. Food is in abundance while happy friendships rule everywhere."

As Toby was speaking Prince suddenly interrupted, "You mean there are no dog wardens, or dog pounds?"

"Such things do not exist," replied Toby, "Indeed in Paradise Valley neither hurt, injury of any kind, nor incarceration of anybody ever takes place. Those humans lucky enough to go there can bring their dogs also. Especially those dogs who loved their masters and were obedient and helpful to them when they were on Earth. But come, we must hurry along if we are to reach our destination."

As we proceeded along I asked Toby how he got his name—Toby of the Braveheart.

"Well, I will tell you," replied Toby, "When I was on Earth I lived with a very happy family by the name of Grace. I was happy there too. They named me Toby Alexander Grace, gave me a lovely lead, collar and disk, and whenever the family went hunting or fishing, I was always brought along too. I had my own chair to sit in and was even allowed to watch television at night with the family. One day the Circus came to Town and we all went to see the show.

While some of the acts were performing one of the lions broke loose from its cage; there was panic everywhere as the humans scattered in all directions. My master's youngest son, Sean, only six years old, got displaced in the panic. The lion attacked him and I immediately rushed to his aid; the lion released him and immediately attacked me. I had no chance against an animal of such superior strength and I died very quickly from the multiple wounds inflicted. The family rejoiced at the saving of their son from death but were saddened that I had been killed in the process. With due pomp and ceremony I was buried in their back garden and a small statue erected over my grave. It was all very sad for everyone.

My spirit was whisked up into the Heavens and eventually into the Kingdom of the Dogs; there I was welcomed by the great Benefactor, and received a hero's welcome. As a reward for my great love, dedication to the humans with whom I had lived on Earth, and particularly my action in saving young Sean's life, I was immediately appointed the great Benefactor's chief representative throughout the Universe, and henceforth designated 'Toby of the Brave heart'. It was a great honour and I was very proud. One of my chief duties is to welcome all dogs into the Kingdom and to advise and explain the rules that apply to those who have come here."

"That must have been a wonderful feeling," cried Prince, "and certainly a great honour—particularly after such a horrible death; you must be very pleased."

"Yes," replied Toby, "I am indeed. Entering the Kingdom of the Dogs has been the happiest day of my life."

Very shortly afterwards—being within a short distance of the Kingdom, a loud noise, like the sound of a trumpet, was heard.

"What's that?" asked Prince.

"Hush, quiet now," replied Toby, "we have just heard the first blast of the guards trumpet signalling our approach. There will be two more blasts, after which the gates will open and we will be welcomed in."

As Toby indicated, two further blasts were heard, the last being the loudest of all—reverberating all around the Universe. Prince trembled with fright as a panorama of light flashed across the sky. Suddenly a pair of large golden gates was visible in the distance; on either side of these were large gold covered walls approximately twelve feet high, and stretching as far as the eye could see. Standing on top of these were hundreds of dogs all barking out a universal chorus of song of welcome as follows: "Woof, woof, woof-woof-woof...woof!" or, in the language of the humans, "a hundred thousand welcomes to Toby of the Brave heart, and a special welcome to his guest and visitor, Prince."

I was flabbergasted as I beheld this amazing scene, and, in my excitement almost fell off Toby's back. Toby, watchful as ever, caught me just in time. The gates now opened and we both proceeded to enter this amazing place. There was a guard of honour present numbering hundreds of dogs, and positioned along each side of the road. I noticed Labradors, Jack Russell's, Bulldogs, Greyhounds, all stretching at their leads and calling out a most enthusiastic welcome to us as we passed in. I was almost overcome with awe. Toby now called upon me to step down from off his back as it was required that we walk the last hundred yards to the great Benefactors house.

It was all so exciting.

Passing along I was awestruck by the facial expressions

of all the dogs there; I did not see an unhappy face among any of them. Further on and stretching into the distance, I saw—both to the left and to the right—an array of gold-coloured kennels, one for each dog and suitably inlaid with decorative materials and a fine-woven mat upon which to rest. Moreover, each kennel had a nameplate over its entrance; there was *Rex*, *Chip*, *Butch*, *Blackie* and many more names besides. Close to each kennel was a small play area for each dog, and, interspersed between the kennels were flower beds, each varying in size and specially marked for the seasons of the year: thus there was the Autumn bed, the Winter bed, the Summer bed and the Spring bed, all clearly marked out. Finally there was located, close to these, specially marked-out trees which enabled each dog attend upon the calls of nature, as required; It was all most impressive.

As we passed along I noticed also a special open area; this was for all dogs that grow old; for in the Kingdom of the Dogs there are no pounds, no lockups, and all dogs are free—so long as they obey the rules.

"You see," said Toby, "unlike Earth we look upon our old and infirm dogs with special regard; none are suffered to be in want for anything, neither food, companionship, medical aid, or any need whatsoever. And when any dog passes on, he or she receives a Cosmic funeral. This takes them to a higher state of being which I cannot go into just now, but which I will explain at another time. These then, Prince, is the rewards afforded to all dogs who live by the Benefactors laws of love."

Lastly, and just before we came to the entrance of the great Benefactor's house we passed a large sign which read: *Welcome to Happy Valley—the last resting place of all dogs who loved and cared.*

With that the front doors of the benefactors house opened, and the great Benefactor himself emerged. I trembled with expectation as to what was to happen next.

Suddenly this amazing sight appeared before Toby and I. It was a great presence of light, roughly seven feet tall by three feet broad, which glowed intensely, yet not in a way that blinded our eyes. It had a warm feeling that flowed out towards us: quite all embracing, yet not intimidating, yet not overpowering. I felt much at ease. Toby stepped forward and spoke. "Great Benefactor! May eternal health, happiness, and peace forever reign with you; may I present my young friend Prince whom I have brought to meet you and to give him an opportunity to visit our great Kingdom."

Just then a voice spoke coming from within the cloud of light, "We are delighted with the return of our great, great representative, 'Toby of the Brave heart', and also to see our young visitor, Prince. Welcome to you both. We trust you had a pleasant journey?"

"Indeed so," replied Toby.

"We had indeed," interjected Prince, "Mister Toby showed me all the great sights as we crossed the Universe; I am very happy to be here, thank you."

"Yes," continued Toby, "young Prince was a great passenger throughout the whole journey, and we had some pleasant conversation."

"Good!" cried the Benefactor, "What you see about you here young Prince are the happy homes of all dogs who led good and obedient lives while on Earth. They were faithful to their masters, love all humankind, even the ones who ill-treated them, showing them no kindness at all. They have now earned their reward and live happily and freely here in the Kingdom; for them there is no more scavenging in side-streets or back lanes looking for food scraps; here we have fields of good, healthy bones and meat scraps, which any dog can visit at his leisure and take his pick. Moreover, all dogs lucky enough to enter the Kingdom have his or her every need catered for: unlike on Earth, there is no fighting, rivalry, or jealousy here. Each dog's chief vocation is to assist in every way the total happiness of his fellow dogs—without regard as to class or colour: would that it were so down among the humans!"

"So, tell me about yourself, young Prince," asked the Benefactor, "Your life on Earth, and whom do you live with? Are you being treated all right? Are you happy on Earth?"

Prince trembled slightly as he replied, "I am glad to say, Mr Benefactor, that the master and mistress with whom I live treat me very kindly; indeed only recently they bought me a new kennel with a nice warm mat inside; I have three friends living beside me—Roger the Turtle, and Alice and Jack—both rabbits. They regularly talk to me and are always telling stories. I like them very much. I am delighted Mr Benefactor to have had this opportunity to visit the Kingdom of the Dogs, and to make the acquaintance of both yourself and Mr. Toby. I hope that when I die I too will come straight to the Kingdom."

"That, my young friend will depend very much upon you," cried the Benefactor, "you are still young and have plenty of time to prove yourself worthy to be brought here. You must return to Earth, now; meantime I am confident that in due time you will earn your just reward. Meantime I have seen what has happened to your friend, Boxer; he is locked up in the Pound; you must take all steps necessary to effect his rescue, else he will die. Toby will assist you if needed. Now I must go; I have much work to do: many animals to look after—many thousands to comfort. Toby you must take Prince back to Earth. See that he returns safely, and that nothing happens either to him or his friend Boxer."

As he finished speaking the doors once more began to open and the light slowly receded back inside the house. Once again three blasts of a trumpet were heard, then silence.

As we turned to walk away my heart felt a little sad as we prepared to leave this place. There were so many happy dogs about, and they gave us both, and me in particular such a warm welcome, it brought tears to my eyes. As we approached the exit gates all the dogs barked their fond goodbyes, while those up on the walls howled and barked loudly wishing us all the best as we went on our way. As we went through the gates a loud blast of a trumpet was sounded, then another; I jumped onto Toby's back and we both began our long journey home. We were just a short distance out when a third blast of a trumpet sounded. It was so loud it reverberated right around the Universe; it gave me such a fright that I fell from off his back. Suddenly I awoke to find myself lying on my back in my kennel! I was back home; there was no Toby; no golden gates; no dogs cheering—it had all been a dream! Or had it?

I peered my head cautiously outside to find that it was a bright, sunny dry morning. I stepped outside to attend upon the calls of nature. As I was returning to my kennel, suddenly, the back door of the house opened, and out stepped my mistress holding what looked like a plate of food. She walked to the kennel and laid it on the ground close to the entrance, then turned and went back into the house.

"Ah," I murmured to myself, "breakfast!"

I immediately tucked in. When finished I returned into my kennel to rest, pondering on what adventures and experiences I might encounter this day. Apart from relaxing in the early morning sun, or strutting about in the back garden, I really did nothing exciting.

I did during the course of the day make the acquaintance of our next-door neighbour's cat, Fluffy. He was a large black male who spent most of his day watching from a safe distance. We talked little, and I think Fluffy knew to keep a safe distance from me at all times. I could not help thinking of my friend, Boxer, locked up in the Dog Pound. Was he suffering? I wondered. I hoped not. I wondered how could I help to rescue him? And what of my dream – or was it a dream? Would 'Toby of the Brave Heart' help? Or was he a figment of my own imagination; was there such a place as 'The Kingdom of the Dogs'? The more I thought of poor Boxer the more depressed I became. About two weeks later I was out being walked by my mistress when an interesting occurrence took place. My mistress happened to meet one of the neighbours, Mrs Grimes. She indicated that she was considering going to the local Dog Pound to see if she could get a nice dog pet for her son, Gerard. After some discussion it was agreed that they would both visit the Pound the following Tuesday

And see what they could get; my mistress said that she would bring me along on the visit: "It would be nice for little Prince to meet and see some other dogs," she remarked. Needless to say I was delighted with this bit of news; perhaps I might see my friend Boxer there? The thought raised my spirits, and I started hopping and bouncing along in a most cheerful manner.

My mistress remarked, "Why Prince, what has cheered you up all of sudden?"

With that I barked—*Woof, woof, woof, woof!*— I could not

contain my excitement. The possibility that I might once again see the pal who had saved my life was almost unbearable; I felt a new air of confidence, and strained at my lead as we went along. Meeting other dogs on the way I took every opportunity to tell them the news. My mistress found it difficult to understand my behaviour, so I wagged my tail repeatedly, at the same time giving her a warm and affectionate look to reassure her that all was well.

The following Tuesday Mrs Grimes, my mistress and myself went to the Dog Pound. We arrived there at 11:00 AM and were welcomed by a Miss Clements, the caretaker in charge. I was very excited about this visit and determined to observe as much as possible of what went on; and of course I hoped that I might see my best pal, Boxer. The premises were not very large; it contained about forty pens—eighteen of which contained dogs of various breeds. As we entered the penned area my mistress lifted me up into her arms; needless to say I became very excited. I saw a Jack Russell that looked a little undernourished. Several of the other dogs started to bark like hell, all pleading to be free. Some were friendly and wagged their tails profusely. How sad I thought that man's best friend should be locked up like this. Meanwhile Mrs Clements and my mistress were in deep conversation; I could see that they did not understand what the barking was all about. I understood and sad indeed was the stories were the stories I heard. A middle aged Collie barked fiercely to catch my attention: he had a saddening tale to tell as follows: "I was once a very happy dog, I had hundreds of friends and lived with nice family in a nice home just on the edge of Town. I was fully trained by my mistress, both in hygiene matters and in house security—both at day and night. I use to carry the paper for her when we would be returning home from shopping, and I got on greatly with the children, giving them jockey-backs very frequently. I was on first name terms with all the dogs on our street. With this family I was very happy. Alas! How that all changed. The master of the house started drinking. He then lost his job. And then, most terrible of all, he started beating the mistress, causing great distress to the children. One night he came home late very drunk; he started to strike young Tommy, his second eldest son, a mere slip of a lad; this was too much for me. I growled fiercely at him, and if the mistress had not intervened I would have torn him to pieces. For weeks afterwards I had to keep out of his way; eventually, despite protests from the mistress, he put me out of the house altogether. There was no proper dog box, and as the weeks passed I got weaker and weaker from exposure to the elements: it was not possible to survive on the scraps of food afforded to me by the neighbours. One day while foraging in the Park I was captured by the dog warden and confined here in the Pound. To be fair to them I would have died on the streets if they had not brought me in. The food is not bad and I'm hoping some kind human will one day offer me a nice home."

As I stared down at him I couldn't help thinking of my pal, Boxer, and wondering if he were here. I conveyed to him through murmurs, flapping of my ears and a restrained series of barks my sorrow for his plight. I told him I would speak to my friend Toby of the Brave Heart, and ask him to find a nice new home, soon. I then asked Rover if he had seen a Mongrel dog, named Boxer, black in colour since he had come into the Pound. Suddenly, and just as he was about to answer, I heard this familiar bark coming from one of the kennels in an outer yard; I became very excited! Those barks sound like Boxer's. Just then Mrs Clements, my mistress, and Mrs Grimes turned and walked out in the direction of the self same yard to see other dogs. As we were walking Rover gave two excited barks—indicating that a dog that I had described was in fact housed out there: I barked back to Rover as my excitement upon hearing this news became more intense. Entering the yard I noticed several breeds housed in various kennels; several became very excited upon seeing us: some barked and howled continuously, scratched at the wire mesh with their paws - all competing to catch our attention. I looked diligently to see if Boxer was present in any kennel; as I did so some of the other dogs cried out to me personally, "please, please, help us get out of here; we don't want to be here! We want to be free." It was all a most upsetting sight; yet what could I do? Nothing. I barked words of comfort to all I saw, promising that if I could help in any way I would.

Meanwhile Mrs Grimes was taking a close look at each dog in turn to see if she favoured one dog more than all the others. A scotch terrier had caught her eye; she moved closer to look. My mistress and I, meanwhile, moved along to look at the rest of the kennels. Again that bark sounded—the one in particular I had found familiar earlier; as I turned my head to look at the direction from which it came—there, to my utter excitement I observed my friend Boxer standing up in a kennel that up to now had appeared empty. I became terribly excited and immediately struggled to break free from my mistress: this I successfully did—and jumping to the ground raced towards Boxer. Well such wagging of tails you never did see! We barked and licked at each other's face through the wire mesh in an ecstacy of true friendship; to meet again the friend that had saved my life—well, it was just wonderful. Mrs Clements, the caretaker of the Pound had become distracted by my leap to the floor and reacquaintance with Boxer; she turned aside, remarking, "why ma'am, your dog seems to be quite taken with that old Mongrel there, almost as if they were old friends." My mistress quickly bent down and picked me up into her arms, remarking as she did, "Indeed that seems so." Meanwhile Boxer and I continued to bark and smile at each other to everyone's interest and curiosity, while Mrs Grimes moved closer to Boxer to have a look. Boxer smiled at her warmly and wagged his tail continuously to engage her attention.

"What a warm, friendly dog he is, Hilda!" she cried. "Indeed," cried my mistress, "they seem quite taken with each other, almost as if they knew one another."

"I like him. How much will you sell him for?" she asked.

"Oh there is no charge," replied Mrs Clements, "we are delighted to give him to anyone prepared to provide a good home. Mind you a small financial donation to help us run our Pound would not be refused! He's yours if you wish to have him."

Mrs Grimes took the hint. Turning to my mistress she cried, "Hilda, should I take him? what do you think?"

"Yes," replied my mistress, "He has a warm friendly smile: I like that in a dog; he's also quite taken with my Prince; they could be good friends together."

Mrs Grimes turned to Mrs Clements, "Yes I will have him; we'll take him right away, if that is alright."

"Excellent," returned Mrs Clements, "He'll make a good companion, so he will."

As all this discussion was going on I continued to keep Boxer informed as to what was happening. This I did by mild barking, and occasional loud whimpers. Boxer was most pleased! He was now removed from his kennel and secured by a makeshift lead as we all headed home together. I was very pleased at this most satisfactory outcome to our visit; having once more met up with the true friend, who had saved my life, brought me great happiness. As we exited the gates I looked back at all the kennels, and with a heavy heart listened to the barks and cries of all the other dogs left behind; I resolved that I would do everything I could to see that as many as possible went to new homes in the weeks and months ahead.

3

Rambles in the park
I make new friends
A sick dog is discovered
His death and burial

IN THE ENSUING WEEKS WE WERE TWO of the happiest dogs in our neighbourhood. Regularly Boxer would come down and slip into our backyard through a gap in the hedge, and if we were not basking in the sun then we were teasing Roger the Turtle or chasing the two rabbits, Alice and Jack. It was all great fun. I had told Boxer about my dream of Toby of the Brave Heart; of the great Benefactor, and of the Kingdom of the Dogs; he listened with great interest, yet, like myself, wondered if it were only a dream, or if in fact it had been a real experience. I couldn't say yes or no with any great truth. "Whether a dream or not," cried Boxer, "it sounds like a lovely place. And those inlaid kennels! And fields of bones! Why, it sounds like Heaven! A place every dog would like to be."

"Well hopefully it is true; it is real: and that one day we will all go there," remarked Prince.

Meanwhile we both played about together enjoying each

other's company, while exploring what new and further adventures we might get involved in.

One day Boxer and I decided we would venture a little further away from our homes, to see what was over the hill, so to speak. I should remind my readers, by the way, that where we lived was close to some fields; indeed there was a large farm called Hazel Oak containing, I believe, over two-hundred acres of land. It was here that I first made the acquaintance of creatures called Cows. Like the pigs in my former mistress's home, they did nothing else but eat all day and lounge about in the sun! Our first stop was a nearby Park called Greenacres, in which there were many clusters of trees spread here and there. Of varying heights and types, they presented a picturesque scene giving character to the Park.

We began to run around playfully, as dogs ordinarily do; I murmured to Boxer, "Lets hope that no dog Wardens are lurking about!" Boxer barked several times, in a laughing sort of way; as we galloped around suddenly we were joined by three other dogs: one was an Alsatian, one a Red Setter, and the other a little Jack Russell. The latter was quite cocky and arrogant and barked at us in a most intimidating manner. I did not like him. As we got to know them better it was all fun and games; there was elegant wagging of tails, ears cocked up—and chirping and barking in the best dog language: it was all very exciting. I kept my distance, not venturing to draw too close to any of them; though I was a Mongrel dog I was very conscious of hygiene standards, and as fleas were known to hop from one dog to another, I was determined to ensure that they did not take up residence on my body!

For the next hour or so we all played and chatted about our individual life's experiences. The Alsatian informed us his name was Rufus, and that he lived on Airdale road, a couple of streets away from where Boxer and I lived. He had no master, he having died some years ago, but the mistress of the house—a most kind hearted person—always seemed sad; she did not go out much, and did not take much real interest in his health. His great consolation was that he had the freedom of the city. He could roam where he liked and often travelled into Town, to back lanes—particularly where meat shops and restaurants existed: here he often found some of the most appetising tit-bits to eat. He related to us how on many occasions he successfully eluded the Dog Wardens, arriving home exhausted after his nights rambling, consoled, as he informed us, by a full stomach!

I noticed that his appearance was somewhat ragged; his coat had a coarse roughness about it, yet he seemed under-nourished; however; he had clear, bright, sparkling eyes, coupled with an air of authority that was impressive.

The Red Setter on the other hand was called Bowser and he looked the picture of health. He informed us he was in residence (his own words!) in the nearby local farm named Hazel Oak. He lived in a fine kennel made of redbrick, suitably furnished with regular supplies of fresh straw, and was fed daily on the best of food. His master had entered him in several dog show competitions in which he had won several honours. Moreover, when the family went on holidays each year, he also, was brought along; an experience he thoroughly enjoyed. I found him affable, friendly, and very curious about everything. He quizzed Boxer and I with endless questions, such as where we lived, had we nice homes, and were we ever sick: a real nosey nosey-parker! I thought he was too pompous.

Myself, though being a mere Mongrel dog, I was not

disposed in this initial meeting at least, to be bursting over with enthusiasm to have him as a friend. Lastly there was the little Jack Russell, called Young Henry, or Henry, for short. Though small in stature he was very high-spirited; he paraded up and down in a cocky sort of manner, giving off continuously a sort of suppressed growl, rather like a dog keen to start a fight! I thought him too arrogant for his size and I advised him to calm down as he was getting Rufus the Alsatian a little annoyed. I was not keen to include Young Henry among my circle of friends.

We all had great fun playing chasing around the park, and our new friends—particularly Rufus and Bowser—were great fun to be with. Not so the Jack Russell, Henry. He was much too reserved for me; even Boxer was not impressed. After a while he drifted off on his own and we were glad to see the last of him. With Rufus and Bowser both Boxer and I shared many happy times together; in the following weeks we would meet regularly in the Park, sharing many and varied experiences together.

One of those experiences involved the case of Alonzo, a dog we befriended for a time. I recall it as if it were only yesterday. It all came about like this: one day there was a great stir in our backyard. As my mistress was bringing me out my breakfast, she noticed that Alice the rabbit was missing. A thorough search was undertaken of the garden, there was no sign of her whatsoever: she had disappeared. Despite enquiries with the neighbours, she was nowhere to be found. Given that our home was close to Hazel-Oak Farm, we concluded that given the time of year it was, that she had been visited by a suitor and encouraged to abandon the homestead. What was upsetting to us was of course how her absence had upset the Mistress, for she loved that rabbit dearly.

A week passed and still Alice was not found. One morning Boxer and I were out in the nearby fields walking; we were in effect washing our feet in the wet morning dew which lay upon the grass, when suddenly we saw Alice bouncing around in the company of another rabbit—a male of the species. Alice, noticing Boxer and me, stood firm; her companion, on the other hand, took fright and fled. She commenced to bounce around in a frenzy of enthusiasm upon seeing us approach. When Boxer and I reached where she was standing she became very emotional; we motioned around each other, given vent to our feelings of happiness at once again being together. I noticed that Boxer was particularly affected, and I could see that he shared in the happiness of this early morning re-union, as Alice began to relate to us her many adventures since she went missing from home. And many and varied they were indeed.

She had been shot at by the humans, chased by wild dogs, and was lucky to be alive. However she had survived all and now enquired how Jack was. I immediately gave her all the latest news including how the Mistress was all upset at her disappearance, as was poor Jack. He was very distressed at her absence. I informed her how on a particular day last week I had looked into his hutch; there I saw tears coming from his eyes! Boxer gave several mild barks to confirm the truth of what I had said, and this news saddened poor Alice no end.

To create some happiness I quickly gave two loud barks signalling that we must be up and away before the humans came out and about—otherwise we would not get Alice home safely. Just before we went on our way Alice went back into the bushes to bid her friend farewell, while Boxer and I kept our eyes peeled for any enemies about. In a short while she rejoined us and we all started for home. After we had travelled a short distance across the field, she turned, stood up on her hind legs and looked back in the direction where she had parted from her friend: it was all quite moving.

On her way home she told us about a dog she knew that was quite ill, and was positioned in a particular part of a nearby field; she urged us to stop there and see if we could help. Boxer and I were quite disturbed to hear this and immediately urged Alice to take us there at once. We set off to the upper end of an adjacent field, where, in a recessed area in a clump of bushes, we saw to our horror a ragged Mongrel dog that looked anything but well. As we worked our way through the bushes the creature tried to rise, at the same time giving off a bark that was barely audible. Alice moved close and looked at him while at the same time flapping her ears in friendship. She then stepped back while I moved forward to enquire what was the matter. I was horrified to hear what came next.

"I am delighted to see you all," he cried, "and particularly my friend, Alice. As you can see, I am quite ill and have been living here for over a week and have had very little to eat."

"You do indeed look anything but well," cried Boxer, "You look like you have distemper."

"And so I have," replied the latter, "But first let me introduce myself: my name is Alonzo—at least that is what I have been called for as long as I can remember. I lived with a family about three miles from here. I was happy there until one day about four months ago the family suddenly packed up moved away and left me behind. For weeks I was heartbroken and had to scrape and forage as best I could for food in order to live. Not only that I was also hounded and chased by the humans, who turned their dogs on me, beat me with sticks so that my very life was continuously in peril. It was horrible. I had to run and hide to wherever I could find shelter, and if it were not for the kindness of an old woman who visits the local park each week and brought me a little food—I would be dead by now. For the last week and a half I have been unable to go and meet her, and being weak with hunger I feel I have now contracted distemper."

As he spoke these words I could see the tears forming in his eyes, and upon his face was the saddest expression I have ever seen; even poor Boxer was visibly affected. He leaned closer to Alonzo gave off several barks of affection and support, at the same time licking him in the face; I was visibly moved at what I saw.

Boxer and I resolved to immediately to help our new-found friend. We decided that some food be got immediately. It was decided that I would return home with Alice and that Boxer would remain behind to comfort Alonzo until our return. Within a short time they both arrived home. They entered into the backyard through a gap in the hedge and cautiously approached the rabbit hutch, Alice moving a little faster than I, and in some measure of excitement. Jack, her friend and partner, was nowhere to be seen.

Alice began to jump and bounce about and make all sorts of noises. This was to attract Jack's attention. Suddenly, from deep inside the hutch, he did indeed emerge to see what was all the excitement. Upon seeing Alice he leapt into the air, raced towards her and they both pawed at each other in a most affectionate manner. They made funny noises and warmed to each other in a manner that would melt your heart. I was touched to witness such expressions of love and affection that bonded these two creatures together. While all this was going on I noticed a tray of food placed just outside the back door; I raced towards it; it contained a nice piece of soft meat among the scraps on the tray. I set aside this for Alonzo, and then set about tucking into the rest. Soon I eat my fill.

After bidding goodbye to Jack and Alice I started back for the Park with my chosen piece of meat. As I was trotting down the back garden the back door of the house suddenly opened, and out walked my mistress. Noticing the plate cleared of food, she began calling me; with my goal foremost on my mind I ignored her call for the present. Noticing Alice back at the hutch she became very excited. She cried out, "Robert, Robert, come quickly—look, Alice is back!"

Robert came out of the house just in time to see my mistress rush forward, lift Alice up, and cuddle her warmly. For Prince this was a most joyous scene to behold.

Jack, meantime, observing Alice in my mistress' arms began to hop and dance about in a most excited manner; my mistress noticing this released Alice who quickly joined Jack. Now they both danced and hopped about the garden making all sorts of funny noises to each other: I could see that they were both overjoyed to see each once again! I would have loved to stay longer and share in their mutual joy; however, Boxer would be waiting for me so I did not delay further. With my precious piece of meat firmly gripped between my teeth I crawled out through the gap in the hedge, and was quickly on my way.

I soon arrived back, much to Boxers delight, and immediately gave Alonzo the piece of meat; he was delighted with it and despite his weakened condition, he chewed it slowly and eventually swallowed it.

Over the next few days Boxer and I continued to bring

him food, and try to cheer him up; however, despite our best efforts, he deteriorated and it was with much pain and suffering we watched him get weaker and weaker. Then, one bright, sunny morning, we arrived on a visit and were shocked to find poor Alonzo—dead. Boxer and I were shattered. We were overcome with grief and sadness: we stood there staring down at him, speechless. This scene of death was a whole new experience for me which I found difficult to understand; Boxer, on the other hand, seemed to cope better; he held his composure much better than I did. I broke down in tears and began to howl and bark to give expression to the great sadness I felt within me; leaning forward I embraced poor Alonzo, as Boxer too began to bark to express the great sadness he felt, also. We could not understand why this terrible tragedy had been allowed to happen. As we looked upon the scene before us I hoped in my heart that the great Benefactor—if he really existed, that he would send down Toby of the Brave Heart to take back to the Kingdom of the Dogs poor Alonzo.

As I reflected upon this, suddenly my attention was drawn to an outbreak of song from four small birds perched on a tree branch just above where Alonzo lay; they whistled and chirped, alternatively looking down where our dead friend lay.

"Why I believe they are singing a funeral song for Alonzo," cried Boxer, "How wonderful."

Boxer and I, as we both listened, were cheered up by the beauty and harmony of their voices; it was an experience I shall never forget. I again had that vision of those golden walls at the entrance to the Kingdom of the Dogs, and the great chorus of song I had heard while in the company of Toby of the Brave Heart; if such a place really existed, then, I hoped that someday poor Alonzo would go there. Boxer and I now pondered on what we should do with poor Alonzo's body? On considered reflection we decided, rather than leave him here in the ditch we would dig out a burial spot in the field, and inter his body there. We selected a spot and immediately began to dig. Soon we had a chamber dug out, and fairly sore paws after our labours. We entered the bushes to fetch the body. As we did so the four birds kept up their singing, while a fifth bird was now perched on Alonzo's head. I have to confess that the scene once more brought tears to my eyes; here before lay this poor dog placed here on Earth with so much love to give, asking nothing in return, yet abused by the humans and left here to die, a forgotten creature regarded as of little consequence; how terrible: how sad—shameful.

Boxer and I now removed Alonzo's body and placed it in the grave we had dug out; we then covered it in with fresh clay: soon our work was complete, yet not so according to the singing birds in the bushes. They were now joined by three other birds who began to carry leaves in their beaks which they deposited on top of the grave; this they done for several minutes: it was all most impressive. With our work finished Boxer and I sat down alongside Alonzo's last resting place. We broke into our own lament. We barked, howled and wept for our dead friend, raising our paws to Heaven with a feeling of great sorrow; again I thought of my dream, and the Kingdom of the Dogs; I thought of Toby of the brave heart and hoped that our dead friend would one day end up there. I had not been long pondering on these matters when I thought I heard a noise. It sounded like a trumpet. I asked Boxer did he hear anything: he replied no. I remarked to him that I thought that it had become very quiet all of a sudden. I noticed too that the birds in the bushes had stopped singing. Boxer now propped up his ears to listen, for he too had noticed the sudden silence. We both looked at each other with mixed feelings, and a deep sense of apprehension.

Suddenly a second trumpet sound was heard—this time in three separate blasts, after which all was quiet again. Then suddenly before our eyes I beheld the great friend of my drea—Toby of the Brave Heart! How he had come there, I had no idea.

Almost immediately he spoke: "And how on this bright, yet sad morning is my friend, Prince?"

"Fine, fine," I replied, as I struggled to gather my thoughts, "fine—but sad in a way."

"I know of your sadness," replied Toby, "and also of the sadness of your pal, Boxer. A terrible tragedy has occurred here this day, and your friend Alonzo has suffered much here on earth. I have been sent down this day to bring his spirit home; all his other dog friends are waiting back in the Kingdom to welcome him home."

I should say at this stage that Toby seemed only half visible, and while I could clearly see who he was, this was not the case with Boxer, who, afterwards questioned whether in fact Toby had appeared—or not. After further brief exchanges with Toby he assured me that a special kennel had been set-aside for Alonzo, and that a great welcome awaited him as soon as he reached the Kingdom. Suddenly there was a stir in the earth where we had laid Alonzo; Boxer and I stood back a little frightened. We next witnessed a most extraordinary happening, for up from the grave appeared our friend, Alonzo! Boxer and I were dumbfounded. We watched him slowly ascend from the grave and climb on to Toby's back.

As he did so he stared at both Boxer and I in a most happy and pleasing manner. He did not bark or cry out and the sheer look of happiness on his face clearly told us that he was very happy to be returning home. We watched them both as they ascended into the heavens; as they did so Toby uttered a special cheerio to Boxer and I, saying at the same time that our kindness to Alonzo would not be forgotten. Our good deed would be recorded in the book of good deeds kept in the Kingdom of the Dogs: in good time we would receive our reward. We watched in awe as they climbed higher and higher into the skies, eventually disappearing out of sight. It was sometime before Boxer and I returned fully to our senses, for this extraordinary event had really stunned us. We were very saddened by poor Alonzo's death, and it gradually dawned on us that he had really been taken up into the Heavens. As we made our way home we spoke little of these extraordinary events of this particular morning.

4

A neighbourhood menace
My courtship days
A cruelty incident reported
The court case

WHEN WE ARRIVED HOME BOXER told me about a new cat
that had moved into our neighbourhood. It was a big Tomcat,
brash, arrogant, and recently was much given to howling
and meowing late at night; nobody could get a decent night's
sleep. Not only that, observed Boxer, but it had now gathered
a number of its friends and they were all engaged in singing into the late hours—that is after they were all finished
rummaging through waste-bins looking for scraps of food!
They were making such a racket, that nobody could sleep
properly at night. Recently I spoke to some of my friends,
particular lyRover the Bulldog and his son, Samson, and we
have agreed to hold a meeting tomorrow night to try to do
something about it. Boxer asked me would I too come, and
of course I agreed at once; indeed I offered to help out in any
way I could. After all, us dogs must have our proper night's
sleep too, so the matter must be redressed.

The following night we all assembled at the bottom of

234

Riordan's lane, where we began our deliberations. Present were myself, Rover the Bulldog and his son, Samson, Rusty the Collie, Dasher the Labrador and Growler, a Mongrel Boxer and I had recently become acquainted with; he brought several of his friends along, something Boxer and I were pleased about. As Boxer was the oldest among us, we asked him to open the proceedings.

Boxer, standing up on his hind legs, spoke thus: "My friends I wish to call this meeting to order. We have a crisis on our hands, which must immediately receive our attention. Recently we have been invaded by a multitude of cats! We know from listening to our masters that the antics of this said cat are becoming a nuisance to the humans; they can't sleep at night! But more important, my friends—it is no longer possible for us dogs to get a decent night's sleep also! This is a most serious matter which we, my friends, have got to sort out. The purpose, therefore, of this meeting is to consider ideas on what is to be done to stop this nuisance; my friends without further ado I now throw this meeting open to hear your views."

Listening to Boxer's opening remarks I felt great pride in being his friend. His age and experience certainly stood to him. He demonstrated command, and a true air of authority; I was sure this problem would be resolved quickly.

With that Rover the Bulldog spoke, "My friends, since that black Tom cat came into our area it is not possible to get a decent night's sleep! Lids of bins are knocked to the ground, waste bags are torn open, fighting, screaming and howling are to be heard every night; worse still, other cats are also coming in after him: something has to be done."

All the other dogs concurred with what Rover had said, each adding their own individual experience in dealing with this new community nuisance. Dasher, normally quiet and reserved, called for the introduction by the humans of a Control of Cats Act, similar to the Control of Dogs Act, which they had brought into law. All concurred in this last point, each remarking on the many ways dogs are discriminated against throughout the country. "Indeed," continued Dasher, "the number of dog shelters provided are totally inadequate for the needs of our people. Why a dog can not attend upon the calls of nature in public—because of the lack of decent toilet facilities! It is a disgrace."

Boxer intervened by recalling that in the most recent year twenty-five thousand of our brothers and sisters had been killed because of this terrible neglect. It could not be allowed to continue!

As the meeting continued, suddenly a noise was heard mid-way down a nearby lane, where a human was seen to be in hot pursuit of three cats. Boxer immediately recommended a suspension of the meeting, "Right lads, I'm suspending this meeting and call on all to go into action at once and let's get rid of these cats once and for all."

"Hear, hear!" roared all present.

"One thing," continued Boxer, "no cats are to be bitten or physically harmed in any way. Chase them—yes; scare the living daylights out of them—yes, but no physical contact or harm."

All barked their approval of Boxer's firm instruction, and without any further delay they raced in the direction in which the three cats had gone, full of determination.

As I reflect back on our meeting that night, I tremble slightly at what was the outcome. We certainly got rid of the cats that did not reside in our neighbourhood, for none have been seen since! As to the cost, well Rusty the Collie unfortunately sustained a broken leg that night, but quickly recovered. In truth the experience was hilarious! We chased at least six cats up and down Riordan's Lane, across to Bay view drive, up Corcoran street, in and out of back yards, over fences, and criss-crossing each other's paths till on one occasion I wasn't sure whether we were chasing the cats or they were chasing us! Boxer and I had great fun; none of the cats were physically attacked and what happened that night was the talk of the neighbourhood for days afterwards.

I shall never forget my first courtship days, or the unforgettable Miss Pearl Brown. She was a Collie belonging to a family that moved into our area for a short time. She had a lovely black and white coat and was in the peak of health. I first made her acquaintance on a summer's morning as I was playing in the local Park with my two friends, Boxer and Growler. All of us were quite taken by her beauty as her mistress was walking her there. We paused from our playing and began staring at her, alternately barking to catch her attention. The sight of her really captivated my heart. For the first time in my life I was in love!

I could see too that Boxer was also quite captivated by Pearl; his ears were cocked while his tail wagged continuously. "Now there, Prince, is a real beauty; I shall have to make her acquaintance soon," he cried.

Both Rusty and Growler, my other two friends, raced across towards her, barking out their enthusiasm and giving every indication that they too wanted to get to know her. I had trotted over closer to her myself, though not so close as to cause concern either to herself, or he mistress; it would be undignified to crowd upon a lady in the situation in which Pearl found herself; I was resolved to cultivate her acquaint-

ance in circumstances better suited to us both. As Rusty and
Growler tried to force themselves on Pearl her mistress was
less than pleased; she threatened them both with her walking
cane, narrowly missing Growler's ear after a forward thrust;
both dogs were forced to make a hasty retreat.

As Pearl and her mistress went on their way Pearl paused,
turned around, and looked directly at me in a most inviting
manner causing a fluttering in my heart: I felt that we would
meet again, soon.

As we strolled around the Park, and just shortly after
getting over our initial excitement of seeing Pearl, our repose was suddenly disturbed by the screams of one of the
humans; the screams came from a lady human who had just
had her handbag snatched. She was lying on the ground and
appeared in a state of shock. The perpetrator of this vile
deed turned out to be one of the younger humans whom
we observed racing away from the scene. Boxer immediately gave chase, with Growler and myself joining in; we
all raced like hell hoping the culprit would drop the bag;
however, when we did catch up with him, instead of dropping it he turned and swung it like hell at all three of us:
we were forced to duck and sway this way and that, yet we
did not give up the struggle. We barked and snarled em-
ploying every tactic in order to force him to drop it, which
eventually he did. Boxer immediately picked it up and like
a triumphant army all three of us ran back to the distressed
human, who now was being assisted by a number of other
humans that had come to her aid.

Boxer immediately walked up to her and dropped the bag
at her feet, while Growler, Rusty and I drew back a short
distance so as not to crowd the situation. We were delighted
to see how happy the lady was having now got her bag back.

The other humans who were assisting her were lavish in their praise of Boxer. "Now isn't that the cutest thing you ever did see," cried one. "Just imagine," she continued, "they ran after the culprit, and recovered her bag!" "Aye," replied another, "and his other two friends gave a great helping hand, too; goes to show that some dogs are very clever, aye, and understanding too."

For the moment we were the heroes of the hour, particularly Boxer. But then I was not surprised, for he, being the oldest and most experienced of us all, also had a very caring and loving heart. The lady herself was not above expressing her appreciation, for she remarked thus: "Next time I come into the Park I will bring a nice bone for you. Yes, and also something for your friends—just like I used to do for my friend Alonzo."

At the mention of Alonzo's name Boxer and I looked at each other, bowed our heads and slowly walked back across the Park towards the main entrance. The mention of poor Alonzo's name had saddened our hearts a little: as we were walking off I overheard the old lady remark "how strange, they all seem so sad all of a sudden: I wonder what can be the matter?"

Of course she could not have known how poor Alonzo had died; we were encouraged to note that at least she had some good nature in her, given that she was a human.

By now I was approaching my fifth birthday, and from conversation I overheard and understood, the Mistress of the house—at the behest of the children, particularly Francis, the youngest—was planning a little celebration for me real soon. I was very excited at hearing this news, and privately hoped that I might be able to invite my friends. I imagined that Alice and Jack, that they would be invited along. Of my other friends, I resolved to ensure that they too were invited.

Over the coming weeks I took careful note of the comings and goings of everyone, both in and around the house. It was now the summer season, and the days were long, bright, and sunny. My Master and Mistress spent much time sitting in the back garden enjoying the sun. Alice and Jack were often let loose from their Pen, and even Roger the Turtle joined in the fun. Ah! Those were happy days: two fine meals a day, a comfortable kennel to sleep in, and surrounded by a family of loving and caring humans who were not only so happy themselves, but also found time to shower love and affection on me, even though I was only a dog. During these happy interludes I gathered from my sense of acute observation that my fifth birthday would be celebrated on a Saturday week, in the afternoon. I was very excited at this news, and, when the Mistress remarked that we must make this a special event—and invite some of my friends—I was doubly excited! I jumped down from my favourite chair in the house, bounced around, barked with excitement, giving every indication that her remarks met with my full approval. "There," she cried, "even Prince agrees with my suggestion, don't you boy?" I was not slow to respond. I barked several times more, wagged my tail continuously in demonstration of my full agreement.

In due course the big day arrived. I had been up very early; indeed I slept very little that night from thinking of this happy event. I had met most of my friends in the previous few days and had invited them around to the back garden to the celebrations. To make sure there were no hitches I made two extra gaps in the hedge which surrounded our garden thus ensuring that they would have no difficulty in gaining access. The Saturday turned out to be a lovely sunny day; everybody was up early: even the birds were out and about singing their little hearts out! There was even a great feeling in the air. The Mistress was out and about looking after Alice and Jack, I got an early breakfast, (though I noticed that my plate was not as full of food as was usual), however, excited as I was I did not feel like eating as much as usual: I was more looking forward to today's events that were to unfold! After breakfast I spent my time lounging in the sun and watching the antics of Roger. Alice was not about, and Roger seemed very excited, and for what reason I couldn't gather; perhaps he too knew it was my birthday and was anxious to share in the celebrations! Mind you neither he nor Alice needed much excuse to join in any celebration! As my companions and neighbours they were always quick to join in games I or my friends were engaged in: they were good companions to me.

About midday the Mistress's youngest son, Francis, joined me in the back garden and we had great fun rolling and tumbling about until we were eventually both exhausted. He was only six years old, and we both loved each other very much. When we were together he would lift me up in his arms—cuddling me in a very loving and almost motherly way. The first thing he would do each day after he would return from school would be to rush out into the back yard, head straight for my kennel, call me out, lift me up and almost cuddle me to death! On occasions I would hide among the bushes just about the time he was expected to arrive, and when he whistled and called I would refuse to come out; this would perplex him considerably! And when I did reveal myself I would race around and around the garden before allowing him to lift me up; in truth we had some great fun times together.

I could tell that he too had a sense that something exciting was to take place, for young Francis was not one to miss out on the fun! It was with some difficulty that I restrained my excitement; to help, I stretched out on the grass and tried to relax. Later that afternoon saw the proceedings get underway, as the Master and Mistress, together with other members of the family came out into the garden to sit and enjoy the afternoon sunshine. Alice and Jack—even Roger the Turtle—took their places, all exhibiting an air of expectation that something important was about to take place. After a short while the Mistress returned into the house but soon emerged with what appeared to be a pot, complete with lid. After a brief few words with the Master she called everybody's attention, then made the following speech:

"Right everybody could I have your attention. You all know that today is Prince's birthday; he is five years old this very day. Now to the outside world this might be viewed as not an important occasion, but to us assembled here, Prince, being part of our family, and over the past five years having giving us all some much happiness, and having been such a loving and faithful friend, we thought it right that we should this day celebrate this important occasion. He has watched over our house and garden—both day and night— and has shown an uncanny knack for cheering us all up whenever we felt down; has never been the cause of any trouble to anyone, got on extremely well with all the neighbours dogs, and even brought Alice back just when we had thought we had lost her. Today we have prepared a special dinner in his honour. Not only that but I have also invited some of our neighbours over to visit. I have asked them bring their dog pets as well. They should be arriving soon. Meantime, as I pour out this luscious meal for Prince, will you all join me in a special toast to a special friend—and a dear member of our family!"

Orange and lemonade drinks were distributed around to all. "To Prince, a true and faithful friend—happy birthday!" cried my Mistress.

Upon hearing this toast proposed in my honour I felt very humbled. It almost brought tears to my eyes. However, as the Mistress went on I was getting hungrier by the minute; she was a terrible woman for chatting, not to mention speech-making! Well I could see that she was only warming up and however well intentioned I could see that unless I dropped her a hint—or some members of the family did, she would ramble on and on. I began to bark, wag my tail and run around.

She immediately interjected, "Now Prince have patience. You will have your dinner soon. As I was saying...Prince has been, rather, I should say, *is* our own special friend and companion, and we all love him dearly, and we know he loves us too."

As she completed this sentence young Francis, toddled over and put his two arms around me and gave me a big hug; I responded by licking his face several times. Meantime the Mistress had concluded her speech, having received a little encouragement from other members of the family! She now set down the pot on a nearby table, and for the next ten minutes everybody sat back amidst an air of expectation as to what was to happen next. Anxious to get my teeth into some food, I was equally anxious to see what was to happen next.

The Master who had earlier returned into the house now

emerged once again holding a tray, which appeared to hold a square cake, lit by five candles. The Mistress meanwhile had removed from the pot on the table what looked like a rich meaty stew; from where I was standing it gave off a delicious smell, which quite got me excited. As the table upon which it was placed was not very high, I was able stand on my hind legs, lean my forepaws against the tabletop and get a full view of what was set out. The Master meanwhile approached the table, set down the tray he was carrying beside the other tray, and called the rest of the family—including myself, to gather around. Next, the Mistress called young Francis, made him put his arm around me, and instructed him—acting on my behalf—to blow out the lighted candles, and call Happy Birthday. It was all very moving and, although I am not human myself, I instinctively felt the deep and warm emotive feelings which pervaded the whole company.

Little Francis, on being called upon by the Mistress, now called out, "Happy birthday dear Prince, happy birthday dear Prince, happy birthday dear Prince, happy birthday to you!"

All around the table joined in the chorus, even Boxer, Rusty, and Alice and Jack. I was very moved, and it all brought tears to my eyes. The Mistress, noticing how keenly I watched the meals, immediately lifted the tray which contained the blown out candles, removed them, and now placed it down on the ground beside me. It contained a large, cooled roasted joint! With great excitement I immediately began eating. As I was doing so I suddenly heard a dog barking; it was coming from the end of the garden. I recognised it to be my pal Boxer! I raced down and met him just as he was coming through the hedge. I invited him up to share my food; however, some of the family members present began to push him away: I immediately barked my disapproval. As the afternoon pushed towards evening, the Master and Mistress, together with the other members of the family all retired inside the house. My pals Boxer, Rusty, and my other dog friends that had come, all barked their thanks for having been invited, declaring how thoroughly they had enjoyed the food; suddenly Jack the rabbit started to hop and jump about in a frenzy of excitement! I sensed that something was wrong, but what? I began to bark loudly to attract my Mistress's attention; she came out of the house almost immediately.

"Boxer," she cried, "what is wrong?"

I turned and ran straight to Jack's hutch. She followed me directly. Reaching it she bent down and looked straight in, but pulled back almost immediately with a look of great excitement on her face. She stood up and called her husband from the house. "Robert, Robert, come quickly," she cried. The Master at once emerged from the house and joined her at the hutch.

"You will never believe it," she cried, "but Alice is after having two young babies!"

Both the Master and the Mistress spent some standing at the Hutch talking and I could tell by the expressions on their faces that they were very excited at this turn of events. As for Jack, well, he kept running in and out of the hutch, cuddling up to Alice, and, as would all fathers on such occasions, demonstrate all the excitement and happiness on the occasion of new family arrivals. Boxer and I all felt part of this happy event; we showed our enthusiasm by given off a series of low barks to congratulate them both: for me personally— on this the occasion of my fifth birthday, the arrival of Alice and Jack's new family, concluded a most happy and exciting day—and one which I shall always remember.

I shall never forget my courtship days, and the many beautiful ladies which had captured my attention and whom I had courted. Some of these were from the locality, some from outside our area. One in particular, Sheba Brown, a Red Setter, had quite bowled me over when I first saw her way back in 1967. I composed a poem for her, which went as follows:

> There was Sheba Brown from way up town,
> who rolled from side to side, whose long brown
> ears and dazzling eyes quite turned my head around.
> Her passionate ways and loving heart I never could
> resist; oh why my Sheba had you to go, and leave
> me here behind? You fairly broke this old dogs heart,
> I truly missed you so!

This beautiful soulmate, upon whom for many weeks I engaged in a passionate courtship, finally left Town with Her Master and Mistress, but not before I had gotten myself into several fights with other dogs on her account, and on one occasion had to crawl home with a broken leg at 3:00 AM in the morning! However, the lady who finally captured my heart in the end was the lovely Pearl. I first met her when Boxer, Growler and I were out playing in the Park. All three of us danced, ran around and barked to engage her attention, but with little success; her Mistress was quite firm in ensuring that none of us got too near. For my part her parting glance to me just as she was leaving the Park made a great impression on my heart; I felt we were destined to meet again.

Over the coming weeks I kept regular watch in and around the Park area, hoping for an opportunity to see her again.

Then one particular afternoon I was out walking on my own and there she was, unattended, and running around loose to her heart's content. Her Mistress, I quickly noted, was seated on one of the nearby park benches: I could not believe my luck! I was determined to engage her attention and give full expression of my feelings on this most opportune of occasions; I raced out to where she was running about, barking out my greetings and lavishing my undivided attention upon her. My sudden arrival caused her to pause and observe me in a restrained, yet excited manner. I detected at once that she was not angry at my arrival; indeed, her coyness and reserve were understandable in the circumstances, given that I was a mere Mongrel; I was not of an upper class breed—not, mind you, that I would be offended to find myself in that category! However, I was a Mongrel dog—and proud of that; we didn't have airs and graces—nor did we have them imposed upon us: we were free agents and came and went as we wished, and consequently we rarely mixed with other dogs held to be of better breeding. On this occasion I had had a good wash in the local canal earlier in the morning; I felt quite fresh and clean, and was determined to press on with my firm resolution to win the heart of Miss Pearl Brown!

I hovered around her—confident of success. For the next few minutes we courted, kissed, sniffed, barked, wagged our tails, and gave such demonstration of filial love to each other as to cause some humans that were passing to stop and stare at us both. Whether in admiration, or just out of plain curiosity, I was unable to determine.

Pearl informed me where she lived, that she had been entered in several dog show competitions, and had won many prizes. She also informed me that she lived in a comfortable home, was fed well and regularly groomed. However she was not allowed to mix freely with other dogs and consequently led a very sheltered and lonely life. I could see by the look on her face that she was indeed sad of heart; it reminded me of the sad faces I had seen on many of the dogs up in the Pound that I had recently visited. Though she was shy as I already indicated, I could see by the gleam in her eyes that we were going to get on very well. I was very excited and determined to make a good impression. Pearl was a true lady and my instinct told me she must be treated accordingly. We began to play about, alternatively barking at each other— communicating in the true spirit in which us dogs do; a form of communication, I might add, barely understood by the humans—if understood at all.

As we played I noticed some of them pausing in their stride and looking at Pearl and myself with interest. Pearl's owner meanwhile was engaged in conversation with another human and this allowed time for Pearl and I to get better acquainted. Together we talked of our many tales and experiences, and she was particularly pleased to hear about Toby of the Brave Heart, and also of the Kingdom of the Dogs; she was particularly saddened to hear of the death of our friend, poor Alonzo. I found her most affable to talk with; she listened with patience and understanding, and though she was a better class of dog than I she did not display any airs or graces in her demeanour towards me: I felt very much at ease in her company.

Unfortunately this brief interlude, so full of happiness to me, came to a sudden end. Pearl's owner came galloping towards us waving a big stick! Obviously she was determined to send me on my way! I was forced to beat a hasty retreat, but not before Pearl and I had agreed to meet again a few days hence. I had pledged to call and see her again as soon as possible. Her Mistress quickly strapped up Pearl again and they both left the Park. Just before they passed out of sight, Pearl turned her head, looked in my direction and barked several times, to remind me to come and see her soon; with the love-light burning in my little dog's heart for this lovely lady, this I was resolved to do—and soon. With that I ran straight for home.

The following day when I met Boxer and Rusty I explained to them all the news about my encounter with Pearl. They both received my news with compelling interest, and I could see that Boxer, particularly, sensed my excitement; like a true friend he wished me well. Rusty of course did likewise, and, given the fresh morning it was we all three set off on our daily ramble in the nearby fields of Hazel-Oak Farm. We were not long on our way when we encountered a most saddening incident. We saw one of the humans, a most unpleasant looking character with an angry scowl on his face; he had a young Alsatian dog on a lead and was repeatedly beating him with a stick. The unfortunate dog screamed and howled for all he was worth, but the beatings did not cease. Not only that but the poor dog was in a most dilapidated condition; its coat was in a most ragged state, and appeared to have been half starved. Boxer, upon observing this scene was furious. He urged Rusty and I to follow him immediately. He rushed straight at the human, barking furiously and set upon attacking him. The human, noticing all three of us rushing forward, turned and started running with the Alsatian towards the nearby road. We continued our chase—determined to teach this most cruel human a lesson he would never forget.

We quickly caught up with them both and the human, in a frenzy of anger, lashed out with his stick at each of us—determined to drive us away. But we were not to be intimidated so, and Boxer, to his eternal credit, snarled, roared, and barked so furiously forcing the human to flee from the field, unfortunately, though, with the poor Alsatian pup, also. As all three of us were somewhat tired from the chase, we did not follow.

In our attempt to rescue our fellow brother we had only succeeded in stopping this barbarous act of cruelty, and felt sure that this would be likely to recur again. Indeed during the chase the Alsatian had pleaded with us to affect his rescue from his cruel Master, and, also to help his two brothers and sister who were housed in most filthy conditions, and were half-starved. Having considered of this matter we were resolved on a plan to do just that. We agreed that Rusty immediately follow this cruel human home to where he lived, and report back to us. We agreed to meet later in the evening to consider what action to take, following receipt of his findings; meantime Boxer and I returned home without further delay.

Later that evening Boxer, Rusty and I meet in my back garden as arranged. Rusty reported on what he had seen as follows. About three-quarters of a mile from where the cruelty incident occurred, he had observed the cruel human enter a house; this was positioned backing onto a field and had a large rear back garden in which was located a large shed. Approaching the rear of the house he heard loud dog noises coming from the same shed; some of the dogs inside were barking noisily calling for food, and also pleading to be released. The garden had a lot of rubbish strewn about, given it a very untidy appearance. As he watched and listened from the rear end of the garden he observed the same cruel human emerge from the rear of the house, a young man accompanying him, and also the young Alsatian dog. He overheard the boy calling the dog by the name of Major. Just then the boy opened the shed door and entered. Immediately there was a loud noise of dogs barking and screaming which persisted for several minutes; then there was silence. The shed door reopened, the Master grabbed hold of the Alsatian and, with great force, threw him into the shed and slammed the door at once.

Then both Master and boy returned into the house from which they had come from. As Rusty related this series of events he paused in his narrative, obviously emotionally upset from recalling what he had seen and heard. He continued: "I resolved to get a closer look at this shed and endeavour to see exactly how many dogs were locked in there, and to see exactly what condition they were in. I squeezed through a small opening in the hedge, which enclosed the garden, and cautiously moved towards it. I was able to proceed unnoticed, thanks to the many clumps of rubbish strewn about the garden, which gave me cover from detection.

Upon reaching the shed I was fortunate in that there was a small hole in the sidewall, which enabled me to peer inside; looking through I was shocked at what I saw and shall never forget the sight that met my eyes. There were six dogs railed off in one corner, three of whom I could see very clearly, and all of which seemed half starved. I was shocked. One dog was stretched out on the ground and seemed half dead; moreover, the floor was filthy and appeared damp and all the dogs had looks of terrible sadness on their faces."

Rusty said that he had spoken with Major briefly, assuring him that we would do everything in our power to help him and the others as soon as possible.

Boxer and Rusty listened with keen interest to their friend's report and, remembering the cruelty they had seen the human inflict on Major, they were determined to rescue them and also to see that this cruel human was punished for what he had done. They decided to visit the house next day to see for themselves where the dogs were housed; having done this they would next plan what action to take. Accordingly the next day they met together and travelled the three-quarters of a mile to where the dogs were held. The house and garden were situated at the end of a long line of terraced houses whose backs faced out onto a field. All, except one, were flanked by a back wall which secured the houses and gardens from intruders; the last house—the one where the dogs were kept—its wall was broken and a hedge had grown up in its place. It was through a gap here that Rusty had gained entry. This opening was a fortunate piece of luck; for it was from here they would gain entry to the shed. They moved closer and peered through, and, having got a good look in they decided to return either during the night or early in the morning, and affect the rescue of Major and the other dogs. With this plan in mind they decided to return home and come back the following morning.

At 5:00 AM the following morning Prince was awakened by several barks from Boxer who, accompanied by Rusty, was ready to go and rescue Major and his family. Prince rose quickly and joined them, and soon all three were on their way. They arrived at the house and proceeded to put their plan into action. Taking turns, while being as quiet as they could, they dug a deep hole sufficiently wide to enable each to pass under the floor of the shed where they discovered a part of the floor broken; this they ripped open sufficient to enable them to climb up into the section where young Major and his family were resting. As they entered, Prince was horrified at what he saw. On the floor was Major's brother, dead. He bore all the marks of having recently received a severe beating which had been the cause of his death. Major's mother and father were huddled close to him, shivering, they themselves in a very emaciated condition. Boxer was shocked at what he saw, and described the scene as a serious case of animal ill-treatment and criminal neglect. All of us held an immediate consultation; we decided to inform those humans whom we knew were kind to animals of what had happened here; meantime Major and his parents expressed delight at the interest we were taking in their situation, and asked us to help them in every way we could. They informed us of the horrible and continuous ill-treatment they were receiving at the hands of the humans that lived in the house, and pleaded with us to help them escape. Having consulted with us for a few moments more we agreed at once to leave immediately and head back to my back garden; I was confident that my Mistress would provide some food and shelter for Major and his parents. Without further delay we slipped quietly away from the shed, and headed home.

We eventually arrived back and settled down close to Alice and Jack's hutch to wait the dawn. As Major's mother was very sick I allowed her to sleep and rest in my kennel for the present. For the next hour or so we sat around and chatted about our individual experiences; Major's dad informed us his name was Butch, and his son was called Henry; they both told how for months this cruel human had been systematically ill-treating the whole family and how they had given up all hope of escape, that is until Major had told them of how we had tried to help him in the Park. As Butch related his story, and particularly as he told us how his other son, Rex, had been beaten and done to death, I could not but notice tears rolling from his eyes; I was so visibly shaken by his description of this most foul deed that I wept myself. Even Boxer could not restrain his emotions: he swore that he would not rest till this cruel human was brought to justice.

By now the dawn began to break and soon my Mistress would be leaving out my breakfast as she normally did each morning. A short while later the back door opened, and, sure enough out she came—a nice tray of food in one of her hands. As she was about to lay it down, she paused, and looked in the direction of my kennel. I immediately raced towards her, looked up into her face and barked several times. She stretched out her arm, patted me on the head, at the same time exclaiming "Why Prince, what have we here? Surely you're not bringing home all your friends for breakfast, also?" She moved towards my kennel to get a closer look at Butch and his son, Major; I kept barking and ran over to stand beside Major. As the Mistress approached Butch tried to rise; however, being too weak with hunger, he failed to get up. My Mistress, who had a kind and loving heart quickly perceived this, and, in response to my barking, said "Prince your new friend looks very ill."

Boxer, sensing her sudden anxiety and concern, now began to bark also; Butch suddenly leaned forward and began to lick her hand. I moved towards the entrance of the kennel, barked fiercely to draw her attention to Major's mother who was resting inside. Bending down she looked inside the kennel, and almost immediately rose up again, turned, and raced back into the house. She then reappeared quickly with two small plates of food, one of which she gave to Major, and the other to his mother resting inside the kennel. I invited Butch and Rusty to share in the plate of food that I had received: they gladly tucked in!

The back door of the house now opened again, and the Master of the house came out; he quickly joined my Mistress.

"This is most terrible," she cried. "Look how ill these dogs are, Michael."

Michael looked closely at them before replying.

"Look, look," continued my Mistress, "why they are half starved."

"I'm afraid you're right my love," he cried. "This is terrible. How did they get here?"

Of course they could not know the circumstances of exactly how they had come to be in the back garden, or the facts surrounding just what had happened. I kept barking to draw their attention to my concern and worry.

"We will have to ring the dog authorities," cried my Mistress, "these dogs must receive medical attention immediately—otherwise they will surely die."

They both now returned back into the house. A short while later my Mistress returned with drinking water and some more food. Meanwhile Boxer, Butch and Rusty left the garden to return home, while I spent the rest of the morning comforting Major and his mother as best I could.

Meanwhile, the local Veterinary doctor my Mistress had summoned eventually arrived to examine Major and his mother. To ensure that none of them would be frightened, I had explained to young Major that the Vet was coming to make them well again. When he arrived he immediately carried out a full examination of both dogs. My Master and Mistress were both present to offer any assistance required. When the Vet had completed his examination he remarked "These dogs are in a terrible state. Do they belong to you folks?"

"We have no idea," replied my Mistress, "they came home with our dog, Prince. When we opened our back door this morning, why, there they were, sitting in our back garden."

I immediately gave several barks of support to my Mistress, confirming just exactly the truth of what she had said. The Veterinary doctor, meanwhile, turned to look in my direction, remarking as he did, "yes, I see this dog seems to confirm what you say."

I then moved towards the entrance of the kennel, gave several more barks, to draw attention to Major's mother inside. The Veterinary doctor took the hint and quickly approached the kennel. Major and I meanwhile began to call her out. Soon she was on her feet and slowly began to come forward; however as she struggled both he and I were near to crying, as we observed the terrible condition she was in: at any moment we feared she would collapse and die. Just as she struggled out of the kennel I noticed something that I had not seen before: she had a collar around her neck attached to which was a metal tag with an address. The Vet noticed it too as he assisted her from the kennel. I immediately noted some small measure of conversation take place between my mistress and he, and I gathered that the upshot of this was that the tag contained an address where Major and his family lived. This was indeed an exciting break for us and I gathered from the conversation that the Vet was to contact the police to investigate this further. Meanwhile, having been administered some medical assistance, they were all taken away to the local veterinary hospital for further treatment. Needless to say I was delighted as to how matters were going; as they went on their way I gave several barks of farewell, noticing at the same time the expression of happiness on my Mistress' face that they would be looked after: For me the whole affair ended for the moment a most traumatic night and I wasted no time in retiring to my kennel for a well earned sleep!

In the days that followed I was delighted to learn that as a result of a police and animal welfare authority operation, resulting in a raid on Major's home address, the cruel human who owned the dogs had been arrested and charged with cruelty to animals—and was to appear in court on a Wednesday morning in two week's time. I learned also that Major's young brother, who had been done so cruelly to death, would be listed in evidence. I also learned that my Mistress would be attending the hearing; I resolved that Boxer and I must endeavour to go also. When the day of hearing arrived my Mistress and I set out for the courthouse which, fortunately, was not far from where we lived. The Master also attended and brought Boxer along. I meanwhile had arranged with Boxer that I would arrange to get him into the courtroom when we arrived there. As luck would have it my Mistress and I had no difficulty getting into the public gallery; Boxer was also sneaked in by the Master— something I was delighted about. We waited with anxiety for the case to begin.

With the arrival of the judge the court was called to order and the clerk of the court called case number 4B to attention. The cruel human was led in and the clerk of the court now read out the indictment.

"Jeremy Bissell you are charged that on Monday, April 26th you did house and keep in a lockup shed at the rear of your house, number 24 Keeper Street, in most filthy and unhygienic conditions, several Alsatian dogs, one of which was found murdered as the result of having received several blows to the head, and that contrary to Part III, Section 17–2 of the Protection of Animals Amendment Act (1965) you were wilfully neglectful of your obligations under the said Act in that you failed in your duty of maintenance and protection—as required by the said Act. How do you plead?"

"Not guilty," replied Bissell, in a somewhat arrogant manner.

Boxer and I were horrified at this response, as indeed were my Master and Mistress, so evident by the looks on their faces. The judge called upon the clerk to continue. First to give evidence was police officer Jenkins. He outlined how upon responding to a call from Jeremiah Scone, the local Vet, both he and an officer from the local society for the protection of animals had made an urgent visit to 24 Keeper Street, where, upon examination of the premises referred to in the charge, they discovered a number of Alsatian dogs in a most awful state of neglect, and also one dog dead. Mr Jenkins also went on to say that in his opinion the condition of the deceased dog represented the worst case of cruelty visited upon an animal he had witnessed for many years. Furthermore, the other four dogs that they had examined were in a most neglected state also. Bissell, who was conducting his own defence challenged the witness, and denied that he had been neglectful of his dogs, that the dog referred too had only recently rambled home to his back garden in very poor health; he had no knowledge of how it had become injured, and that it did not belong to him. The judge interjected, "Come now Mr Bissell, surely you don't expect us to believe that the injuries this animal received were inflicted elsewhere?"

"I did not kill that dog," retorted Bissell.

Then suddenly a loud dog bark was heard in the courtroom. The judge, who was making notes suddenly stopped writing and looked up.

"What's that?" he cried. "Is there a dog in my courtroom?"

"Really your honour, a dog in the courtroom!" cried the clerk of the court. "I assure your worship there is none."

The judge was indignant at the clerk's comment. He replied brusquely, "Do you think my ears deceive me? I just heard a dog bark."

Needless to say Boxer and I had to keep perfectly still in the public gallery and, ably supported by my Mistress, we remained undiscovered.

The bailiff meanwhile conducted a search of the courtroom and reported to the clerk that there were definitely no dogs about. The case now continued and Boxer and I listened with renewed interest as more evidence was heard. We could not understand where the dog barking had come from; we both looked at each other in puzzled amazement. Meanwhile Miss Murphy in her evidence confirmed that all the dogs belonged to the defendant and that her Association had on a number of occasions in the past responded to telephone calls from concerned local residents about the ill-treatment of the Alsatians; despite repeated calls to gain access to the premises and inspect the animals, they had no success: indeed the accused had on a number of occasions verbally abused their officers when they called to the house.

As the hearing continued more evidence was offered

which clearly underlined the guilt of the accused; indeed, each time Bissell denied the charges of wrongdoing, a dog was heard to bark in the courtroom!

On the last occasion when the barking dog was heard we noticed the judge turn slightly pale! We feared that he might suspend the proceedings because of this. We were glad that he did not do so.

Meanwhile it became increasingly obvious that the dog barking was very much upsetting Mr Bissell; he became very agitated and pale as death. He fiddled with his hands as he stood there in the dock, and appeared quite nervous.

Finally when all the evidence had been given the judge delivered his judgement as follows, "Mr Bissell, having considered all the evidence presented here this morning I find that you are guilty of the charge laid against you in the indictment; that you are guilty of extreme neglect and cruelty resulting in the death of one of those animals which were in your care. I fine you 1000 Euro and ban you from keeping any dogs in your care for the next ten years.

From the evidence of such wanton neglect and cruelty which I have heard here this morning you can count your self lucky that I am not sentencing you to a term in jail!"

Boxer and I were delighted with this result, as indeed was my Mistress—evident from the smile on her face. That firm justice had been given to this most cruel human truly elated our spirits. Interestingly, just as the judge delivered his verdict several dog barks resounded around the courtroom as follows: *Woof! Woof! Woof! W-o-o-o-o-f!*

The judge, upon hearing these barks, turned slightly pale and immediately made a hasty retreat from the bench; while Bissell was seen to race towards the courtroom exit in a most agitated frame of mind!

It was then that Boxer and I were to discover where the barking was coming from.

As I stood to leave I observed just over the dock area where Bissell had been standing, was my friend, 'Toby of the Brave Heart,' together with Wacker standing behind him! They were very visible, almost as you would see them in daylight. I motioned Boxer to look quickly so that he could see them too; however as on the occasion of poor Alonzo's burial when Toby had also appeared, Boxer couldn't make out the images; being an old dog his sight would not have been the best. I assured him they were there. They now moved towards us and as they passed over our heads they both smiled down at Boxer and I, and I could see that they were very pleased as to how we had acted in this whole affair. Coming out into the early morning sunshine Boxer and I were very happy also and looked forward to more happy days together in the weeks and months ahead.